W·CLARK
PUBLISHING
A STATEMENT IN LITERATURE

THIRSTY

THIRSTY

A novel by

MIKE SANDERS

Wahida Clark Presents Publishing, LLC
134 Evergreen Place
Suite 305
East Orange, New Jersey 07018
973-678-9982
www.wclarkpublishing.com

Thirsty
ISBN 13-digit 978-0-9818545-4-0
ISBN 10-digit 0-9818545-4-0
Library of Congress Catalog Number 2009921479
    1. Urban, Charlotte, North Carolina, Hip-Hop,
        Women, African American, – Fiction

Cover design and layout by Baja Wakiri Ukweli
Book design by Jonathan Gullery
Edits and layout by Nuance Art.*.

Printed in United States

2 1

Dedications

This book is dedicated to someone whom I love totally and unconditionally. The one person who pushed me into pouring all of my blood, sweat, and tears into this novel and making it come together. Thank you SOOOOOO much!!! So without further ado, I would like to dedicate this book to MY DAMN SELF!! Yeah, I said it!!

Acknowledgements

First and foremost I would like to thank the Most High for all things imaginable!

Mikai, LeCrecia, and Skylar, words can't begin to describe the way I feel about my princesses. Thanks for your unconditional love! Daddy is finally home and it is ON!!!

My caring and loving family, without your support and encouragement I would have crashed a long time ago. Thanks for throwing me a life line when I was drowning!

No, I'm not going to waste neither my energy nor my acknowledgment space naming all of you who shit on me in my time of need because you know who you are. If you're not sure if I'm talking about YOU just speak to me and see what type of reaction you get.

Kinya, it's only right that you get your shine because you have been pivotal in this process and a true "friend." Although you, too, at one point turned your back, it's still love! Thanks for continuing to be there when I needed you most.

To those who showed love when I came home (Corey, Barry, Rez, Dirt, Big Will, Sum, and Big B. the Guyanese) I really appreciate it. I see that real people really do real things! That's what's up!!

To all of my readers across the nation, thanks for your support! Here's another banger for you! Can't wait to meet all of you on tour very soon!!

Thanks to all of the book clubs that read *Hustlin' Backwards* and *Snitch* and posted reviews. Ms.Toni from OOSA, good lookin' for everything. I really appreciate it.

To everyone on lock, keep ya heads to the sky!! Change is gonna come soon!!!

Thanks to everyone at WCP! Wahida, Tobias, Hadiya, Keisha, and everyone who contributed to getting *Thirsty* into print. This is only the beginning!!

You can get at me at: queencitysbest@yahoo.com, myspace/ queencitysbest and wclarkpublishing.com.

QUEEN CITY STAND UP!!!!!

THIRSTY

PROLOGUE
JUSTICE

As I nervously climbed those winding stairs with my baby .380 clutched tightly in my sweaty palms, I could feel beads of sweat trickling down between my breasts. With each step I climbed, my heart beat like jungle drums and felt as if it would leap from my chest at any given moment. Regardless, I knew I had to still my nerves, but I also knew there was no turning back! I'd decided that *today* would be the day I'd make this nigga pay for all of the pain and anguish he'd put me through.

As I neared the door to his home office I could hear the familiar melodious sound of his money counting machine as it rhythmically spit out bill after bill. I was hoping that I'd rocked him to sleep during our time together so he'd be totally oblivious to what I was about to do. I was also hoping that he'd gotten so comfortable as to have left the door unlocked. He knew I had never disturbed him while he was in this room handling his business because I knew a man needed his space from time to time. But today, *his* space was about to become *mine* as well.

When I was directly in front of the large, oak door I stood there and silently prayed my nerves would allow me to carry out my task. Hell, it's not everyday a sistahh's about to catch a damn *body*!

A million and one emotions began to well up in me all at once. So suddenly, that it felt as if they were colliding and toppling over one another. I tried with all the restraint I could muster up to hold back the tears, which were fighting to be released, but it was to no avail. My eyes lost the battle and the water sprang free. Mascara streaked down my chiseled cheekbones as the tears flowed freely.

Just the thought of how easily the man beyond this door had come

11

into my life and turned it upside down, made me really grasp the concept of what could happen when a man catches you at a vulnerable stage. I witnessed first hand how a woman's mind can really get twisted.

After taking a deep, nervous breath I reached for the cold knob and was thoroughly surprised to find it *unlocked.* I paused for a moment to muster up the courage I needed. With a trembling hand, I twisted the brass knob and hurriedly pushed the heavy door open just in time witness this nigga's eyes almost pop out of their sockets as he looked up from his desk where he sat.

"Justice," he called out my name while staring in astonishment as I stood there in his doorway brandishing a pistol, looking like a crazed woman.

CHAPTER ONE

How It All Began...

Located downtown on South Summit Avenue was club Nine Three Five, and everybody who was somebody was up in the house tonight. Charlotte's hottest nightclub was off the hook for its first annual "Grown & Sexy White Party." All patrons were dressed immaculately from head to toe in all white. From a distance it looked angelic. It was showtime for real. Dope boys competing with the celebrities and the girls competing with each other.

DJ Incognito was pumping the latest Mary J. Blige hit. The sound of the bass invaded my soul as I sat slightly swaying my hips on the barstool and observing the packed mirrored dance floor. The whole while I was keeping a close eye on the VIP.

Carolina Panthers' Julius Peppers held down the VIP section with several of his teammates along with a few members of the Charlotte Bobcats basketball team. Panthers' star wide receiver Steve Smith was celebrating his birthday and champagne was flowing like it was mere tap water. Security was thick like Obama himself was trying to get a drink. But that didn't stop the hundreds of groupies from begging for VIP wristbands and trying to get in. Charlotte's most elite nightclub was packed to capacity and it was a wonder that the fire marshals hadn't yet come and tried to shut things down.

It is a known fact that whenever the ballers came out to party, so does the "baller chasers." Needless to say, every chick who thought they had what it took to snag one of those niggas was hovering around the club in the skimpiest outfit they could squeeze into, lurking like vultures waiting for the kill.

Money attracts women, so for every one male there were at least three women and the men were taking complete advantage of the three to one ratio. Most of the men were well groomed and looked as if they had just stepped out of the barber's chair. But there were a few who looked like they had just finished going ten rounds with Mike Tyson. Most of these niggas were hustlers whose chips were not stacked as high as the ball players, yet and still, together they flossed enough ice to build a three-family igloo.

My girl Sapphire and I were seated at one of the two bars on the first level of the club basking in the limelight. We were enjoying our drinks and grooving to the smooth sounds that were pouring from the sound system. I was in my zone and feeling hella good! Guys had been checkin' for us all night, but Sapphire and I were unfazed by all of the attention we had been receiving. One by one, we had been shooting niggas down left and right. But that didn't deter a few who were still relentlessly determined to holla. Evidently, quite a few seemingly assumed they had what the next man didn't because even well into the night they were still approaching.

We hadn't been out in quite some time so we were truly letting it all hang out tonight. Being the object of most men's desire was nothing new to us. We were accustomed to stealing away most of the other chicks' spotlights wherever we went. This night was no different.

Sapphire and I were what most people would refer to as *mysteries* because no one really knew a whole lot about us. Men *loved* us because they couldn't have us at the drop of a hat like most other chicks, and women *hated* us because they couldn't figure us out. The hate never really bothered us because we were aware of the fact that it is human nature for us to fear and oftentimes hate what we don't understand. For that reason, our circle always stayed as tight as a nun's pussy. Besides the two of us, we didn't have any female friends because bitches are just *too* jealous.

As I swiveled around on my stool to face the bar I was startled by a presence that had sidled his way between me and Sapphire. Evidently, this nigga had spoken to me while I was checking out the VIP, but I hadn't heard a word he'd said.

"What!? I can't hear you," I shouted over the loud music to, yet, another brother whom had invaded me and my girl's space for what seemed like the umpteenth time since our arrival at the club. This one definitely had *no* chance whatsoever. His face was decorated with the kind of pimples I hadn't seen since junior high school and his so-called dreads were so matted up they looked like a throw rug. The instant deal breaker was his dental work. He was displaying my ultimate turn-off—platinum teeth! I hate to see metal in a grown man's mouth.

"I said can I buy the beautiful lady a drink?" Dreadlocks repeated himself slightly louder than he'd done the first time.

"No thank you, sweetie. I'm straight," I replied casually, trying not to be rude. I picked up my XO from the bar and took a sip just to make sure he saw that I had a fresh drink and didn't need his assistance. Dreadlocks kept trying to holla but I had already tuned him out after the word "drink" had escaped his lips. I was so not feeling this nigga! I turned my back to him and started talking to Sapphire while he stood there looking angry and dejected.

"Oh, so you gonna just turn ya' back to a nigga while he talkin' to you?" Dreadlocks asked with his burnt lips a little too close to my ear. He was so close I could feel one of his dreads grazing my neck. I could also smell his breath, which reeked of alcohol and cigarettes.

At this point I felt as if Dreadlocks was being a slight bit disrespectful. This caused the tiny steel ball in the center of my tongue to start clacking against the insides of my top front teeth. Clacking my tongue ring was a predisposition that happened anytime I'm angry or annoyed. And it happened every time without fail!

I continued to ignore him until he finally got the message that I wasn't going to give him any rhythm. He sauntered off in search of another potential victim. But not before calling me a "conceited bitch."

"Oooooh, no-the-hell-he-didn't!" Sapphire commented in disbelief as she watched the guy walk away. "Rude ass nigga. Right up *your* alley, huh, Justice," she teased with a pearly white smile. Her soft voice was straining to be heard over the roaring music.

"Bitch, pleeze. Smelled like he had a lil' man wit' shitty boots on walking around in the back of his throat. I almost passed-the-fuck-out!" I had my nose turned up as if I could still smell the guy's breath.

Sapphire and I always got a kick out of teasing one another. We were *the shit* and we knew it. It had once been stated that, "A beautiful woman armed with a load of confidence is considered to be a dangerous woman!" Me and my girl definitely oozed with exuberant confidence. We were two bitches with class, sass, *and* ass! A helluva combination.

I sat my drink down and glanced over at the mirror behind the bar where the liquor was stacked and caught a glimpse of my reflection. I was dressed in a pair of leather Dolce & Gabbana white shorts that accented my well toned butter scotch thighs and a silk blouse that was unbuttoned down to the crease of my breasts. I wasn't wearing a bra, so I knew men would be drooling over my perky breasts every time the silk shirt grazed my nipples.

With one fluid motion I uncrossed, then crossed my legs again, placing the opposite leg atop the other so all of the lustful-eyed niggas could get a quick flash of thick thighs. I also did it so all of the jealous chicks that I knew were watching could get a good look at my expensive Guiseppe stiletto thong boots.

I looked over at Sapphire and saw her give me one of those, "Gurl, you a damn trip" looks as she twisted her lips into a half-smile because she knew exactly what I was doing. Not wanting to be outdone, Sapphire flipped her jet-black shoulder length tresses backwards over her shoulder so the platinum diamond earrings she was wearing could sparkle for everyone to see. She glanced down at her cleavage and discreetly adjusted her ample ebony D-cups so that they looked as if they were about to pop out of the top of the white Prada dress with spaghetti straps. As I watched my girl vie for attention, for the first time that night I noticed how well the dress she had chosen to wear was clashing perfectly with her chocolate skin.

Although Sapphire is a pound or two slimmer than my voluptuous frame she is still a far cry from being petite. Nor does she have my slanted eyes, but she is still as fine as wine in her own right. On a daily basis I continuously get compared to that Kimora Lee chick because of my "Asian-like" eyes and the uncanny resemblance we bare. Sapphire on the other hand had been told a time or two that she could pass for a thicker version of Gabrielle Union—all the way down to the dimples.

While grooving on my stool to Anthony Hamilton's latest joint, I unconsciously thought about how much my girl Sapphire has meant to me for years. I conceded that she was truly the sister I never had. Although I loved my friend to death, there were times when she could be a tad bit nerve wracking with her naïveté. At this time, I was twenty-two, only nineteen months older than Sapphire. However, that age gap seemed so much broader because I'd been exposed to so much more shit.

I had never really lived what one would call a sheltered life and I've always had street smarts. There's absolutely nothing slow about me but the way I walk. Therefore, sometimes it took a true vet such as myself to school Sapphire on certain aspects of life, especially when it came to trifling ass men. Nevertheless, no matter how many times I would try to tell her about those dogs, she would fail to take heed; leading her to a broken heart every other week.

For example, a few weeks ago Sapphire had caught her so-called boyfriend Travis getting his tiny ass dick sucked by her cousin. Her trifling ass first cousin Joy had been on her knees giving him dome in his living room while he sat there on the sofa with his pants around his ankles. He hadn't even had the common sense to take the liberty of locking the damn door when he knew Sapphire could pop up at any given moment. I would have kicked both their asses. She just calmly walked back down the steps to the parking lot and keyed his Benz.

I had even tried to warn Sapphire that Travis's dog ass was no damn good and how he had even had the audacity to try *me* when she was not around. However, Sapphire wouldn't listen and had to find out the hard way.

Nevertheless, I have always felt compassion for my girl. The two of us had been as thick as thieves for years. We had met years earlier when my mother had moved me and my younger brother Monk to Charlotte, North Carolina, from Chicago in search of a "better life," so she had said.

When our family had first arrived in Charlotte we ended up living next door to Sapphire and her mother in Piedmont Courts housing projects (one of the worst projects in the city at that time). Sapphire's mother and my mother became friends, so naturally, Sapphire and I spent a lot of time together. Back then Sapphire's mother had an abusive boyfriend named Ty and I often noticed bruises on Sapphire's arms and legs, which she always claimed to come from falling or bumping into things. School counselors also noticed and questioned her, but she continuously convinced them that nothing was wrong at home.

One night Sapphire's mother and Ty were arguing so loud that it woke me up out of my sleep. Next thing I heard was a gunshot followed by shrill screams. Two minutes later, Sapphire's mother was banging on our door, screaming and crying hysterically. She was yelling that Ty had shot himself. She was trembling so hard that she couldn't have dialed 911 if she had tried. So, my mother called the police for her.

I was sitting up in my bed, listening to my mother try to calm Sapphire's mother down when my bedroom door slowly opened. Sapphire stood there in her bed clothes. Her eyes were lifeless and she looked like she had seen a damn ghost. I got up and pulled her into my room and shut the door.

"What happened?" I asked.

She didn't respond. I think she was in shock.

Sapphire finally climbed into bed with me like she always did whenever she spent the night. She curled up into a ball and just stared up at the ceiling. My nosey ass wanted to know what had happened to Ty, but Sapphire was not telling. The next morning it was all over the news and all over the neighborhood that Ty had shot himself in the head. It was ruled a suicide. But later that day, after my best friend made me promise to never repeat what she was about to tell me, Sapphire broke down and told me what *really* happened.

Ty had been molesting Sapphire for two years right up under her mother's nose. Sapphire wouldn't tell because he had said he'd kill her and her mother if anyone ever found out, and she believed him. The night he died Sapphire's mother had caught him sneaking out of Sapphire's room and zipping up his pants. An argument ensued and Sapphire's mother asked her what Ty was doing in her room. Sapphire finally told on him. Sapphire's mother must've temporarily lost her mind and went to get Ty's gun from their bedroom drawer. She blew his brains out right before Sapphire's young eyes.

For all these years I've kept my promise to my girl and no one will *ever* know about that night unless she told them because I intended to take her secret to my grave!

Ever since Sapphire had caught Travis she had been a little down in the dumps. So, I figured a night out at Nine Three Five was just what the doctor ordered to get her mind off of things.

"Look," said Sapphire while nodding toward the dance floor. "Shabba Ranks still tryin' to get at you." She was referring to the guy who had called me a "conceited bitch."

I turned towards the dance floor and spotted Dreadlocks dancing with a heavyset light-skinned chick. He was staring at me with blood-shot eyes. I held his gaze for a second, then sat my drink on the bar and raised my right hand to my lips. I blew a kiss in his direction while displaying my best fake smile.

Sapphire took a sip of her Mimosa and almost chocked when she saw what I'd just done. She choked back a cough and wiped her lips with a napkin.

"Why the hell you do that? You know he gonna come runnin' his lil' happy ass back over here."

"I want him to catch that and kiss my ass wit' it. I got his 'conceited bitch'," I replied while picking my drink back up and resumed to sip and groove.

"O-Kaaay," Sapphire teased as we both laughed and raised our hands high for a high-five, then commenced to slap hands in midair.

I looked around the smoke-filled room and saw several big time hustlers. Some I recognized, others were new faces. They were all sipping champagne and trying to holla at anybody who they thought would fall victim to their prowess. My eyes wandered to one of the many pool tables in a far corner of the room where two fine ass brothers were shooting a game. It was obvious to me that they were not ball players because they just had that "street" appeal that made my spine tingle. The jewels they were draped in were shining so brightly I could see the sparkle of different colored stones even from where I was seated. It's safe to say that they looked very appetizing.

However, I had to check myself because I'd sworn off fucking with hustlers. I absolutely refused to go down that avenue again. I'd had entirely too many close brushes with danger while fucking with those types of men in my past. I must admit though, I definitely enjoyed the benefits I'd reaped from playing my role with them, but the reward was not worth the risk.

Back in the day I had never really understood why most women were always attracted to the niggas who would have rather hugged the streets than hug their woman. That chronicle had always been somewhat a mystery to me until one day I met a street nigga named Carlos who turned my ass out! Had me running behind him and even searching for his ass in broad daylight with a flashlight. Had a bitch sprung.

I had met Carlos at a nightclub downtown in the Adam's Mark hotel a few years back and it had been on since the day I first laid eyes on him. He was the only man who could handle me and my wild ways. He kept me laced in the latest fashions and I never wanted for anything when I was with him. But I got tired of being so dependent on him and wanted my own shit and he didn't like that. That's when the problems started and we ended up going our separate ways. We stayed cool, but it was never like it was in the beginning of our relationship.

Since dealing with Carlos, I had begun to understand why a woman would act that way over those types of niggas. But for the life of me I still couldn't seem to explain it. Personally, there was just something about a nigga dressed in baggy jeans with a mean swagger and a permanent screw faced expression that made my thong sticky upon first sight.

And God forbid if the nigga had a baldhead, I'd have to wring my panties out like a wet dish cloth. Like a fool, I thought I could change a hustler. That is, until I began to see a continuous pattern of those men eventually changing *me*. Since I'd reformed from getting seriously involved with street niggas I still couldn't let go of the sex. I absolutely had to have me some of that "thug dick" from time to time.

It's true what they say about thugs. They've got the best dick game! Whoever had coined the phrase "thug love" must have had experienced some of that same "I can't walk straight 'cause dis nigga done fucked me 'til my pussy was raw" type sex that I've endured with a few street niggas, especially with my ex Carlos. Sex between the two of us had always been earth shattering!

Lately I'd been setting my sights higher and I was determined to make my dollars graduate. For instance, all of those ball playing niggas who were in the club tonight were all fair game. A little challenge has never hurt anyone before. Besides, I have always been thirsty for guap, a thirst that will never be quenched.

I finally looked away from the pool table where the hustlers were and fixed my gaze on the dance floor, then over to the second bar area hoping to spot a potential victim. No one caught my eye. I then gazed toward the area where the VIP was located and saw the familiar faces of several well-known athletes who were surrounded by groupies. While observing these tricks, I sucked my teeth and rolled my eyes at those cheap ass hookers who were fucking the game up for "real" bitches such as myself. I knew half of those heifers would fuck for a mere buck and the other half would do something real strange for a little piece of change. They had no idea how to get real money from those niggas. That thought alone had me seething with anger.

Sapphire must have did a CAT scan on my brain and read my thoughts. "Girl, what you over there thinkin' 'bout?" she asked.

"See that." I pointed towards the VIP area. "It's hoes like that who be in the way and blockin'."

Sapphire turned on her stool in the direction in which I was looking. She teased, "Don't hate. Participate."

"Chile pleeze. Them hoes can't even smell my panties, let alone fuck wit' my game. I'll run circles around them square ass bitches."

I looked at my girl and realized she didn't have a clue as to how treacherous I was.

I thought, *If you only knew.*

A little while later, the drinks I had consumed throughout the evening had finally begun to catch up with me. I felt my bladder expand a little. Tiny beads of sweat began forming on my forehead indicating that I was a little tipsy. I reached for a napkin on the bar, dabbed my forehead and decided that now was as good a time as any to make that dreaded trip to the ladies' room.

"Watch my drink. Gotta tinkle," I told Sapphire as I grabbed my Chloe handbag from the bar and rose to my feet. As soon as I had stood up I realized I had a better buzz than I'd originally thought. When the lightheadedness finally subsided I headed towards the restroom, which seemed as if it was a mile away. I got stopped by at least six different guys while en route. While fanning my way through the thick clouds of cigarette and cigar smoke I only said "Hi" and kept it moving. It was hard as hell still trying to be cute while I was about to piss on myself.

The bright lights in the bathroom helped me shake a little of my high off. Surprisingly, the bathroom was clean despite so much traffic in and out all night. Even the air didn't smell half bad inside. I guessed all of the trifling chicks had stayed home this night.

After finally relieving my aching bladder I decided to touch up my lip-gloss and reapply my mascara. While in the mirror minding my business I saw two of the groupies come sauntering in. They were the main two I'd seen hanging all over the ball players in VIP. The two girls, one high yellow and the other pecan tan, were visibly twisted.

The skirts they both wore were so short you could see a hint of ass cheeks hanging out. Apparently they had no shame whatsoever because they began bragging candidly about how they were going to meet up with two of the football players at the Embassy Suites hotel after the club. They even mentioned room numbers. I didn't know if the two girls were trying to impress me or if they were just that oblivious to my presence. But I managed to keep my game face on and was filing all of that pertinent info away in my mental rolodex.

The groupies were in the middle of discussing stopping by the Waffle House before joining the players at the room when I'd decided I'd heard enough. I was packing up my things and getting ready to leave the restroom when I saw the high yellow chick pour a line of coke onto a compact mirror and they both shared a hit. Afterwards, they engaged in a passionate uninhibited kiss. Other chicks were coming in and out of the restroom and acted as if the two girls' actions were normal. No one commented, no one stared.

"Dust head, dyke bitches," I muttered under my breath in disgust as I began to make my exit. My mind was doing cartwheels and somersaults and my mental cash register began *cha-chinging* like crazy. Only if those girls could have read my thoughts at that instance. My devious mind was working full-throttle!

I left the two groupies in the restroom and headed back to my seat at the bar. I almost managed to make it back without too much harassment from the hardheads. That shit is so annoying. As soon as I made it back to my seat, I saw Sapphire's trifling ass cousin Joy and one of her girlfriends approaching the bar area near where we were seated. I nudged Sapphire with my elbow and nodded in Joy's direction so that she could take notice. When Sapphire spotted her cousin, I saw fire jump into her eyes. I was halfway hoping she would take out her earrings and slap some Vaseline on her face old school style and beat that hoe down. But for the moment Sapphire managed to maintain her composure.

Joy sashayed her narrow ass over to where we were seated. The baggy pants suit she was wearing seemed to swallow her small frame. The shoes she had on were so ran down it looked as if she had been running track in them. Her micro braids were frizzy as hell and her eyes held that glossy, *ex* induced look. Just one glance is all it took for me to tell that she was "rollin'." Her big-boned girlfriend was right behind her looking twice as jacked up as Joy was.

Joy looked at me and rolled her eyes with one hand on her skinny ass hips and the other clutching a half-empty Heineken bottle. She turned to Sapphire and before she could fix her mouth to speak, Sapphire spat, "If you ain't comin' to tell a bitch that your triflin' ass got the Ebola virus and finna die within the next twenty-four hours I suggest you not open your mouth! 'Cause I don't feel like hearing *shit* you gotta say! 'Cause I'm about two seconds off your ass! I really feel like gettin' all up in yo' bizness right about now!"

It was obvious that Sapphire was having flashbacks of walking in on Joy sucking Travis's dick. And the more she thought about it the more heated she became.

Joy stood there with a dumbfounded expression glued to her face while Big Boned stood behind her looking like she had something to say. I sat there stunned because I had never seen Sapphire this heated before, but I guess she had good reason to be. The way she was looking all fiery-eyed and screw faced almost led me to believe she was about to invite Joy out to the parking lot. She knew I had my "baby .380" in the car, and judging from the size of this chick Joy had with her, we would have definitely needed it for her swole ass. Besides, I was just *too* cute that night to be taking an ass whippin'.

Joy looked at Sapphire with a scowl and turned to walk away. Before she walked off she stated a defiant "Fuck you!"

Hearing this, Sapphire rolled her neck ghetto-style and returned, "Nah, fuck *you!* You bum bitch!" Sapphire put her drink down and started to rise up off her stool. I grabbed her arm and stopped her. I looked around and saw that we were getting a few unwanted, inquisitive stares from individuals who had evidently heard the berating between the two cousins and were undoubtedly expecting a catfight.

After Joy and her friend had left I tried to calm Sapphire down. I patted her thigh and said, "Girl, fuck Joy. She can't help it that she's a nympho. All that bitch think about is dick. Dick, dick, dick. If it ain't on her mind, it's in her mouth."

Sapphire looked at me sideways.

"Okay, bad choice of words. But you know what I mean. Let that bitch have sloppy seconds. You know she wasn't doin' nothing but tastin' you when she was suckin' Travis's dick."

I watched Joy as she snaked her way through the crowd.

"Up in here lookin' a hot ass mess," I added as I saw Sapphire trying to surpress a smile. I could tell she was lightening up a little.

"I know right? Did you see the shoes that hoe had on?" Sapphire added as we shared a small laugh.

A few minutes later, the atmosphere had calmed down a little. I looked over at Sapphire and tried to figure out where that sudden violent streak had emerged. Ever since I'd known Sapphire she had always been the cool, peaceful type. Only this night I saw something in her that made me look at her in a totally different light. I thought for a moment that maybe my girl was finally ready to get down with my hustle and roll with a bitch. Then on second thought, I rationalized that she was not yet ready to jump out there with an ocean full of sharks. For the simple fact that some of the shit I was into was so devious and conniving that it had my own conscience fucked up at times. I concluded that she was definitely not ready.

While I was in deep thought I happened to see the same two groupies from the restroom saying their goodbyes to the players. I couldn't quite figure out which two of the players they had planned their rendezvous with but then again, it really didn't matter because they all had dough, and I definitely wanted some of it.

"Gotta go do somethin' right quick. Be right back," I told Sapphire as I fished my phone out of my purse and quickly headed toward the club's exit.

Once outside, I stood a few feet away from the exit door and punched in digits on my cell. I was trying my best to ignore the "Yo, ma" and "What up, shorty" from the niggas who were milling around and loitering. They truly acted as if they had a lack of anything better to do.

I stood on the curb with my phone glued to my ear and my eyes were trained on the club's exit waiting for the two groupies to emerge. I was hoping they'd come right out behind me so I wouldn't have to be outside too long. Although it was still summer, the night air was chilly and my arms were starting to form chill bumps.

I listened as the line rang three times before it was eventually answered. Coincidentally, as soon as the line was answered I spotted the two chicks coming out of the club giggling and staggering slightly. As I watched them stroll through the parking lot, I spoke into my phone. I kept my eyes on them until they reached their car, a late model Honda Accord. That was all I needed to see. I then turned my attention away from them and resumed my conversation.

After a few minutes of idle chatter I finally ended the call with my younger brother Monk and attempted to re-enter the club. Just before I reached the entrance I felt a hand on my arm. The vulgar comments and crazy ass looks from niggas I could deal with, but putting your hands on me without my permission is a straight-up violation!

Instinctively, I spun around with all intentions of checkin' whoever this nigga was that had the audacity to put his hands on me. I turned on my heels with my mouth open, ready to go off. However, I was repressed when I came face to face with one of the finest pieces of masculinity I'd ever seen! My demeanor immediately softened as I blinked twice in succession to make sure my eyes weren't playing tricks on me and to make sure the liquor didn't have a sistah hallucinating.

The first thing I noticed was his complexion. His skin looked as if someone had dipped him into a bowl of creamy chocolate, then sat his ass out in the sun to dry. I was loving that! Purely out of habit, starting with his shoes I gave his attire a quick once-over as my eyes scanned his body like a bar code. He had on spotless white on white Prada sneakers and Mek jeans. He also had on a button-down shirt that was unbuttoned, revealing a broad chest covered by a white tee. I couldn't even front, I was feeling his appearance. I realized that he must not have been inside the club because he wasn't wearing what the dress code had required. I wouldn't have been able to miss all of *that* up in there anyway.

He looked to be at least six-three because I stand at five-seven without heels and this night my heels had four inches on them. Even with the heels on he was still towering over me by at least three inches.

And, oh-my-God, his head was as smooth as a baby's naked ass!

"Excuse me, can I have a minute?" His voice boomed with so much baritone-like bass that it made my nipples tighten up! I wanted to say "A minute? Hell, for you I got a whole lifetime." However, I folded my arms across my suddenly erect nipples and responded, "Maybe. Depends."

I was demurely biting my bottom lip, trying my damnest to look sexy while continuing to hold his gaze.

He flashed a Taye Diggs-like smile displaying even, pearly whites, then he casually stroked his well-trimmed goatee before extending his hand to me

"I'm J.T."

"Justice," I blurted out. Then I flinched at the realization that I'd just given him my real name. That was something I very rarely did upon first introduction.

Damn I'm slippin', I thought as I allowed him to take my hand. He raised it to his luscious lips and blessed it with the most seductive kiss I'd ever felt. I had to shake my head in an attempt to snap out of the spell this nigga had put me under.

This nigga got a bitch straight trippin'.

I took back possession of my hand while further observing this Adonis in human form standing before me. Because of his height I concluded that he was probably a "hoop nigga." Then on second guess, the edginess he was exuding screamed "street nigga." I had really been trying to leave those types of niggas alone, but J.T. had my ass ready to backslide!

While we were having our moment, a jet-black Hummer with a set of big ass chrome rims pulled alongside us and stopped. The windows were so heavily tinted the only thing I could see was quick flashes of light, which was radiating from several TV screens inside the truck.

Suddenly the driver's side window slowly descended and a voice came from within. Had a bitch almost ready to hit the deck, thinking it was a roll-by or something. Can't just roll up on black folks all slow with dark ass tinted windows like that. I'm from Chi-town and I've seen it happen entirely too many times in the past. One minute a vehicle would creep by all slow and shit and the next thing you knew everybody would be running and ducking bullets. That shit is not cool!

My heart raced like crazy until I heard the driver's words, "Yo J.T., let's be out 'fore I haveta straighten one o' these niggas and make light shine through one o' they asses for not mindin' they fuckin' bizness out here."

When I was finally able to see who that voice belonged to I noticed that he was a light-brown skinned guy wearing a backwards fitted cap. He had an oversized platinum chain draped around his neck. When he stuck his hand out the window to thump ashes off the blunt he was smoking I saw that his wrist was wrapped in an ice-encrusted timepiece. I also noticed that his pinkie was laced in some nice sparkly shit as well.

Yep, street niggas, I thought while shifting my gaze from the driver back to J.T.

"Simmer down, nigga. I'm comin," J.T. replied to his boy just before the driver's side window went back up. He turned back to me. "I'm about to dip, but I wanna holla at you later. Like perhaps tomorrow…if you're not too busy. So, why don't you…" He paused to take out his iPhone, then said, "Your number would really make my night complete."

I thought for a brief moment, contemplating on whether or not to give him my number. After a few hesitant seconds I decided against it. I flipped my cell back open and replied, "Why don't I just get yours instead."

J.T. wasted no time in relaying his number to me as he watched me punch his digits into my phone and save the number.

After saying our goodbyes, with promises of hooking up in the near future, I watched as he strolled around and climbed into the passenger's side of the large truck.

I thought, *I gotta have me some of that! I hope his dick is as long as his dollars!*

While observing him walk away I noticed that he walked with a swagger that bordered the thin line between that of confidence and that of arrogance. Either way, that walk turned a sistahh on.

Minutes after J.T. had left, I was back inside Nine Three Five, retreiving my girl so we could be out because there was money to be made.

CHAPTER TWO
JUSTICE

I pulled my silver Chrysler 300 into the Waffle House on Sugar Creek Road in search of the Honda I'd witnessed the two groupies leaving the club in. If a person didn't know any better they'd think a block party was in progress outside of the restaurant. Women were prancing around as if they were in a fashion show and the niggas had their trunks popped open, blasting music. It was chaotic!

I slowly cruised through the crowded lot, ignoring the niggas who were motioning for me to stop so they could holla. I didn't see the car I was looking for so I assumed that the girls had probably gone to the Waffle House on South Boulevard, the one closest to the Embassy Suites hotel. I was silently hoping that the girls would indeed stick to the itinerary that I'd overheard them discussing in the bathroom earlier. If not, a monkey wrench would've definitely been thrown into my plans. After slowly maneuvering through the melee I exited the parking lot and pulled back onto the main road.

"I'm kinda hungry. Why didn't we go in?" Sapphire asked from the passenger's side. She had no idea that at that moment I had ulterior motives for going to the restaurant and that food was the farthest thing from my mind.

"It was too crowded out there. We goin' to another one."

I got onto the Interstate and pushed it, making the "Ghetto Bentley" purr as we cruised down 1-85.

A little while later we were cruising through the parking lot of the Waffle House on South Boulevard. This one was a lot less crowded and the parking lot was quiet and serene. It was nothing like the fiasco on Sugar Creek that we'd just left. As I rode past the front of the restaurant

I immediately saw the two groupies inside. They were seated in a corner booth with menus, talking and laughing heartily.

I pulled around to the side of the building and spotted what I'd been searching for. Bingo! There was the Honda. To my satisfaction, it was parked away from all the other cars. By parking in such a secluded area the girls had made phase two of my plan a lot easier than I'd anticipated.

I parked on side of the restaurant, out of view of the patrons whom were inside and far enough away from the street so that no one could see us. I instructed Sapphire to go inside and order some carry-out.

"Get me one o' those patty melt things with extra pickles and an iced tea."

I dug into my hand bag for some money, handed her a few bills, and waited for her to get out so I could execute phase two.

Sapphire grabbed her bag, opened the door, and exited the car. I watched as she headed for the entrance of the restaurant. Once she was inside I reached over, opened my glove compartment, and searched for the tool I needed to carry out my task. After moving my .380 aside and rummaging through a few scattered papers, I finally found what I'd been looking for. I quickly grabbed it by the handle and clutched it tightly in my palm.

Moments later, my door was open and I was out of the car with my eyes scanning the area like a surveillance camera, making sure no one was watching me. Satisfied that no eyes were on me, I moved swiftly towards the Honda. My heels were click-clacking on the pavement with each step I took. When I reached the girls' car I looked around again just to be certain I wasn't being watched. Flicking open the switchblade I had in my palm, I bent down in those tight ass shorts and jabbed one of the back tires twice. The air rushing out of the rubber sounded like a nine hundred pound man was taking a fart. I waited for a few moments to make sure the tire had completely deflated before I moved inconspicuously back to my car unnoticed.

After about five minutes of being seated back inside my vehicle I saw Sapphire exiting the restaurant, carrying two boxes and trying to balance two large drinks. I looked past her and took a quick glimpse back inside the restaurant at the two groupies. I saw that they were busy eating the meals they had ordered. They were totally oblivious to what I had just done.

Sapphire started whining as soon as she opened the door.

"Girl, you could've at least tried to help me carry this shit." Once inside she closed the door, then blurted out, "Oh, shit, wait a minute."

She opened the door and retrieved one of the drinks from the roof of the car.

"So, what's the plan?" Sapphire asked while I was pulling out of the lot. She opened one of the boxes that was resting on her lap and took a bite of bacon, then licked her fingers. The aroma of the food was starting to make my stomach growl a little.

"I gotta go meet my brother," I told Sapphire as I watched her munch on her food. "But first we gonna go eat this food."

I was tapping my French manicured fingernails on the steering wheel in tune to Jamie Foxx's CD as I drove.

"Oooh, that's my shit!" Sapphire stated as she reached down and increased the volume on my stereo while snapping her fingers and grooving in her seat.

I rode for a few blocks until we were near the hotel where my latest gold mine lay. I pulled the Chrysler into the parking lot of a Mini-Mart that was directly across the street from the Embassy Suites hotel. Next to a pay phone is where I parked and killed the engine while allowing the radio to continue to play. Sapphire looked over at me and shook her head. I knew she had questions as to what I was up to. Only she didn't ask because she was used to seeing me do sneaky shit on occasion.

We sat and ate our food while talking about a few of the fine ass men who had been at the club. I didn't want to leave the club as early as we had, but my motto is M.O.D. (Money over Dick). Therefore, a bitch had to do what a bitch had to do!

I commented in between bites of my patty melt, "You know if I didn't haveta handle this binness with Monk we could've hung out a little while longer."

"Hell, I ain't up for that shit tonight anyway." Sapphire paused. "That shit wit' Joy threw me all the way off my square."

Thinking back to the confrontation that Sapphire was referring to, I remembered the way she had checked her cousin.

"Lemme find out you tryna get all gangsta an' shit all of a sudden," I teased while peeping her demeanor.

Sapphire looked up from her plate and smirked. "I ain't sayin' all that. I'm just tired of people taking my kindness for weakness."

Her voice was hushed.

As an afterthought she added, "I might not be all 'gangstress' like your ass, but I can hold my own in any situation, *thank you*." She had a twinge of sarcasm in her voice as she spoke.

"Oh, is *that* right?"

"Yeah, that's right. You betta ask somebody." Sapphire was smiling.

I was watching the hotel's entrance as we continued to talk.

Sapphire peeped my shifting eyes and finally asked, "Girl, what the hell are we up to? Why we sittin' out here in this damn parking lot eating? And *why* yo' ass keep watching that damn hotel?" Her words were strung along like one big run-on sentence.

"I told you I gotta meet my brother," I left it at that. I changed the subject back to the guys at the club. "Met somebody tonight."

"Who and when?" Sapphire asked. She was curious to know when I'd had time to meet somebody. We had been together all night and she couldn't remember me giving anybody more than fifteen seconds of my time.

"A guy named J.T. And it was when I stepped outside to use the phone. Talking about fine? This nigga was that with a capital *F!*" I was still watching the street as I spoke. "Then his boy pulled up in a damn Hummer! Now, this nigga here was laced! All I needed to see was his wrist and how icy that chain was that was swinging from his neck. Girl, I think I was talking to the appetizer while the entree was sitting in that damn truck."

"You mean to tell me them niggas was doin' it like that and you didn't come get me? Oooh, you know you dead wrong for that."

"Girl, you know I'ma put a bitch on," I assured my ace. Just then, I spotted what I'd been looking for. "'Bout damn time," I stated more so to myself than to Sapphire as I wiped my lips with a napkin and started the car.

Sapphire looked up from her meal and followed my gaze toward the vehicle that I was referring to.

"Who dat?" She squinted her eyes in an attempt to recognize the car.

I told her it was Monk as I was pulling away from the pay phone and back out into the street. I blinked my lights at the Mustang, and then I followed my brother to a nearby Amoco gas station. I pulled in and parked parallel beside Monk so that my window was right next to his. Both our windows descended at the same time. Immediately, my nostrils were attacked by the strong weed smell that was emanating from inside the Mustang.

"What up big sis?" my younger brother spoke. Due to his habitual weed and cigarette smoking his voice was kind of husky for his nineteen years of age. He was slouched down behind the wooden steering wheel with a black fitted cap pulled down past his eyebrows. His slanted eyes were barely visible.

"You got that?" I asked, not wanting to waste time with small talk.

"Do Fluffy got fleas?" He was being sarcastic, causing his two passengers to laugh. "Hell yeah we got that. You know not to question that. You know I'm 'bout my binness," he stated arrogantly.

Then he reached down in his lap and handed me a wad of crumpled bills through the open window while the guy on his passenger's side spoke to Sapphire.

"Wuzzup Phire? You act like you don't know a nigga. You can't speak?"

Sapphire craned her neck and looked around me to see who was speaking to her. When she recognized who it was she spoke back.

"Oh, hey, D.C., I didn't know that was you over there." She sat back and gave me a weird ass look.

34

I looked down at the crumpled bills in my hand and addressed my brother.

"Monk, y'all betta quit playin' and break a bitch off. I *know* ya'll got more than *this.*" I was holding up money. It looked like a few gees but I knew they had come up on ten times that amount.

"Girl, quit trippin'. You know a nigga got you." Monk pointed at a plastic bag that was resting in D.C.'s lap. "As soon as we get rid of this shit right here, I'ma hit you off again."

I leaned out the window to get a closer look at what was in the bag. What I saw made me smile. I settled back into my seat and opened my bag to stuff the loot inside. There was a dark-skinned boy in the back seat of the Mustang who I didn't recognize. His thick wavy hair was cut short and neat, and his beady eyes were bloodshot red from the weed. He was watching me with lustful eyes, staring all in my grill and making a sistah kind of uneasy.

I looked at him, then back at my brother and asked, "Monk, why your friend keep starin' at me like he knows me or something?"

D.C. passed Monk the L from which he took a toke, then exhaled a thick cloud of smoke. He turned his head, glancing at the dude in the back seat and then looked back at me with low eyelids. Without looking at the guy, Monk addressed him by name.

"Yo, Cross, why you sweatin' my sister nigga?" He was just teasing but Cross couldn't tell.

Caught off guard, Cross snapped out of his daze.

"I ain't sweatin' her." He lied. "I'm just trippin' on how much she look like that broad Russell Simmons used to fuck wit'." His voice was raspy as he spoke. I wasn't fazed by Cross's comment because I was used to hearing it regularly.

Without responding to Cross's remark, I asked Monk, "You gonna get at me tomorrow with the rest of that, right?"

I noticed how Monk kept glancing up at the rearview as if he was expecting someone.

"Ice," Monk called me by the nickname he had given me when we were kids. Although it spelled the last three letters of my name, he said he called me that because I was so "cold hearted"! "Have a nigga ever shit on you before?" He was looking at me with a serious expression glued to his features. "It might not be tomorrow, but a nigga got you."

"Monk, I'm just sayin'—"

"You just sayin'," he cut me off. "You need the dough and yotty, yotty, yotty. Yeah, yeah, I know. Same song, different CD." He then looked at me and smiled. "I. Got. You."

He offered me the blunt he was smoking, but I declined. He looked past me and held the cannabis-filled leaf up so that Sapphire could see it.

"Phire, wanna hit this?"

Sapphire leaned forward to see what she was being offered. Seeing the weed, she turned up her nose, "Nah, I'm straight."

She sat back and finished polishing off her meal.

"Sapphire, when you gonna let a nigga holla at that?" D.C. asked from the passenger's side with a smirk. His neatly twisted dreads framed his youthful, almost hairless face. D.C. and Monk were the same age so I regarded him as a little brother as well. Way too young for my girl.

"Boy, pleeze," I scolded D.C. "I done told y'all young ass niggas about that."

Monk and his hardheaded ass friends already knew that it wasn't even going down like that.

"I wasn't talkin' to you. I was talkin' to Sapphire. You her mamma or something?" D.C. was smiling again.

Just as Sapphire opened her mouth to respond, we all heard sirens off in the distance headed in our direction.

"Yo, that's our cue baby girl," Monk said while once again looking into the rearview mirror. He looked over at me with those chinky eyes. The weed had his already slanted eyes so tight I could barely see the slits.

At that instance, I noticed how much Monk looked like our father whom we hadn't seen since our mother's funeral years earlier. They shared the same high cheekbones, that thick curly hair and those thick ass eyelashes.

"Make sure you try to get at me tomorrow," I told him.

He just nodded and put the Mustang in gear, then slowly drove off. As I watched the Mustang exit the lot and ride off into the night I said a silent prayer for my brother to stay safe.

I finally pulled off and headed in the opposite direction of which my brother had gone. Thirty seconds later, Sapphire started with the interrogation, which I knew would come.

"Now, correct me if I'm wrong, but I know that nigga D.C. is out here wildin'. Now he hanging with your crazy ass brother?" Sapphire's eyebrows were raised. "The two of them together don't spell anything but "death wish" 'cause somebody gonna do something to them crazy ass niggas! Now how the hell did *you* end up in that retarded ass circle? What y'all got goin' on?" Sapphire was staring at me with a knowing look. "And don't sit up here and say y'all ain't got nothing goin' on, 'cause I just seen Monk break you off."

She pointed at my bag where I had stuffed the money Monk had given me.

"You gonna holla at your girl or what?"

I stopped at a red light, looked over at my friend, and wondered if I should've told her what I was up to or not. I really doubted if she could handle my scandal if I were to tell her, so I opted not to. Besides, I wasn't quite ready to put her up on my game just yet so I kept my mouth shut. I figured silence would be the best defense. I looked back towards the street, turned up the volume on my stereo, and began singing along with the radio while ignoring Sapphire's inquisitive glare.

Sapphire reached over and turned the volume back down.

"Oh, so it's like that?"

She was waiting for me to answer, but I continued to ignore her.

"It's aiight, you ain't gotta tell me. You know the streets can't keep no secrets. What's done in the dark..." she let her voice trail off as she turned back toward the window and stared out. She already knew I would eventually tell her because she was my girl, but I was hesitant to make the revelation so soon. Sapphire was as square as a pool table and as green as the cloth on top of it, and I didn't want her to start looking at me sideways once she found out. So, I stalled.

I pushed a loose strand of hair out of my face where it had fallen and promptly tucked it behind my ear while letting a deep sigh escape my lips.

I told her, "Look, we'll talk when we get to my place, all right?"

Sapphire looked semi-appeased for the moment. She turned the volume back up and sat in her seat with a slight smirk, satisfied that she'd gotten her way.

The rest of the ride to my place was pretty much quiet and uneventful. Twenty minutes after leaving my brother I was pulling into my condominium complex on W.T. Harris Boulevard. As I passed the security gate, I waved at Otis, the graying, obese security guard who was sitting in the booth. I was surprised as hell to see him still awake. Normally around this time he would've been snoring and slobbering on himself. He waved me through the gate and winked flirtatiously at me and Sapphire as we passed.

As soon as we entered my condo I disengaged the alarm and headed straight for my bedroom while Sapphire disappeared into the guest room.

Sitting on my large canopy-post bed, I untied my boots and kicked them off so I could rub my aching feet. I wiggled out of those tight ass shorts and breathed a sigh of relief. As I sat on my bed I glanced at my nightstand and saw the gold-plated picture frame with a photo of my mother in it. Staring at the photo made me remember that my mother's birthday was three days away. She would have been turning forty-six.

As I thought about my mother, wet clusters began forming around my eyes. I didn't want Sapphire to see me crying like a baby so I went into my bathroom, which was connected to my bedroom, and took the photo with me. I hit the light switch and once the room was filled with light I stared into the large vanity mirror at my reflection. I saw how weary my eyes looked and how it looked as if someone had pushed the fast-forward button on my life. Time had been going by fast as hell because it seemed like just yesterday when my mother had passed. It definitely didn't seem like five years had passed.

I rubbed my fingers across the smooth surface of the picture as if I could feel my mother's soft cheeks. As I observed her Filipino features I noticed how much we resembled. The only difference was the fact that my skin was darker and my body more voluptuous; traits that I'd inherited from my father's side of the family.

My mother, Kimoka Pasca, was a full-blooded Filipino who could barely speak English when she'd met and fell in love with my no-good ass father, Tyson Dial, while he was serving active duty in her country as a marine. Eventually, they married and he moved her to the U.S. where they settled in his hometown of Chicago. I was born a few years after their arrival to the States, followed by Monk. Tyson's side of the family, the black side, is where I'd inherited my tanned skin and brazen attitude from. But it had been Kimoka who had passed down my exotic features.

Lung cancer had taken my mother away from me only a week after I'd finished high school. I was so glad I'd gotten that chance to fulfill her last wish of seeing me walk that stage. She had also made me promise that I'd take care of Monk and make sure he didn't fall victim to the lure of the streets like so many other young black males. If she was still living to see how her baby girl and her son had turned out, lung cancer wouldn't have killed her because she would have surely died from a broken heart. I missed my mother more than any words could possibly describe.

As I continued to stare into the mirror, I whispered a hushed, "Girl, yo' mamma pro'lly turning over in her grave right about now."

I dreaded to think about how Kimoka would react to what my brother and I were doing. I silently wondered if all the materialistic things I had accumulated from getting street money were worth getting "caught up" for.

I had to give it to myself, at age twenty-two I had it going on. My ride was tight, pockets phat, and crib was laced. Not to mention that my wardrobe was full of Prada, Gucci, Louis Vuitton, you name it I had it. I probably could have started a small boutique with my clothes alone.

My home itself spelled *luxury*! I had spared no cost at decorating it with Italian furniture, expensive art, and a few whatnots. I still had a headache from the cost. Thank goodness my brother kept up with boosters who had a few stolen cards that helped with the appliance area. Entering my home, most people marveled over the Victorian style mantle that stood out in my living room. Even though I didn't have carpet I still wanted my guests to remove their shoes while walking on my cherry wood floors. The collection of books that lined the wall of my study was a conversation piece. And for those who were lucky enough to sleep on my canopy post Renaissance-style bed, couldn't figure out if it was the silk Versace sheets or the mattress that made them sleep so well.

As I continued to observe my appearance in the mirror I heard Sapphire milling about in my bedroom just outside my bathroom door.

She yelled, "Where's that scarf I left over here last weekend?"

I took a deep breath and wiped my wet eyes. I sniffled one last time, then yelled back, "Look in the bottom drawer where I keep all of mine."

I began scrubbing my face with a sponge to remove the light touch of foundation I'd been wearing. Then I figured Sapphire would never find her scarf amongst all of mine so I yelled again, "Just use one of mine if you don't see it."

While I was washing my face I was debating whether or not to put Sapphire up on my game or if I should leave her in the blind a little longer. I was undecided. Then after giving it a little more thought I decided that I would not broach the subject and would only discuss it if Sapphire brought it back up.

I dried my face with a towel, grabbed my mother's photo, and exited the bathroom. Sapphire watched me as I placed the picture back onto the nightstand but she didn't comment. Instead, she wasted no time getting all up in my mix.

"So, wuzzup? Put me on," she smiled.

She was sitting on my bed Indian-style wearing a pair of *my* gym shorts, one of *my* old T-shirts, and her hair was wrapped up in one of *my* scarves.

I looked at her and joked, "Lemme find out you got on a pair of my panties too."

"You know you don't wear this old stuff. You oughtta be glad it's goin' to good use."

I slipped on a pair of my favorite sweats and a wife beater. Grabbing the remote, I flicked on the 62-inch plasma that was mounted on the wall across from the bed. I was hoping to catch the late news. As I flopped down on the bed Sapphire let out a long sigh. She was looking at me with an exasperated glare. I knew she was getting impatient with me.

Tired of being brushed off, Sapphire sucked her teeth and stood to leave the room. Frustration was evident in her features.

"Okay, Okay, damn, you act like a lil' baby sometimes," I stated sarcastically while wrapping my hair in a scarf. "Hand me my bag." I pointed in the direction of my dresser. She walked over to the dresser and tossed my bag at me.

"Excuse you. You *do* know that this is a Chloe," I said, holding up the purse.

"Whatever," she responded.

She was watching me with curious eyes as I took out the money I'd gotten from my brother.

"Count this." I handed her the wad. She took it from my hand and sat back down on the bed and began counting.

While Sapphire was counting my money I looked at her and stated with all seriousness, "Look, what I'm about to tell you, you betta not repeat. You hear me?"

"Yes, maam," Sapphire sarcastically replied while continuing to count the bills.

"I'm serious! I ain't tellin' you nothing until you promise me you ain't gonna tell nobody." I was sure she could detect the graveness in my voice.

"Damn you act like this some top secret type shit you got goin' on." She was tallying up the last of the bills as she spoke.

"You better treat it like it's some top secret shit, 'cause if I hear this shit get repeated we gonna fall-the-fuck-out! Seriously!"

Sapphire placed the counted money in one neat stack, then looked up at me. "Aiight, you got my word."

"Good 'cause I'm graveyard serious about what I just said."

"Didn't I just say okay?" She pointed at the money, which was lying on the bed. "By the way, it's thirty-three hundred."

I could tell she really wanted to know why I had just gotten over three grand from my brother. I thanked her for counting the money for me, then I began to explain my hustle to her.

"See, me and Monk and nem got a little binness deal worked out."

Sapphire was looking at me with inquisitive eyes that were full of unasked questions. All of a sudden her eyes widened and her mouth sprang open as if she'd gotten hit by a bolt of lightening. The words jumped from her lips.

"Oh, shit! You sellin' drugs ain't you?" She was almost sure of the impending answer.

"Would you just listen?" I snapped, almost becoming impatient.

"My bad. Go ahead and finish."

Just then, as if on cue, a news brief was flashing across the television screen. Sapphire started to speak again but I hushed her and pointed to the television indicating that she should watch for a minute.

We both listened as the news reporter stated: *"Authorities were called to the Embassy Suites hotel on South Tryon Street just over an hour ago in response to a call made by the manager, stating that an armed robbery had taken place in one of the suites occupied by two members of the Carolina Panthers football team. No one was injured, however, the assailants managed to get away with an undisclosed amount of cash along with several pieces of expensive jewelry. Police are on the lookout for three black males believed to be in their late teens to early twenties. Representatives for the Panthers are refusing to release the names of the two victims and are...*"

The reporter's voice trailed off as Sapphire sat there and stared at the television, looking as if she were lost in thought. Her eyes widened again, this time with astonishment and slight confusion.

She pointed to the television in disbelief and blurted out, "We was just down there! What...I mean...How did..."

I was watching my girl's demeanor to see if she had actually figured out what I'd been trying to tell her.

Already speculating the answer, Sapphire asked, "So that's what you had to meet Monk and nem for?"

I was still watching the television as police cars surrounded the Embassy Suites.

I pointed to the tube. "That right there was *my* work. I did that." Sapphire was looking confused so I added, "I overheard these two chicks talking about meeting those football players at the hotel and I even heard them mention room numbers. So, me being the bitch that I am, I put my lick down and beat them hoes to the punch."

I went on to explain how I had peeped which car the girls had been driving while I was outside the club talking to Monk on the phone. I even told her about how I had slashed the tires to immobilize the girls so they wouldn't be able to show up at the room while Monk and his boys were there handling their business. When I'd finished telling Sapphire about what I'd done I was thinking she'd look at me indifferently or try to give a bitch the third degree. But to my surprise, Sapphire was more so *intrigued* than anything else.

"Damn, all you doin' is settin' that shit up for Monk and nem? I mean, you ain't gotta go with them or nothin' like that?" Sapphire had become enthralled.

I took a deep breath, "Sometimes they might need a female to help them gain entry 'cause you know a nigga'll let a fine bitch up in his spot any day before he'll let a hard-head in. So, in situations like that all I do is get 'em to open the door, then the rest is on Monk and nem, 'cause a bitch be *out*. I ain't never stayed around while they handled their binness. Tonight I didn't even have to be with them. I just called Monk and gave him the details I'd overheard the girls divulge at the club."

"And them niggas be breakin' you off like *this,*" Sapphire was holding up my wad of cash. "Just to get them inside?" she was in disbelief.

"Yep. They owe me some more after they get rid of the jewelry they took from them niggas."

I was trying to catch the last of the news report while she spoke. I was hoping they didn't have any suspects for the robbery. After hearing that they didn't have any, I was finally able to relax.

"Jewelry?" Sapphire asked.

"You didn't see all that ice Monk had in that plastic bag when he showed it to me at the gas station?"

"Guuuurl, you gotta put a bitch on," Sapphire stated while looking at the bills in her hand and smiling wickedly.

"I'on' know, Phire, this shit ain't as sweet as you think it is." I was trying to deter her.

Sapphire got up off the bed and walked around to my side where I was seated and got all up in my face.

She was smiling when she stated, "Bitch, cut me in or cut it out. You know we go back way too far for you to be leaving me outta shit like this. Damn, I thought we was better than that."

"Girl, you know we still got each other's backs like chiropractors, and we still as deep as them dimples in yo' cheeks. But, I'on' know 'bout this."

"Justice, put me on. I'm serious. Girl you know a bitch needs some damn money."

Toying with her emotions, I lay back on the bed and nonchalantly stated, "I'ma think about it."

I licked my thumb and started slowly flipping through the bills of cash like a drug dealer counting his stacks.

"Yo' broke ass need a loan?" I asked.

"See there you go wit' that ole bullshit," Sapphire stated as she playfully swung one of my pillows at my head.

"Gurl, you betta chill. You know you playing with authentic Versace and your "I need some money" ass can't pay for it if you rip it. Matter o' fact, get an umberella 'cause I'm finna make it rain on your broke ass." I tossed the three Gs toward my ceiling and watched as they fell onto Sapphire's scarf-covered head. We both laughed at my antics.

Sapphire and I stayed up well into the night talking about the many capers I'd been on with my brother and other stick-up kids. I told her about the lick I had set Monk up with two months back. I'd put him on a hustler who had been fucking with this stripper I knew who danced at Onyx. I also told her about several other hustlers in Charlotte I had set up over the years. I told her that the nigga J.T. was currently in my crosshairs, and that it would be only a matter of time before he felt my wrath!

The more I talked the more she wanted to be down. I told her I would link her with Monk and his boys as long as she promised to keep *everything* confidential. She said that she fully understood the seriousness of it all and she was more than ready to get her feet wet.

That night, I drifted off to sleep with racing thoughts. I was silently wondering if I had done the right thing by putting Phire on or if I had very well made a grave mistake.

CHAPTER THREE
CARLOS

Surveying my smoke-filled playroom, which I call the "Men's Lounge," I took in the scene. FOR TRUE PLAYERS ONLY read the neon light that hung on the wall over my fully stocked bar. The still image displayed on the projection TV screen was from the Playstaion 3 being paused. Two arcade pinball machines sat idle in one corner and a professional length pool table occupied the other corner. There were only a selective few that knew this room existed, my connect and my street team. It was also a safe spot to meet without having to worry about unwanted niggas and bitches being all up in our mix. We met here once a month to unwind and get blitzed.

My two youngans, Lil' Joe and Dave, were shooting a game of pool for a hundred dollars a ball. Dave was nineteen and Lil Joe was twenty. Lil Joe was the youngest and the biggest of my soldiers in the room. Standing six-four and weighing in at two-seventy, he looked like a college linebacker. Dave was the smallest of my men. He was five feet six inches of pure gangsta. Together they ran several crack houses for me on the west side of Charlotte and served weight to other dealers in that same area. Because of their size difference, I often referred to them as David and Goliath.

After rolling up and refilling their drinks, Face and Supreme unpaused the Madden football game on the Playstation 3. The table stakes were five hundred dollars a quarter and from the looks of things Face was losing. Face was medium height, medium built, and light brown skinned with a grotesque scar that ran from his right temple to just below his chin. The scar was the reason he had been given the nickname Scarface.

Supreme was a rail thin brother with long, thick dreads that hung down to the middle of his back. His complexion was dark brown and he had cold, beady eyes. His lips were just as dark as his complexion due to chronic cigar and weed smoking. Preme claimed to be a Five-Percenter, a religion a lot of niggas claim to pick up during one of their many trips to the penal hotel. He called himself a God Body, a natural-born god whom had the power to give and take life. If someone were to ask me I'd say the nigga was an angel of death. Preme and Face were my two hit men whom once used to murder just for the sport of it. They enjoyed it so much they were actually doing it for free...until I had come along. Then they were getting paid more than generously for doing what they loved.

Lastly, there was Ali. Ali was my lieutenant and trustworthy side-kick who had always been down for whatever. Ali and I had grown up in the same housing projects, Boulevard Homes on West Boulevard, on the west side of the Queen City. We had both gone through the same struggle of trying to make it out. I made it out of the hood first and as soon as my pockets got right it was without question that my man got right too. We had known one another long before all of the money had come into our lives, explaining the reason why he was second in command.

Standing an even six feet tall and weighing in at a solid 190 pounds, Ali and I were almost identical in size, only I'm an inch taller. Whereas, I'm a deep dark brown, Ali was a shade or two lighter. Like me, Ali also sported a low cut with sea-sickening waves. Because of his name, many thought my nigga was Muslim. However, he'd received the moniker at an early age because of his acute ability to box so well. He was a dangerous man with his hands. Ali could scrap with the best of them. Now that he was older, he let his pistol handle most confrontations.

I truly trusted the five men in my presence with my life. I paid them all well and treated them as equals rather than as employees. For that reason, they all respected me to the fullest. It was a known fact that if you kept a person dependent upon you they would remain loyal, and it was plain to see that I was these men's bread and butter. For me, loyalty was worth more than any amount of money imaginable. Money was no object and fear was nonexistent. Each of us had money to burn and wouldn't hesitate to do whatever or *whomever* to keep it that way.

I sat off in one corner of the large game room clutching a half-empty bottle of Armand de Brignac (Ace of Spades) champagne from which I'd been swigging. I was high as shit from the blunts that were being passed back and forth throughout the room. Jumping up from the money-green leather sofa, I spilled champagne on my Mek jeans. So I headed to the bar to get a paper towel to wipe myself off with. I noticed Ali on the phone and I could tell he was talking to a broad. I sat on the stool next to him and motioned for him to end the call so we could get down to business. I needed to holla at him about something that had been bothering me for the past couple of days. Checking my Audermars Piguet, I noticed that it was almost midnight.

"Damn," I mumbled to myself thinking about all the pussy I was missing at Nine Three Five tonight. Thursdays was Ladies Night. But then I said fuck it because them hoes would be there the following week and the week after that and so on. We needed to handle this business.

After making plans to hook up with the girl he had been talking to, Ali ended his call. He turned on the stool to face me.

"What's good Los?" He had a half-smoked blunt dangling between his lips.

I slowly swiveled around on my stool and looked out at the four men enjoying themselves. Without looking at Ali, I asked, "You know a nigga named Cross?"

Ali relit the blunt, then asked, "You talkin' 'bout that nigga who be robbin'?"

I swigged the remnants of the champagne bottle I was holding.

"Yeah, *that* nigga."

I reached for the blunt Ali had just lit and took a long, slow toke inhaling the 'dro. I added, "I just got word that him an' two other niggas was the ones who did that *kick-door* last week. They had a bitch wit' 'em too."

I was referring to the robbery that had taken place a week earlier at one of my stash spots. No one had been hurt, but the robbers had managed to get away with eighty-three grand of my dough. I'd heard that they were in and out so fast it was like they were on a professional bank heist. Initially, no one had known who had been responsible for the robbery. However, the entire universe knows it never takes long for the streets to start whispering. This nigga told a bitch, who'd told some more niggas, who happened to tell another bitch, who ended up telling me. Same shit, different toilet. It always happens like that.

"Say word!" Ali was looking at me with perplexity as if he couldn't grasp the finality of my last statement.

I didn't respond, as I was lost in thought about how bad I wanted those niggas to suffer. I passed the blunt back to Ali, arose from the stool, and walked behind the bar to retrieve another bottle of champagne. After popping the cork, I leaned on the bar towards Ali.

"In all of my twenty-four years on this earth, I'on' think I ever wanted somethin' as bad as I wanna see them hoe-ass niggas shed blood." I had venom in my voice.

"So how we gonna handle that? You gonna let Mark take care of it?" Ali asked, then blew a cloud of smoke towards the ceiling.

"Mark? You serious? That was *my* dough them niggas took."

I looked out at Supreme and Face and knew exactly how I was going to handle the situation. But I had to be smart with this hit because I had been picked up on several occasions and taken to Homicide for questioning. No witnesses, no evidence, no charges. I was too sharp for their asses. I always stayed two steps ahead of the game. I knew one slip up could cost me my freedom and everything I had hustled hard for. Therefore, I knew I had to handle this situation with Cross with extreme caution. Since so many people knew my spot had been robbed I knew I'd get the blame if the niggas who had done it suddenly wound up bodied. I just had to sit back and wait for a minute before moving on them.

I looked out at my boys and spoke up loud enough to be heard over all of the shit talking and berating throughout the room.

"Yo! Yo! I need y'all to check this out for a minute!"

I reached for the remote to turn the surround sound down, which was pumping Lil' Wayne's new joint. I waited until I was sure I had their undivided attention before continuing.

Lil' Joe and Dave both turned to face me while holding the customized pool sticks in their hands. They leaned back against the expensive pool table side by side looking like a black Arnold Swartzeneggar and Danny Devito in that old school movie *Twins*. Lil' Joe was towering over Dave by almost a foot.

Supreme and Face paused the video game again and craned their necks so they could see what all the fuss was about. Face was apparently agitated because I'd just interrupted his game and he was losing fifteen hundred dollars.

"Nigga, you can't wait 'til we finish this last quarter? It's almost over." Face had a thick blunt between his burnt lips as he spoke.

"It ain't gonna take long. I just wanna put y'all niggas up on the reason why we all here tonight." I was standing behind the bar speaking as if I was standing at a podium. "Y'all know a nigga been tryin' to figga out who them niggas was that tried me like that last week, right?" I saw everyone nod in agreement. "Well, I found out who one of them snakes is."

Preme was the first to speak up as he sat the controller pad down.

"Yo, god, you know all you gotta do is give a nigga some names an' we'll toe tag them bitches." He had a one-track mind—*murder*. I knew Preme was ready to put in work but this situation wasn't as simple as just murkin' a few niggas and calling it a day. This one had to be handled with delicacy.

I told Preme, "I wish it was that easy, my nigga." I took a deep breath, "but it ain't. Y'all know how them investigators keep harassing muthafuckas about unsolved murders an' shit?"

I didn't wait for a response.

"Well, my name keeps comin' up." I knitted my brow as I remembered something I'd heard a while back. I added to my previous statements, "Oh, and that bitch-made ass nigga Junior told Face that some niggas in the county jail was talkin' 'bout I had somethin' to do wit' slumpin' them two niggas in North Charlotte a couple of months ago."

The group looked at Face as he nodded in agreement to what I'd just said. I sat the bottle of champagne on the bar and looked out at Supreme.

"Now, Preme, tell me," I tilted my head to one side, "how the fuck a nigga know I had somethin' to do wit' that shit?" My voice had unconsciously risen.

Supreme's brows furrowed in confusion as his mind replayed the incident in which I was speaking about. He had went on that mission alone and had slumped those two dudes in a parked car in a dark parking lot on Pegram Street, execution-style. He hadn't left any witnesses and no evidence. All the police had found when they had arrived at the scene had been two dead bodies and thirteen .9mm shell casings with no prints on them. As usual, Preme hadn't uttered a word about the hit so he truly had no idea how someone could have come to that conclusion.

"Come on, Los, you know damn well I didn't let that shit leak." Preme made that statement with all seriousness.

"See, that's what I mean, lucky assumptions like that'll get a nigga a *forever* sentence!"

Felony murder charges were getting niggas fried in the courtroom. I knew some niggas who had gotten so much time that their future PO hadn't even been born at the time they were being sentenced.

After a moment of silence, "That nigga Cross was the one who robbed Mark last week. Him, two more niggas, and a bitch. I don't know who the other two niggas and the girl is just yet, but best believe I'ma find out. And for real, it really don't even matter 'cause when we do this nigga, we doin' every muthafucka in his presence at that time. I'on' give a fuck who it is!"

I paused to take a swig. All of my boys had begun talking amongst themselves but I quieted them when I begun to speak again. This time my tone was a little calmer.

"I'on' give a fuck if his mamma, his grandma, or whoever is around when we go get this nigga. I hate it for 'em. Consider 'em guilty by association. We gonna teach muthafuckas that when you around snakes, you get bit!" My words lingered in the air as my niggas waited for further instructions, but there weren't any.

I had learned years ago that if a person wasn't part of the solution then they were more than likely part of the problem. I knew the only way to solve a problem is to eliminate it so that it has no room for manifestation. This nigga Cross had definitely become a *problem*.

We were all ready to deal with this nigga, but I knew better than to jump the gun. I made sure each of my boys understood that nobody was to make a move until I gave the word. I knew each of my boys wanted to get at this nigga for different reasons. Ali wanted him dead because he had tried me, and trying me was just like trying him. It was like taking food off of his own table when my money had gotten taken. If I took a loss, then so did he.

Lil' Joe and Dave wanted to get at the nigga because they knew if Cross had tried *my* stash spot, then he definitely wouldn't hesitate to try theirs sooner or later.

Face and Preme wanted to nod him just because they hadn't murked a nigga in a few weeks, and they were starting to get bored and restless.

I'd always believed that an enemy left alive is like a half-dead serpent that you nurse back to life. Consequently, his bite will become more venomous with time! I felt like these niggas were testing my gangsta when they'd robbed my spot. So I was determined to make an example out of their asses.

Everyone stood in agreement that Cross was a walking corpse that refused to lie down in the casket.

CHAPTER FOUR
MONK

It was a blazing Sunday evening, which meant Hornet's Nest Park on Beatties Ford Road was off the hook. On Sundays in the summer Hornet's Nest was the place to be! It was like the club before the club. It was a place where niggas flossed their freshly detailed whips and chicks flaunted the shortest shorts or skirts they could find. On this evening, the park was so crowded it looked like a concert was taking place. Niggas had their doors open, blasting music while the chicks stood in groups gossiping amongst themselves. I was enjoying the view of all those bitches that were dressed as if they were in search of a stage to get naked on. Ass and titties were everywhere; the only thing missing was the pole. The best part was being able to watch these hoes for free. I was also taking in the sights of all those dope boys who were flossing their jewels like Liberace at a piano recital. Ice was in abundance! This was definitely a stick-up kid's heaven.

My T-shirt was draped over my head. I was only wearing a wife beater and still burning up. It felt like July in a microwave oven and my skin felt like it was frying.

What I'd give for an ice cold beer.

But Charlotte PD was patrolling too thick to take a chance with drinking alcohol.

Me, D.C., and our new partner in crime, Cross, were parked side by side on our motorcycles with me in the middle. D.C. and Cross both owned Kawasaki's. Their chromed out custom-painted ZX-13s were tight to death. But they couldn't fuck with my shit. My preference was the Japanese-made Suzuki Hayubussa 1300. My bike was chromed out and painted with that candy chameleon shit that changed colors with the light. I loved it because it came in handy when fleeing from the Jakes! One minute they would be searching for a green bike and the next minute they would be searching for a blue joint! Kept them muthafuckas confused.

We were situated in a corner of one of the large parking lots just off the strip so we could have a clear view of everyone entering and exiting the park. Since we had robbed so many niggas and had accumulated so many enemies we had to be on point, especially when we were out like this. We were parked so we could watch the crowd because we didn't need any surprises. We needed to be able to see everything that was moving.

"Hey, Chinaman. Can a bitch ride wit' choo?" I looked up from my bike and saw that the voice came from a young redbone who looked no older than sixteen in the eyes, but twenty-two in the thighs. She and two of her girlfriends were walking past us looking like younger versions of the video models Vida Guerra, Buffie the Body, and Ice T's white wife, Co-Co. The confusing thing about the trio was the fact that the white girl had the fattest ass.

I wrinkled my eyebrows as I watched the three young girls stroll by smiling at us. My eyes were glued to the snow bunny's backside.

Where da fuck white girls gettin' all this ass from these days? I thought.

The redbone saw me staring at her friend. She looked at me, then followed my gaze to her friend's ass and commented with a knowing smile, "Oh, so *that's* yo' flavor, huh?"

I snapped out of my trance and sarcastically replied while puffing on a Newport, "Ain't y'all a little too young to be out here without a chaperone?"

They had gotten a nice distance away but they still heard my comment. The redbone looked back, rolled her eyes and swung her ass even harder as she walked off. The skirt she was wearing was so short it barely covered her shapely ass cheeks. My remark must have irked her because she didn't look back again. They disappeared into the throng of niggas who were gaping and foaming at the mouth like hungry wolves waiting to devour them.

"Yo, why didn't you holla at shorty?" D.C. asked while laughing.

"Man, you see how these hoes sweatin' a nigga like we celebs an' shit. Why should we *run* down the hill and fuck just one sheep when we can *walk* down an' fuck 'em all?" I looked over at D.C., "Slow ya roll, nigga, we got all day."

After the girls left, we sat there and kicked it for a few minutes. The park began to get congested with cars and bikes. I was on my cell talking to Justice when I heard Cross's raspy voice call my name. When I looked over at him he was pointing towards the park's entrance where I saw a midnight black 760i with dark tinted windows turning into the park.

"You know dem niggas?" Cross asked, sounding just like the rapper Jada Kiss.

"Not yet," I replied. I told my sister I'd call her back. I snapped my phone shut while we all watched the sleek Beemer sitting on 24s slowly cruise up the strip in the slow moving traffic that were attempting to enter the parking area. I didn't know who these niggas were, but I was itching to find out.

As we watched the BMW finally park approximately fifty feet away from where we were, we waited to see who would exit. When the doors finally opened, we were surprised to see two females step out. The passenger was a pecan tan Amazon and the driver looked to be Hispanic. Both women were dimes, hands down, and they seemed to possess air sophistication about them. They both stood next to the car wearing dark sunglasses as they laughed and conversed amongst one another.

I looked around and saw every nigga in my vicinity staring at the two chicks. Even a few females were checking them out and pointing in their direction. I knew most of the niggas who were watching the pair was more than likely thinking about trying to fuck. However, *my* mind was *way* in the gutter! I was thinking about the actual owner of the vehicle the two girls had just emerged from. I had a gut feeling neither of the girls owned that joint and I was willing to bet money that it belonged to a dope boy.

The jack-boy in me always made me look at things beyond the surface. What can I say? It was like second nature for me. My enjoyment of taking shit from people almost ran as deep as my enjoyment of busting a nut. Maybe it was the sense of power I felt whenever I aimed my burner at a mark and watched as they trembled with fear and anxiety. I loved that shit!

From an early age I'd had a fetish for jackin' niggas. Ever since I was a youngster in the "Wild Hundreds" back home in Chicago I'd been running with stick up kids. Most of which were Gangsta Disciples and Black Disciples who used to terrorize housing projects like Argyle Homes and other spots around the Hundreds. The Hundreds were the most ruthless streets in the Southside of Chicago from the early 70s to this very day. Famous gangsters like Al Capone once roamed the Hundreds, reeking havoc.

Thinking about Chicago, I took a deep breath and looked off in the distance and thought about my family and friends back in the Midwest. When my mom had first moved me and Justice to N.C. I was homesick as hell! I had immediately started missing everything about Chicago, especially my niggas, who I used to run with. And my favorite hangout spots like Harold's Chicken on 89th and The Underground club downtown. Of course, I was too young to get inside the club, so me and my niggas used to rob niggas in the parking lot. We knew they didn't have any burners on them as they exited the club so we caught those niggas on the way to their cars. Those were sweet come ups. Eventually I'd gotten over that homesickness when I had started meeting all of these southern bitches who seem to get mesmerized by a nigga's chinky eyes and slick ass tongue.

I had even started meeting a few jack boys. One of whom turned out to be my nigga D.C. We'd met through a bitch we had both been using to set niggas up. We eventually hooked up and started robbing niggas together. Since we'd hooked up we had robbed countless niggas and had been involved in enough gunplay to make those niggas over there in Iraq look like fuckin' boy scouts!

We hooked up with Cross one day when we had a lick that would take three niggas to pull off. Cross was dating D.C.'s cousin at the time, so we propositioned him and he had agreed to come along. That was our first caper with Cross, and those bitch ass football players at the Embassy Suites who Justice had put us up on had been the second.

When I rob a nigga I'd give him an ultimatum: "Give it to me or give it to God! I can do more with it than He can!"

Most took my advice of giving it to me, but there were those who had tried to buck and I usually kept my promise of making them give it to God. God rest their souls!

Most of our licks were quick and efficient—in and out like ghosts. But there were those few times when a nigga would have to put in some work. The sweetest lick we'd been on yet had by far been those football niggas. Those niggas were sitting ducks. Imagine their surprise when they thought they were letting in two bitches only to find out they had let in three *monsters*!

Those niggas were so drunk and horny they just opened the door without hesitation. We took everything them niggas had. Cash, plastic, jewels, you name it! When I went at niggas I was coming for it all! I wouldn't leave a nigga with shit. I'd take a nigga's socks, doo-rags, T-shirts...I wanted it all!

That night I had even taken those football niggas' towels, sheets, and blankets, and had thrown them into a laundry cart at the end of the hallway. The news had failed to mention the fact that they had found those players duct-taped and ass naked. That shit was funny as hell to me. After that night, I couldn't even watch a Panthers' game with a straight face anymore.

Shaking those thoughts and returning to the present, I looked back over at the two chicks standing near the BMW looking like their shit didn't stink. They were brushing niggas off like cats shaking fleas. I saw them shoot down at least six different niggas and that alone made me even more determined to try my hand. I thumped my cigarette butt to the pavement and looked over at D.C. He was still watching the women as well.

I told him, "A closed mouth don't get fed, homie."

I arose from my bike and hung my helmet on the handle bars. D.C. followed suit then he told Cross, "Watch our shit for a minute."

"No doubt," Cross replied.

We all smelled an imminent lick. Now it was time to put in work. Besides, a nigga might've even gotten lucky and ended up getting the pussy as well. Now that would've been a nice bonus! I put my T-shirt back on and draped my towel around my neck as D.C. and I walked toward the women. I had to keep pulling my shorts up a little as we walked across the parking lot, not because they were too big but because the pistol I had in my back pocket was heavy as hell. While we were approaching the BMW we saw two other niggas already trying to holla. We sat back and patiently waited for those clowns to be dismissed. As soon as they were gone we moved in.

I stepped to the driver with my confident swagger and charming grin. I noticed she had her mouth turned up into a scowl. When I was directly in front of her, I commented, "You shouldn't be frownin' like that, baby girl."

"Excuse me, I shouldn't be doing what?" She spoke with an up North accent, which was tainted with just an iota of Spanish. I was thinking maybe she was a Puerto Rican from New York. She dropped her head slightly so she could look over the top of her sunglasses as if she were trying to get a better look at me.

"I said you shouldn't be frownin' like that. 'Cause you never know who might fall in love with yo' smile," I told her with a grin. "Besides, it takes more muscles and more effort to frown than it does to smile."

She cracked a slight smile at my remark and glanced over at her girl to see if she'd heard my comment also, but D.C. had the passenger's full attention.

I leaned against the BMW and stuck my hand into the pockets of my shorts while checking her out. Her curly auburn hair was streaked with blonde highlights and hung well below her shoulders. Her skin was the color of freshly whipped cocaine and I could tell she had a tan because a line was barely visible on her right shoulder where her

58

blouse strap had fallen. A beauty mark decorated the right corner of her mouth just above her pouty top lip like that actress Eva Mendes. She was dressed a tad bit more conservative than the rest of the girls who were running around like pigeons. However, her jeans were so tight it looked as if someone had poured her into them. I figured her to be about five-two or five-three and she was thicker than Government cheese. This bitch was fine as hell! Her friend was pecan-tan, tall as hell, but as equally fine.

"Who gave you permission to lean on my whip?" the driver joked.

"Damn, my bad, ma." I pulled the towel from around my neck and pretended to wipe the spot where I'd been leaning. While clowning around I was discreetly trying to get a good look inside the Beemer.

I heard her say, "Five-speed, wood grain steering wheel, bucket seats, peanut butter interior. Find what you're looking for?"

She'd peeped me.

"So, this is *your* ride, huh?" I was now walking around the BMW, openly admiring it while trying to pick her for information.

"It's mine while I'm drivin' it," she returned.

Just as I'd figured, it belonged to someone else and I wanted to know who that someone else was.

"Ya nigga trust you to bring his whip out here? You must be somethin' real special. A lota niggas wouldn't do that. Hell, I wouldn't do it. You wouldn't be out here flossin' in my shit. 'Cause for one reason you gonna draw too much attention and two, it's gonna be a smooth ass nigga like me tryna get at you and I wouldn't be havin' that."

I was smiling at her. She didn't respond to what I'd just said, she was being cool. I changed tactics.

"What's ya name?"

She looked towards me with those dark ass shades with the double Gs on the side and just stared for a minute.

"It's Tan. Why? You takin' a census or somethin'?" She was being sarcastic.

"Damn, why you so hostile?" I teased. "I just like to know who I'm talkin' to, that's all."

"Well, that makes two of us."

She was letting me know I hadn't introduced myself.

"I'm Chink." I lied while digging into my pocket for my pack of cigarettes. I lit one and asked, "What part of New York you from?"

She corrected me and told me that she was from Jersey, Newark to be exact. I also found out that she was Dominican and not Puerto Rican liked I'd assumed.

She in turn questioned my nationality as well and I told her, "I'm half-African American and half nigga."

She laughed.

She looked at me and stated, "I figured you to be part Asian or somethin'."

She reached for my necklace and caressed it as if she were appraising it. She raised her sunglasses and squinted, trying to make out the charm.

She finally asked, "What is it?"

I lied again. "It's a face."

Actually, the charm was a white-gold, diamond encrusted ski-mask.

"Nice ice. What do you do?" she asked nonchalantly as she readjusted her Gucci frames.

"I direct traffic," I replied, exhaling smoke.

"Say what?" She sounded confused.

"I make sure certain niggas stay in they lane, ya dig?"

She looked perplexed as hell, missing my meaning. However, I didn't bother to clarify myself. We conversed for a few minutes before I ended up giving her my number. She wouldn't give up hers, a clear indication that she more than likely had a man. If her man was the owner of the BMW, then I definitely wanted to see that nigga, just to make sure he was in the right lane.

I walked back to my bike to rejoin Cross while D.C. continued to holla at the passenger.

After I'd climbed onto my bike Cross looked over and asked, "Who them hoes?"

"Some bitches from Jersey. The driver is...is...damn, I done forgot the bitch's name already. Um...um, damn!" I was snapping my fingers, trying to remember the girl's name. "She just told me. I know it's a color. Beige? Nah, that ain't it. Oh, yeah, Tan! That's it, Tan. Damn, a nigga need to quit smokin' so much weed. That shit's fuckin' wit' a nigga's memory."

Cross shook his head with pity as if he wanted to say "that's a damn shame."

Just then, D.C. was smiling as he walked back over to where we were parked.

He said, "Yo, I don't know who them bitches fuckin' with but whoever it is gotta be holdin'. Did you see them diamonds on them bitches' fingers an' shit?" D.C. was climbing back onto his bike as he spoke.

"Yeah, I peeped that," I replied. "You come up?" I was hoping he'd gotten the girl's number.

"You know I did. Hell, I knew *you* wasn't," D.C. responded, laughing. He waved a piece of paper. "You know I got the gift of gab, nigga. A bitch don't stand a chance if she sit there and listen to me for more than five minutes."

It was a good thing he had come up with the digits because we would surely need a way to contact the girls if we planned on getting at their niggas. While we were talking about the broads in the Beemer we heard the sound of motorcycles with loud ass pipes coming down Beatties Ford Road, nearing the park. The bikes were so loud it sounded like a thunder storm was headed in our direction. I looked around and tried to pinpoint the noise and I saw four bikes being stalled near the entrance of the park. The two bikes in front were painted with that candy shit that looked like it was dripping wet. The two in back were flip-flop painted and all four were Italian-built Ducatis, the most expensive bikes on the market.

The sound of Cross starting his bike made me look over at him. He was putting on his helmet as he watched the four bikes slowly progress up the strip in the slow moving traffic.

He looked at me and D.C. and said, "I'm about to bounce. Y'all comin'?"

D.C. and I looked at one another.

"I ain't goin' nowhere; it's too much pussy floatin' 'round out here," D.C. answered.

Cross then looked over at me with raised eyebrows.

"Hell nah I ain't ready either," I answered.

Cross continued to watch the strip before abruptly pulling off. As I watched his bike with the new paint job he'd recently gotten I realized how much differently his joint looked. It looked like a totally different bike.

"Paranoid ass nigga," I mumbled to myself while watching Cross pass the four Ducatis as he exited the park.

"What that nigga goin' through?" D.C. asked.

"He act like he geeked up." I replied while watching Cross disappear around the corner.

Moments after Cross had left, the four Ducatis were pulling up next to me and D.C. Once they were all parked they killed the engines and removed their helmets. I looked over at D.C. and saw him looking the niggas up and down. The driver of the bike that had been leading the pack spoke first. He looked over at D.C.

"What it do Dark Cloud. Or is it Dick Cheney? I never know what D.C. stands for from day to day. Is it Don Cornelius today?" His partners laughed.

"Nah, it's Dying to Creep, 'cause I'm waitin' to catch a nigga slippin' today," D.C. replied with a serious expression glued to his face.

The nigga turned to me and said, "What up bruh-in-law?"

It was Carlos. He had an arrogant smirk on his face. I looked at him and responded non-chalantly.

"Fuck you think's up? A nigga's hot, frustrated, and here y'all come fuckin' up a nigga's aura." I was waving my arms around as if they could really see some type of aura going on. I was also bobbing my head to the beat of someone's stereo that was bumping loud as hell off in the distance.

Ali spoke to both me and D.C. while Supreme and Scarface played the back and sat there mean-mugging like Carlos' little watchdogs.

"Aura? Nigga you can't afford an aura!" Carlos stated as he pulled a knot of hundreds from his front pocket. "Want me to buy you one?" He was laughing.

He stuffed the money back inside his pocket and moved his wrist back and forth so I could see the diamonds sparkling in his platinum watch.

"Seriously though, you got my number. You and D.C. sniper get at me when y'all ready to stop playin' *Robbin' in da Hood* and ready to make some real guap."

He reached over from where he was seated on his bike and held my ski mask charm in his palm for a second, then let it fall back to my chest.

With much sarcasm he laughed and told his boys, "Aw, that's so cuuuute."

He pulled his chain from inside the neck of his t-shirt and held up his platinum Versace charm, which was flooded with baguettes.

He pointed at mine once more and said, "Look, y'all, my chain had a baby."

I laughed and told him, "Fuck you." I knew he was only clowning as he always did with me and D.C., but it was entirely too hot for that comedic shit.

After another joke or two, Carlos and his crew pulled off burning tires, leaving thick clouds of white smoke in their wake. I fanned the smoke from my face and coughed up a few fumes while slowly shaking my head at their feeble attempt to show off. They rode over to where the girls in the BMW were parked and they all greeted one another like they all knew each other.

After they'd left I thought about that nigga Carlos and just how much street money he was out there getting. Carlos was known for holding more weight than the scales at a Jenny Craig convention! He was also rumored to be a millionaire, but I didn't know if that rumor had any truth to it. He was an arrogant ass nigga but we had always gotten along, except for one time.

I thought back to the day he had put his hands on Justice. They had a little lovers' spat and he ended up smacking Justice. Needless to say, I was beyond heated. Fucking with my fam' is a definite no-no! True enough, I'd heard about Carlos' reputation and the bodies he'd supposedly had under his belt but I wasn't fazed. I'd stepped to that nigga with my "problem solver" and checked his ass. And low and behold, Ice was right back with him a week later. Since that little incident had occurred I made it my business to stay out of their domesticated rifts. A woman gets her ass beat, leaves the nigga, and then ends up going right back to him? I still couldn't figure out the logic in that shit. Women can be simple-minded as hell!

Carlos knew I was a robber and he said he respected my hustle as long as I "Never try *him*."

Never try him? This thought caused me to chuckle to myself because I wondered who had died and made his ass God. That nigga actually believed that he was Mr. Fuckin' Untouchable!

After Cross had left the park, D.C. and I stayed and hollered at a few girls for about an hour or so before heading to my sister's place to give her the rest of her money from the Embassy Suites robbery. I'd finally sold the jewels we'd taken from those football niggas and we ended up with a nice stack.

Me and D.C. left the park with a few numbers from some bad bitches, but D.C. had the most important number of them all in his pocket. It was a number that we would undoubtedly put to use in the near future. It was the girl's number from the BMW.

CHAPTER FIVE
JUSTICE

It had taken Monk a few days to get rid of the jewelry that they had taken from the football players but he ended up breaking me off real proper-like just as he'd promised. I had to admit, I was thoroughly satisfied with my share. I was thinking that maybe I could sit my ass down for a minute and possibly find a real job for once.

The money I'd accumulated from the streets would've lasted long enough for a sistah to go to school and acquire some kind of bankable skills. Besides, all I knew how to do was find a way to get something for nothing. I had no idea what field of work those skills would be useful in other than some type of criminal activity. The only legitimate job I'd ever had was at Neiman Marcus as a cashier years earlier. However, when Sapphire had gotten stopped by security with over two thousand dollars worth of clothing and a receipt showing that she'd paid only fifty dollars for it my days as a cashier had come to an end. That had been before I'd gotten a taste of how sweet and how addictive that street money could be. Needless to say, I hadn't done anything legit since.

That same day Monk had come through to break me off Carlos had called and asked if he could "stop by for a few." I was no fool; I already knew what time it was. He wanted some punanny. I don't know *why* I kept falling into that trap. It was as if Carlos had some sort of sexual spell over me because I could never refuse him. The dick had me whipped! No matter how hard I tried to resist him, I just couldn't do it.

I told him he could come over but only for a brief moment because I had some things to take care of. He knew I was lying and didn't really have anything to do because I could see that damn smile on his face all the way through the phone.

After showering and lotioning myself in apricot body oil, Carlos' favorite scent, I decided it was time to tighten up—literally. I reached beneath my sink in the bathroom way behind the Massengils, tampons, and other feminine items and grabbed my secret weapon. I called it my "Rebirth" because after using a teaspoon of it with my douche, the kitty would be almost as tight as it was when I'd come into the world. This coochie tightening cream had by far been my most rewarding purchase from my favorite on-line sex shop.

With a few "Oooh, Daddy, you so big," "Ouch, you hurtin' me," and "It's been a minute since I've done it," a man'll think he struck gold. The best thing about it was the fact that it was tasteless and odorless. Vinegar and water didn't have shit on this concoction. Yep, tricked many niggas with this one!

After becoming "born again," so to speak, I threw on the tightest pair of gym shorts I could find and donned a wife beater. I didn't even waste time putting on panties or a bra because I knew I wouldn't have them on long anyway. I let my still damp hair hang loosely over my shoulders and I put a thin coat of gloss on my lips before taking a seat on my living room sofa to await Carlos' arrival.

I curled my feet up under my butt and clicked on the television with the remote. I tried to get my mind off Carlos and that good lovin' that was on its way over, but my coochie seemed to have a mind of its own as it continuously throbbed with anticipation. I had to place a pillow between my thighs to try to temporarily soothe the sudden ache.

I'd been on the sofa for only a few minutes before my telephone rang.

My first thought was, *This nigga's on that BS. again.* I thought it'd probably be Carlos calling with some tired ass lie as usual that would have him running another hour or so late, or would have him not able to show up at all.

Without looking at the number, I snatched up my cell with an attitude, "See, I knew this shit was gonna happen. I'on' know *why* I keep on fall—"

"Guuurl, what the hell is wrong with you? Who pissed in yo' coffee dis morning?" It was Sapphire.

"My bad, sis, I thought you was Los, callin' with another lie. You know how dat nigga do." I softened my tone as I inserted my Bluetooth.

"Lemme find out you still messin' wit' Carlos? I thought you cut his ass off."

"A bitch still got needs."

"A bitch *needs* to leave his tired ass alone," Sapphire stated, then added, "You always tellin' me about no good ass niggas, but you won't even take your own advice. Practice what you preach sometimes." She was speaking in a sisterly tone.

"See, the difference between me and you is the fact that I know where to draw the line at and you don't. Love ain't nowhere on my agenda! I'm just gettin' my thang off. When I cum, they go! Simple as that." I paused, and then added, "And best believe a nigga definitely ain't gettin' ready to be getting no keys to this spot."

I let that sink in for a minute because Sapphire knew I was calling her out about her choice of men.

"I ain't never gave but two men the keys to my house before. And in both instances they was my *man* at the time."

"Yeah, yo' *man* who dogged yo' ass out. One stole everything that wasn't nailed down and the other used his dick as a thermometer to check your cousin's temperature." I was laughing. I was thinking that the shoe must've fit because she definitely stuck her foot into it.

"See, you wrong for that," said Sapphire. She took a deep breath and added, "But you tellin' the truth though."

"I know I'm tellin' the truth 'cause you and I both know..." I paused because I heard the sound of Carlos's loud ass motorcycle nearing my building. I told her, "Lemme call you back, Los out there."

"Alright. Don't you hurt that nigga up in there wit' yo' freaky ass," Sapphire joked.

"Bye, bitch." I laughed along with her while ending the call. Just then, my intercom buzzed and I heard Carlos's deep voice telling me buzz him in.

After a few short minutes my doorbell rang and I hurried to my bedroom to check myself in the full-length mirror to make sure I was flawless before answering the door. Glancing through the peephole, I saw Carlos standing there dressed in baggy shorts and an Ed Hardy T-shirt with his helmet in his hand. He was looking just as edible as the first day I'd laid eyes on him at C.J.'s nightclub years earlier.

I couldn't stop throbbing!

When I let him in I tried with all my strength to ignore the undeniable chemistry that had always brewed between the two of us. I was testing myself to see how long I could hold out before falling weak. However, as soon as he walked in the smell of his Prada cologne had a sistah ready to crawl into his arms.

He took a seat on my sofa and I plopped down beside him. I tried to avoid looking at him I but couldn't help it. As usual, he looked like he was fresh from the barber shop. His thick waves were spinning out of control and his beard and goatee was trimmed to perfection. Before I could stop myself, my hand had moved on its own. I was reaching over and tracing his wave pattern with my fingers. That was something I used to have a habit of doing back in the day when we were together.

Carlos looked at me with those sexy ass eyes and flashed that smile which always made me melt.

"So, what's been up, ma? How you been?" he asked. He was still smiling, knowing he had me.

I turned away and looked at the television while still stroking his head.

"I'm good, I'm good. How 'bout you?"

"I'm aiight. Niggas been tryin' to carry me like a duffel bag lately, but other than that I'm straight." He shifted a bit before pulling a pistol from his waist. He placed it on my coffee table as he usually did whenever he visited.

"What you mean 'niggas been tryin' to carry you'?" I asked.

"You ain't hear 'bout them niggas kickin' Mark's door in?" He was surprised that I hadn't heard the news.

"Huh-uh, what happened?"

He started telling me about the robbery. "Some bitch tried to get Mark to open the door but he peeped game. But some niggas still ended up kickin' it in and duct taped him and his girl. They took Mark's jewels and a lil' bit of dough. But it's all good though."

Carlos was acting nonchalantly about the incident, but I knew him well enough to know he had revenge on his mind.

"You don't know who did it?" I was rising from the sofa and heading towards my kitchen area to fix a drink.

"Yeah, I know who one of 'em is. A lil' bitch ass nigga from Lake View. You pro'lly don't know 'em." Carlos was watching my ass as he spoke.

I changed the subject and asked if he wanted something to drink. I was bent over with my ass in the air while looking through my refrigerator.

"What kind of beer you got?"

"Corona," I replied while grabbing him a cold one and closing the fridge behind me. I walked over and handed him the beer, then started to go back into the kitchen to fix myself a drink. As I turned to walk away from him I felt his hand smack my ass.

"Boy, you betta quit."

I tried not to smile but the stinging sensation sent a shiver up my spine. He knew I loved having my ass spanked. I switched my ass harder than usual as I headed back into the kitchen area. I knew he was watching and it would only be a matter of time before he made his move. I looked over the bar and saw him rise from the sofa and head towards the kitchen where I was now standing. I was on my tiptoes reaching for a glass in my cabinet so I could mix myself an apple martini.

As soon as I reached up for the Vodka I felt one of Carlos's hands running through my damp hair and his other hand was circling my waist. I tried to turn so I could face him, but he kept me with my back to him as he moved my hair aside and begun kissing and licking on the nape of my neck, just like I liked it. I felt another shiver creep down my spine when his hands moved over my bare stomach and up to my breasts. He always knew exactly how to caress my titties with just the right amount of pressure to make a sigh escape my lips. With one fluid motion, he raised my wife beater and freed my breasts, causing my nipples to stiffen as soon as the cool air from the overhead ceiling fan kissed them.

While cupping a breast in each hand he teased my erect nipples and continued to kiss my neck. The sensation caused my hips to instinctively push backwards with hopes of feeling the bulge of his erection through his jean shorts. And just like I'd figured, his probing dick was poking out in his shorts and tapping me on my ass. This nigga was *really* making my kitty purr with anticipation. My eyes closed involuntarily due to the exquisite sensations I was experiencing.

I was gripping the countertop with one hand to steady myself because Carlos was making my knees weak. My other hand was reaching up and caressing the back of his head as he continued to kiss my neck and upper back. I felt his hand slide from my breasts back down to my stomach. Then I felt him venture further south until he was stroking my kitty through the thin fabric of my shorts. I knew he could feel my wetness because with each slight movement of my legs I could feel the sloshing between my nether lips.

I moved my hand from his head and moved it down to his hand, which was between my legs. I helped him stroke my pussy just the way I liked it to be stroked until I got lightheaded. As I stood there with Carlos grinding his crotch against my ass while strumming me like a violin, I wanted him *so bad!*

Moments later, we were heading to my bedroom while shedding articles of clothing along the way. By the time we reached the room I was completely naked while Carlos was still undressing. I lay on my bed, propped up on my elbows and watched as Carlos took off the remainder of his clothes. He was watching me watch him with that sly smirk on his arrogant ass face. After stepping out of his boxers he approached the bed and positioned himself on top of me. He kissed me, searching my mouth with his tongue while his hands rubbed, squeezed, and caressed my body. I was running my hands along his back, feeling the muscular contours as he began to kiss and lick my breasts with aggression.

A whispered, "Oooh shit," escaped my lips when he took one of my nipples between his teeth and bit down gently. This nigga had me *soaked!*

When I felt his hand glide across my hairless vagina, I instinctively parted my legs so he could have better access. He tickled my clit with his skillful fingers, which sent tiny tremors vibrating through my stomach for a brief moment. His fingers were drenched with my juices when he raised them to his lips and sucked them clean. Nothing turns me on more than a man who loves to eat pussy. Carlos definitely had a knack for the acquired taste and I was more than willing to whet his appetite.

He slid his body down mine until he was face-to-face and lip-to-lip with my kitty. He spread my throbbing lips so delicately you'd think diamonds were about to drip from that spot where my thighs met at the V.

Carlos stuck his tongue so deeply into my tight hole it felt as if a baby snake was slithering around in there.

"Oh, yeah, baby. Mmmmmmm, shit."

He had me moaning and gyrating my hips. I grabbed his head and tried to force his entire skull up into me.

He paused momentarily and looked up at me, "Damn, ma, you really enjoyin' this shit huh?"

He was smiling with wet lips. He replaced his tongue with two fingers and I flinched a little from the sudden intrusion because my pussy had really tightened up. He continued to probe with his digits, loosening me up a little as he attached his lips to my sensitive clit and began to suck away.

"Oh, shiiiit! I'm cummm, I'm cummm." I couldn't even finish the sentence because his swirling tongue felt like a million tiny men doing a rain dance on my swollen nub. I lost it! I came with violent, thigh quivering tremors as Carlos continued to lick me low.

He rolled me over onto my stomach and spread my ass cheeks so he could eat the pussy from the back. He knew this always sent me over the edge. He placed a pillow under my stomach so that my ass was slightly elevated and both holes were exposed. I loved being in such a vulnerable position. I felt Carlos make a wet trail with his tongue from my asshole all the way down to my clit. He did this again and again until I felt like I would pass out from the pleasure of it all. After only a few minutes of this I had to make him stop before he caused a bitch to have a damn seizure!

Once I was able to regain my senses I took the liberty of returning the favor. I sucked him into a frenzy until he was at the point of near-explosion! But I was determined not to let him cum without penetrating me. I stretched a condom over his rigid dick and climbed on top so I would be able to control the depth and speed of our thrusts. I slowly guided him into my tight, dripping hole while lowering myself an inch at a time until my ass was resting on his thighs. His penis was stretching my walls beyond belief and I didn't even have to use my internal muscles to squeeze him for that snug fit. I leaned down and licked his chest, letting my tongue ring graze his nipples. I loved to watch the expression on his face while we fucked so I looked into his eyes while caressing his abs. I saw the pleasure he was feeling as my pussy gripped him like a glove.

Carlos began to thrust his hips upwards causing his member to penetrate me deeply.

"Oh shit! Ummmph, ummmmph, oh yeah! I love this big dick baby! Oh, Looooosss."

I was loving it! Carlos gripped my ass and rammed his stabbing dick up into me with such force it tapped my G-spot, sending me into a whirlwind. My head whipped side to side as my hair swung all over the place like a mad woman!

"Oh, yeeeeah, feels...so...goo...gooo...Oh my God!"

I was about to come again when Carlos suddenly lifted me up off him and lay me on my back with my legs thrown over his shoulders. He entered me a second time. He beat the pussy up so bad from this angle it felt as if he were trying to re-arrange my uterus. It was a little uncomfortable for about all of ten seconds, and then it felt as if a large water filled balloon inside my womb was aching to burst. The pressure started building, and building, and building…until all of a sudden… the damn thing burst! All of my love came raining down on him!

"Oh, shiiiiit, don't stopppp!" My body felt like one gigantic nerve as I climaxed, creaming Carlos's condom-clad dick with my juices. My thighs were shaking and I couldn't control my breathing.

Seconds after my climax, I heard Carlos grunt as he climaxed also. The thin barrier that was preventing skin-to-skin contact was instantly filled with his seed.

As I lay there with Carlos still between my thighs, sweating and panting, I absolutely *hated* this nigga for knowing my body so well. However, in the same instance, a part of me *loved* him for making me feel so damn good.

Street niggas, I thought as I lay there stroking Carlos's back, which was glistening with sweat. *I really need to put an end to this shit,* was my last thought before drifting off into a sex-induced slumber.

CHAPTER SIX
SAPPHIRE

I rolled over and glanced at the digital clock on my nightstand. 2:46 A.M. was illuminated in red digits. Once again, the left side of my large bed was empty. This was really no disappointment to me because since I'd kicked Travis to the curb I'd gotten used to sleeping alone.

Laying in my King-sized bed staring up at the ceiling in the dark, I threw my champagne-colored satin sheet off my naked body and sat upright. I'd always slept in the nude, even when I was a little girl because I'd always enjoyed the unrestricted feeling of having no garments on. This night my skin glistened from a thin sheen of perspiration that covered my body. My nipples stood on end from the sensation of the sudden cool air as I climbed out of bed. I strolled to the nearby lounge chair in a corner of my bedroom and snatched up my bathrobe.

As I entered my bathroom, I switched on the light and walked over to the sink to turn on the cold water, letting it run over my hands. Glancing to the right, I looked over my toiletries, which were scattered about the counter top. My facial creams and scrubbing products along with a box of unopened tampons sat proudly in plain view. I didn't have to worry about Travis being there nor did I have to worry about him popping up anytime he damn well pleased.

Although he'd had his own place, he still used to have a key to my house and could come and go as he pleased. But Joy had put an end to all of that! After all of those months of sharing my space I finally had my bathroom to myself again. If I wanted to leave my panties hanging on the shower stall and not feel embarrassed by it, I could. If I wanted to piss with the door wide open, I could. And if I wanted to prance around all day ass naked without feeling self-conscious, I could do that too. Constantly seeing wave brushes, doo-rags, and beard trimmers in the bathroom was a thing of the past, because I'd thrown those things out along with the man who'd owned them.

I splashed the cold water on my face and immediately tensed up from the shock of the freezing liquid that dripped from my chin. Many times I'd conducted this routine of waking up in the middle of the night and splashing ice-cold water on my face so I couldn't fall back asleep. Yet, I still hadn't gotten over the instant shock syndrome the freezing water always caused. It didn't matter, as long as it kept me from returning to my nightmare. While staring at my dismal reflection in the mirror I began to ponder over the nightmare that no other soul on this earth knew about. It continued to creep its way into my existence night after night without fail. Several years earlier, something had happened in my life that has been tearing at my conscience ever since.

I had never been what one would call a wild child, but during my senior year of high school I decided to have a little fun before graduation. So, going against my better judgment, I allowed a guy I'd only known for a few days to take me to a motel room. That night we drank liquor heavily and smoked weed that unbeknownst to me was laced with cocaine. I'd never even smoked regular weed before, and this stupid ass nigga had the nerve to lace that shit and thought it was funny!

By the time I'd realized what had happened it was too late. I became paranoid as hell and demanded that he take me home. The guy refused to take me and said he wasn't going to let me leave the room unless I had sex with him. I was no virgin at the time and I'd already had plans to give him some when I had agreed to go along with him to the hotel room. Nevertheless, he'd blown that when he did that stupid shit with the weed. It wasn't going down! He started walking around the room, talking reckless and demanding I give him some pussy. I was scared as hell and I knew I had to get out of that room. I started to regret not telling anybody where I'd be that night, but nobody knew where I was. I was with a lunatic! I'd stood up from the chair where I'd been seated and tried to make it to the door but he grabbed me. He threw me onto one of the twin beds and started choking me while trying to pull off my jeans!

He squeezed so tightly around my throat that I'd begun to lose consciousness. The laced weed had my thought process scrambled beyond imagination but I knew my ass would be in trouble unless I reacted quickly. So, I attempted to reach for my purse, which was lying on the small table beside the bed. On my first attempt, I ended up sending the alarm clock crashing to the floor! My second attempt, I finally managed to reach my purse. I snatched it open with one hand while clawing at this nigga's face with the other. I had flashbacks of my mother's boyfriend Ty and all those times he had molested me. At that very moment in my mind the guy on top of me became Ty!

I frantically retrieved the switchblade from my purse that I'd stolen from my cousin two weeks prior and flicked it open with one quick movement. At this point my attacker was foaming at the mouth like a deranged pit-bull with a dazed, faraway look in his eyes. He never noticed what I'd retrieved until it was too late! Scared almost to the point of going into shock, I jabbed him once....twice....and continued to jab him as if I'd lost control of my own body until I eventually lost consciousness due to him choking me.

When I had finally come to I could barely breathe and my head felt like it was about to burst from lack of oxygen flowing to my brain. At first I couldn't remember where I was or how I'd even gotten there. I lay upon the disheveled bed staring up at the dingy ceiling, trying to adjust my dreary eyes. I reached up and rubbed my watery eyes until the fog in my head cleared, then I noticed some caked up blood on my hands, which startled me!

As I sat up, I noticed more blood on the bedspread and even more spots on the floor leading to the bathroom. All of a sudden, memories of what I had done came crashing down on me like hurricane Katrina.

"OH-MY-GOD! Please, don't let him be dead! Please don't let him be dead," I quietly prayed over and over as I slowly climbed off the bed. I was rubbing my bruised throat. It felt as if I'd swallowed a golf ball. In a daze, I followed the red droplets that led me to the nightmare I've been living with ever since.

I'd found the guy lying on the bathroom floor in a puddle of his own blood with his eyes wide open as if he were staring at something. As I looked down at the bloody body on the floor it didn't take a rocket scientist to figure out that he was dead. I felt my stomach's contents rising in my sore throat as I lunged for the toilet. I called "Earl" until I had nothing left in my system to throw up. I was so dazed and confused that I didn't know what to do. I kept trying to remind myself not to panic but damn, a bitch had just killed someone.

As I knelt over the cold toilet I couldn't control the sudden stream of tears from cascading down my cheeks. I pondered over whether or not to call someone, maybe Justice or even the police. However, I immediately dismissed that idea with thoughts of jail creeping into my mind. I kept saying to myself that it was self-defense and although I had the bruises to prove I'd been attacked I still didn't want to chance someone finding out what I'd done. I knew it was stupid of me not to tell anyone but I was young and scared shitless!

I looked down at that dead body once more and briefly thought about something my father had once said. He'd once said that if a man dies with his eyes opened, he probably deserved it. I wasn't quite sure if this guy had deserved it or not and I definitely hadn't had any intentions of killing him, I'd only wanted him to leave me alone and stop choking me. But he wouldn't stop.

I turned away from the lifeless form, contemplating on what to do. After a long moment of debating I decided to clean myself up and wipe away any traces of me ever being there. I took a towel and wiped down anything I could remember touching since I'd entered the room. I cleaned that room better than any maid could've ever done, and I was exhausted as hell when I was finished.

After being certain I'd gotten rid of all possible prints I grabbed my things, including the murder weapon and fled the vicinity. I was so glad I hadn't told anyone that I would be with him that night. No one had seen me enter or exit the room either. Two days later, the incident had been reported as a senseless homicide with no possible suspects and no motive. However, a sistah was still petrified because I'd watched enough C.S.I. to think that someone would still find out..

I ended up graduating, and to this present day I still have flashbacks of that fateful night whenever I as much as simply *smell* weed. I still haven't told anyone about that dark secret. Not even my best friend in the world, Justice. Although she knows about what my mom did to Ty, I could never bring myself to tell her that I too had taken a life. Justice had always thought I was this naïve little chick who has never done anything wrong except getting busted with those clothes at Neiman Marcus, and making a few bad decisions when it came to men. Only if she and everybody else knew.

Recently, I'd been rather content with my life. I'd finally gotten the energy to kick Travis's no good ass to the wayside and had finally gotten a job in which I could cope with as a real estate agent's assistant. It wasn't much but it paid the bills and kept me clothed. I was gonna miss all that dough Travis used to break a sistah off with, but I'd rather have been broke and happy than a paid fool.

My money situation had been the main reason I had told Justice to hook me up with Monk and D.C. My cup was running dry and I sure could use those few extra dollars on the side. For that reason, I was more than ready to get down for my crown with them. Setting people up to be robbed was not something I was proud of, but it was all in the game and a sistah had a helluva thirst to be quenched!

My life was far from perfect, but then again whose life isn't? I'd gotten totally comfortable in my own skin and was satisfied with myself. Nevertheless, dead bodies continued to haunt a sistah beyond imagination.

In my bathroom, still standing before my mirror, I tried to shake all those thoughts and return to the present. I reached for one of my towels so I could dry the water from my face. After wiping away the freezing water, I opened my medicine cabinet and browsed over all of the different types of sleep aides that occupied the shelves. I opted for the Valium. I popped two of the potent pills followed by a glass of tap water before re-entering my bedroom area. The pills usually allowed me to fall asleep in a dream-free, comatose-like state and I was hoping this night would be no different. The sleep aides kept me from dreaming about anything, especially Ty and the murder that I had committed years earlier.

I crawled into my large bed and wrapped myself up in the satin sheets like a butterfly inside a cocoon. My eyes closed and I let the Vs bring about Zzzs.

CHAPTER SEVEN
CARLOS

You mean to tell me that nigga was at the park Sunday?" I was in disbelief while listening to what Dave was telling me.

"That nosey ass bitch Sabrina who Joe be fuckin' said she saw him and two other niggas on bikes out there but she didn't say who the other two niggas was. I'on' know how you missed that nigga," Dave replied as he counted the last stack of my dough. He wrapped it in a rubber band and placed it inside a duffel bag with the rest.

Dave, Lil' Joe, Ali, and I were sitting in Dave's living room conversing. Ali and I had stopped by to collect the money that Joe and Dave owed me for the fourteen kilos I had fronted them a week earlier. We were in the middle of discussing possible locations for another stash spot when Cross's name had come up. I couldn't believe this nigga had been at the park the same day I'd been there and I'd missed him. God *had* to be watching over that nigga!

Dave placed the duffel bag on the sofa next to me and yelled in the kitchen to Lil' Joe.

"Yo, Joe, call that bitch Brina back and tell her Los wanna holla at her!"

I was thinking that was a good idea because I really wanted to speak with her.

Dave relaxed back in his Lazy Boy and asked me, "How many more of them joints you workin' wit?"

He was inquiring about how many kilos I had remaining. Before I could respond Ali took it upon himself to respond for me.

"We got eight and a half more and that's the last of it." Ali was puffing on an apple-flavored Black & Mild as he spoke. He kicked his feet up on Dave's coffee table and relaxed as if he were at home. He added, "It's gonna be next week when we re-up again."

I just sat back and enjoyed the cool air that was circulating throughout the room and let Ali handle my business. After all, he was the lieutenant and that's what he got paid to do. I was lost in thought about that nigga Cross. I was itching to find out who the other two niggas were who'd been at the park with him. I was willing to bet money that it was them snake ass Lake View niggas. I'd had a run in with some niggas from the Lake View neighborhood a while back and ended up having to check one of them nigga's temperature. So, I just knew it was them niggas.

Joe was speaking on his cell phone when he walked into the living room.

I heard him say, "Tell Sabrina I said holla at me when she get back. Yeah, you know who this is, one." He ended the call and told me that Sabrina wasn't home but he'd be sure to get at me as soon as she returned his call.

We kicked it for a little while longer before I decided it was time to leave because me and Ali had more stops to make and more money to collect.

I arose from the sofa and told Dave and Joe, "I'm 'bout to be out."

I gave them dap. Ali followed suit while grabbing the duffel bag with the money in it.

"Don't forget to holla at a nigga if B get back at you," I told Joe over my shoulder on my way out the door. I was speaking in reference to Sabrina.

As I stepped out onto the front porch I heard the sound of Joe's cell ringing.

I was almost at Ali's Escalade, which was parked in the driveway, when I heard Joe's voice, "Yo Los, hold up!"

I turned to see Joe's large frame almost taking up the entire doorway. He was holding up his phone.

"It's Brina!" he stated.

I strolled back up the walkway and met Joe halfway as he handed me the phone and kept walking past me to holla at Ali. I spoke into his phone, "What it do!"

"Hey, Carlos," Sabrina's voice crooned through the phone.

"What up, ma? You got somethin' to tell me?" I was getting straight to the point.

Sabrina didn't respond so I spoke again, "Hello?"

Silence.

"Brina?"

"Yeah, I'm here." I heard her sigh deeply. Anxiety was evident in her voice when she spoke again. "I told Joe I didn't wanna get involved in this shit."

"What shit? Who was wit' that nigga Cross?" I asked with raised eyebrows. I was anxious to find out who this nigga was hanging out with; because nine times outta ten if they were robbers as well I'd basically found the niggas who had jacked my spot. When Sabrina spoke again her words stung me like a wasp!

Hesitantly, she reported in a hushed voice, "D.C. and Monk."

"D.C. and Monk? Fuck Nah!" I tried to control my anger, but the words just leapt out of my mouth involuntarily. I told Sabrina, "Good lookin'."

I closed the phone, disconnecting the call.

Ali and Joe walked up to me because I was still standing there, looking off into space with a dazed expression on my face. It was as if Sabrina's revelation had stricken a nerve so deeply within my core that I had momentarily become paralyzed with anger. I stood there with my head down and Joe's phone pressed against my forehead.

"What she say?" Ali asked.

I didn't answer him because I knew as soon as I would've repeated what Sabrina had just told me, Ali and Joe would have surely jumped the gun. Carelessness was something I definitely didn't need.

"What that bitch say, my nigga?" Ali repeated himself.

I ignored him and handed Joe back his phone. I simply walked over and climbed into the passenger's side of Ali's truck.

"Let's bounce," I told my lieutenant as he climbed behind the wheel and started the engine. I let my window down and told "David" and "Goliath" I'd be in touch with them as soon as I had gotten some more work. They both stood in the driveway and watched as we pulled off.

Once Ali and I were out of Dave's driveway I let the window back up and reclined my seat. Then I adjusted the two air conditioner vents in front of me so I could cool my head. Ali reached over and turned down the volume of his sound system so that Young Jeezy could play at a decent level. My nigga knew me well enough to know when I didn't feel like talking, so he kept quiet and allowed me to think.

I'd always known that 85 percent of communication is non-verbal and that eye contact and body language speaks volumes. But I never actually understood exactly how much truth was really behind that philosophy until at that very moment, I was sitting in Ali's Escalade staring up at the roof.

I had seen D.C. and Monk at the park and they'd acted as if everything was gucci. I had also peeped the way they'd eyeballed me and my niggas, and how nervous they looked when we had rolled up on them.

Fuckin' body language and eye contact.

I was wondering how in the hell I'd missed Cross. I know all three of them had to have seen us coming, but where the fuck was Cross when we pulled up? And Justice, that grimy bitch! I fucked her trifling ass that same day and she'd acted as if she didn't know anything about that shit.

Mark knew Justice so I knew she wasn't the one who had knocked on the door, but I bet that bitch was in on it! If Monk did it; Justice was down with it too. That's how they got down. I swore on everything I loved that if that bitch had something to do with that shit or even knew anything about Monk doing it, I was gonna make sure her and her snake ass brother had double closed-casket funerals. All at my expense! Then I'd ship their punk ass daddy some flowers to Chicago to show my condolences. They just didn't know—they'd fucked with the right one this time!

While I was lost in thought about Justice and her brother, my cell phone rang. I looked at the caller's number and saw that it was Face.

"Yo, lemme hit you back," I said as soon as I answered the phone. When I ended the call I looked over at Ali and asked, "You know how I always say to watch the crease between a nigga's brows when he talkin' to you?"

I was pointing to the crease between my own eyebrows for emphasis.

I added, "And remember how I always tell you to watch his facial expression when he shakes your hand?"

"Yeah, what of it?" Ali replied while bobbing his head and keeping his eyes on the road.

I told Ali, "Well, Monk and D.C.'s handshakes don't match their smiles." He looked over at me with knowing eyes. I was letting him know that those two niggas were playing the game sideways.

"You *gots* to be kidding," he stated. He looked like he was hoping I was joking.

"Nah, I'm dead serious."

"So that's what Sabrina said, huh?"

"Yeah, but this ain't nothin' but a reality check for a nigga though. I'on' put nothin' past a thirsty ass nigga like Monk anyway. So a nigga should've halfway expected that shit from him. And I'd already told that nigga that if he was to ever try me I'd send his lil' ass to hell."

I sighed deeply as I leaned back against the headrest and listened to the music that was playing just above a whisper. I was thinking about what had to be done.

True enough, this situation was a reality check for a nigga but deep down inside I was halfway hoping that check would bounce. Me and Monk had our minor disputes in the past, but I had stayed off his ass on the strength of his sister. I'd been good to him and Justice for as long as I could remember and this is how they'd chosen to repay me?

Fuck being Mr. Nice Nigga, I thought.

I'd always known that certain muthafuckas had a tendency of mistaking kindness for weakness. But an old head once told me to, "*Pick up a bee out of 'kindness' and learn its limitations. It won't be long before that bitch turns her ass to you and releases that stinger!"*

As I sat back and pondered over this I realized that it was time for a certain clique to get stung.

CHAPTER EIGHT
MONK

Dressed in all black, D.C., Cross, and I were riding down 1-77 in the Chevy Caprice that D.C.'s little cousin had stolen for us. We were headed to Rock Hill, South Carolina, which was only twenty minutes outside of Charlotte. Me and D.C. had finally hooked up with the girls from the park who were driving the BMW. The girls' names were Tandora and To'Wanda. Tandora was the one who had been driving and To'Wanda was the passenger.

D.C. and I had met the girls out on dates twice since that day we'd met them, both times at expensive restaurants. They had never invited us over to their place because I figured they were trying to be discreet about where they lived. But what they failed to realize was the fact that they were dealing with habitual stick-up kids, and it was our *job* to find out things like that!

We'd followed them home on several occasions to try and find out who their men were. But as it turned out, the two women were roommates and didn't even have men. The mini-mansion, the BMW, and even the two matching Range Rovers were *theirs.* These bitches were PAID!

From my observation, I determined that Tan was more than likely the one who was handling most of the business because we'd witnessed two Hispanic-looking dudes whom I presumed to be Dominican also visit the house regularly. They came like clockwork on Tuesday and Friday nights baring briefcases and only staying for brief periods of time. I assumed that they were more than likely picking up, dropping off, or stashing either money or dope.

If the dudes were dropping off or stashing, we knew we could wait for them to leave, then run up in there and rape them chicks for whatever was in the briefcases and whatever was in the house. But if they were picking up, we'd probably be assed out if we waited for them to leave. So, we came to the conclusion that we'd fall up in there on the two girls and wait for the dudes to arrive, and then make them all get naked. It was the only way to guarantee we wouldn't miss anything.

We already knew the girls were at home this Friday night because D.C. had spoken with To'Wanda earlier in the evening and she'd made it clear that they would both be staying in. D.C. had called under the pretense of trying to get them to meet us out somewhere for drinks. If the girls hadn't been home when he called, D.C. had suggested that one of us hide under one of the girls' vehicles until one or both of them arrived. Then we would force them into the house at gunpoint. I looked over at D.C. as he sat on the passenger's side loading the clip to his .45.

I laughed and told him, "Of all the things you ever lost in your lifetime, I *know* yo' mind is what you miss the most." To me, his idea of hiding under the car was ludicrous as hell, but he was dead serious!

"Why my idea gotta be so crazy? I kinda liked it," D.C. stated.

Cross interjected from the back seat, "Man that's some ole *Dead Presidents* type shit. That shit only works in the movies."

"Dig this, I got it all figured out," I stated while keeping my eye on the speedometer because we definitely didn't need to be getting pulled over for speeding.

I didn't have a valid driver's license; we were all dressed in black with black gloves and ski masks, plastic-tie handcuffs, duct tape, and pistols on us. We looked like we were headed into combat. Therefore, getting pulled over surely wouldn't have been a good look.

I told my niggas, "Since them hoes at home, all we gotta do is fall up in there."

"What we doin', a *kick-door*? 'Cause I seen them heavy ass double doors and they don't look like they tryin' to budge," D.C. stated.

I looked over at him and arrogantly conceded, "Nah, we gonna *walk* up in that bitch."

"Oh, so them bitches just gonna open the door and let in three niggas with ski masks on?" Cross asked with sarcasm in his raspy voice.

"Look back," I told D.C. and Cross and watched as they both turned in their seats. "See that car that's been followin' a nigga?"

"Yeah, who is that? I ain't wanna seem paranoid, but I been peeping that car ever since we left West Boulevard. They 'bout to get it."

D.C. was still watching the car as he cocked his pistol, ready to fire.

"Simmer down, nigga, that's my sister and Sapphire. Y'all already know what it is!" I said, smiling.

When we reached the girls' neighborhood, I rode past their house and saw both Range Rovers and the BMW parked in the circular driveway, indicating that they were both home. I drove to the end of their street and made a right at the stop sign. The tree-lined streets were peaceful and the neighborhood was so quiet that it was almost eerie. I pulled over and waved my sister around so that she could pull up next to me. I spoke briefly to Ice just to make sure she and Phire knew their roles. Ice was a vet at that shit but Phire was a rookie and we didn't need any fuck-ups.

After our conversation my sister and I went separate ways. I drove back down Tan's street and parked a few houses away from their's. We jogged back to the house while Justice pulled right up in the driveway in the rental car as if she belonged there. She waited for us to get into position before she and Sapphire exited the car. Once she saw that we were situated they waltzed directly up to the front door as if they were visiting old friends.

I was ducking down behind a large granite statue of Cupid just off the side of the walkway, which led to the steps to the front doors. D.C. was posted up directly across from me, behind an identical statue, while Cross was hiding just beyond the porch where the two large double doors were located. All three of us had put on our ski masks and our pistols were cocked and ready! It was understood that once we gained entry, Cross would do all of the talking because we didn't want to take the risk of the two girls recognizing me and D.C. We also made sure D.C.'s dreads and the tattoo on my neck was concealed because those would have been dead giveaways.

While I waited I was looking around at the dark, elegant neighborhood and wondering how much dough a nigga had to have to live there. This neighborhood reminded me of the Ballentyne neighborhood in Charlotte. The cheapest house in this neighborhood was probably five hundred stacks at the least.

I glanced toward the front door and noticed the attire Phire and Ice were wearing. They were both dressed like they were headed to a party. They had on expensive looking skirts along with stylish heels. I'd told them to dress for the club because after they were finished playing their parts that's exactly where I wanted them to go. They needed to be seen for alibi purposes in case something was to go sour.

Phire rang the doorbell using a handkerchief to avoid leaving prints.

Moments later, the porch light above the double doors came on and I saw To'Wanda glance out of the curtains in one of the front rooms. Ice waved at her from the porch.

"Hey, girl! Where Sissy at? Y'all ain't goin' to the party?"

My sister was acting like she was looking for an old friend.

Seconds later, Tan joined her friend at the window and I saw Phire wave at her and motion toward the front door as if she were telling the girls to come and let them in. I watched as To'Wanda momentarily left the window while Tan stayed there looking out.

Damn, Tan's gonna see Cross! I thought as To'Wanda opened the front door to speak with the two girls on their porch, letting them know that they were at the wrong house. As soon as one of the doors opened Cross made his move!

Pushing my sister and Sapphire aside, Cross forced the door open. This caused To'Wanda to trip and fall backwards inside the foyer. Just as I'd figured, as soon as Tan saw Cross, she fled from the window!

"Damn!" I mumbled under my breath.

D.C. and I both emerged from our hiding places at the same time.

We rushed past Phire and Ice and into the house with pistols drawn!

As soon as I stepped through the door I saw Tan heading for the spiral staircase, running full-speed! I stepped over Cross as he subdued To'Wanda while she kicked and screamed. I chased Tan toward the stairs with my pistol aimed at her. When I finally reached the staircase Tan was halfway up the flight, screaming at the top of her lungs. I knew I had to catch her and shut her ass up before a nosey ass neighbor could hear her. I took the stairs two at a time until I was only a few feet away from her. Tan was moving swiftly and she was now only steps away from the top. I reached out and half-lunged, half- dived and grabbed a fistful of her hair, snatching her head backwards as hard as I could! She screamed as her head snapped rearward, but she didn't stop running. She kept it moving.

"What the fuck!?" I mumbled while looking at the clump of hair in my hand that I'd snatched out of Tan's head. Realizing it was weave, I tossed it to the floor and continued to chase her into one of the bedrooms. When I reached the room she had entered, she was attempting to close the door. I rammed it with all the strength I had and ended up knocking her on her ass inside the large bedroom.

In an instance, I was on top of her like a WWE wrestler, holding her down with my weight. I slapped her twice and raised my index finger to my lips in a gesture of silence. Once it was understood who was in control I reached into my pocket and retrieved the plastic cuffs and duct tape. I taped her mouth, and then commenced to cuff her hands behind her back as if she were under arrest. Just then, D.C. entered the room and gave me a "thumb's up," signaling that there were no further occupants inside the house.

I snatched Tan to her feet and motioned for D.C. to take her back downstairs with Cross and To'Wanda. As he ushered her out I began to search the room, starting with the closet. On my way toward the large walk-in I looked over at the nightstand and saw a chrome .25 automatic pistol lying next to the alarm clock.

"Oh snap! That bitch was tryin' to get to her ratchet," I said aloud as I walked over and picked up the small handgun.

I held the tiny pistol in my palm and admired the custom-made pearl handle. I laughed at the idea of Tan wanting to shoot me with that little ass shit. I was still laughing as I placed the burner in my back pocket and stepped inside the spacious closet. I looked about in amazement and was shocked at how much it looked like a mini-boutique inside. These girls had minks, expensive dresses with the tags still attached, and racks upon racks of shoes that were still in boxes like they'd never been worn. Looking at all of that expensive shit had me regretting the fact that we hadn't brought a fucking U-Haul truck with us! Nevertheless, I knew my sister and Phire would enjoy the free shopping spree.

While searching the closet I noticed a small storage chest situated in the corner behind a few hanging dresses. My first thought was *safe;* so I walked over and bent down to open it. As soon as I lifted the lid my eyes were treated with a surprise.

"Well I'd be damned," I said to myself with a broad grin spread across my face. Just one look and I knew I'd just opened *Pandora's Box!* Inside the chest were tons of sex toys. Most of which were strap-on dildos and vibrators of all sizes. There were costumes, whips, hand-cuffs, anal beads, lubrication gels; you name it these bitches had it.

"These bad ass bitches is dykin'," I laughed aloud at the revelation of Tandora and To'Wanda being bisexual.

Then the more I thought about it the more things were beginning to add up and make sense. These girls were doing their thing and getting *paid,* so I guessed they felt like they didn't need a man for anything. However, at that very moment while they were being bound and gagged I was willing to bet anything that they were both wishing they had a man in the house to try and protect them from niggas like me.

I closed the freak box and continued to search the closet, then on to the rest of the bedroom. After coming up empty, I exited the room and headed downstairs to join the rest of my team. I wanted to inform Justice and Sapphire about all of the free gear and shoes Tan and To'Wanda had just donated to them.

On my way down the hall I heard a non-descript sound coming from behind one of the closed doors on my right, just beyond the large bathroom I had just passed.

I thought Cross and D.C. already searched these rooms up here, I thought.

I crept closer to the door with my pistol aimed and ready to squeeze! When I reached the door I stood off to the side and listened for a minute. Slight shuffling could be heard beyond the door and at that instance my adrenaline began pumping like crazy. I reached out and tried the knob to see if it was unlocked, and to my surprise it was!

Hesitantly, I slowly twisted the knob. As soon as the door was ajar I quickly pushed it open and had no idea of what I'd meet with on the other side.

"OOH SHITT!" I gasped as one of the biggest pit bulls I'd ever laid eyes on rushed out!

The beast was foaming at the mouth with bared teeth and lunged directly for me as if he was about to have supper. I threw my arm up in a gesture of defense as I stumbled back against the wall just before I let off two quick shots, striking the dog in its head. It was dead instantly!

Moments later, I was stepping over the lifeless K-9 and was met with Cross as soon as I reached the top of the staircase. I was sweating beneath the mask and my adrenaline was still pumping!

"What the..." Cross started. He looked past me and saw the bloody dog. He let out a deep sigh when he realized that the gunfire hadn't been anything serious. "Oh, yeah, I forgot to tell you. It's a dog in that room."

He was laughing and pointing at the room where the dog had emerged from.

"Fine time to tell a nigga." I just shook my head. I breathed a sigh of relief and whispered, "Where my sister at?"

"They bounced already," he answered while still looking at the bloody dog.

After I gathered my composure we both headed back downstairs to where D.C. was watching over the two girls. Tan and To'Wanda both lay on the floor sobbing behind the duct tape. I nodded at Cross, letting him know it was time to handle business. Without hesitation, he started with the demands.

"Where the money at? As soon as we get it, we'll be out and leave y'all alone." He raised his pistol and pointed it in the girls' direction and added, "Make no mistake about it, if y'all wanna play hard and make a nigga have'ta look for that shit we torturing both you bitches! Give it to us or give that shit to God. It's your choice!"

I looked over at him from where I was standing and I saw him look up at me. He was getting a kick out of using my line.

I bent down and peeled the tape off of Tan's mouth and noticed my handprints on her face from where I'd slapped her.

As soon as the tape was removed she sobbed while confessing, "It's out back in the tool shed in the wooden chest next to the tool locker. The key is in the kitchen in the top drawer next to the dishwasher."

I saw To'Wanda look over at Tan as if she was mad because she had given up the location of the stash. Tan was looking at To'Wanda with tears streaming down her cheeks.

"I'm so sorry. I just didn't wanna see them hurt you," she cried with trembling lips.

I put the tape back on Tan's mouth as Cross entered the kitchen and went straight to the key. He came back and showed the key to Tan and she nodded, confirming that he had the correct key. These girls had actually thought we were going to leave once we cleaned out the stash, but little did they know, we were waiting for the "big fish" to arrive. We were waiting for the two Hispanic dudes with the briefcase!

Cross went back through the kitchen and exited the back door. He was headed for the tool shed, which was approximately fifty feet or so away from the house. I walked over and looked through the kitchen window and saw him open the door to the shed. As soon as he was inside I heard a series of beeps coming from what seemed to be twenty different locations within the house. I rushed back into the living room area where D.C. and the girls were and saw that D.C.'s eyes were as big as saucers. He was frantically looking around and trying to pinpoint the location of the beeps as well. Seconds after the beeps had started, reality dawned on me all at once. These sly ass bitches had set us up. The beeps were coming from an alarm!

I dashed through the kitchen and out the back door to get Cross. I had to let him know that we had to abort our mission. When I reached the tool shed I saw Cross hastily throwing empty boxes out of his way as he continued to search for the never-existing "treasure chest."

I told him, "My nigga, we gotta bounce! You tripped an alarm!"

"That stankin' ass bitch lied! Ain't no money out here! She thank a nigga playin' wit' her ass!? I'ma torture this hoe for real for tryin' me like that!" Cross had venom in his voice.

He was still looking for the chest and acted as if he hadn't heard a word I'd just said. When he was satisfied that there was no stash he exited the shed and was headed back toward the house. D.C. was coming out the back door.

"Yo! You heard what I just said? A muthafuckin' alarm is goin' off, nigga! Fuck dem bitches! We gotta go!" I grabbed Cross's arm as he attempted to re-enter the house with fire in his eyes. I managed to pull him away from the door and gave him a shove, which started his stride as we all fled from the large house.

When we made it back to the car we peeled out and made it out of the neighborhood unnoticed. We drove back to Charlotte feeling like damn fools because we knew we'd just fucked up what should've been a sweet lick. I was behind the wheel once again as Cross rode shotgun D.C. sat in the back. They were both heated!

As I drove, I was having mixed emotions about what had just happened. I was angry as hell because we hadn't come out of the house with anything but a fuckin' .25 automatic. But at the same time, I had a little admiration for how much heart Tandora and To'Wanda had displayed. We had underestimated those bitches and in return, they had caught us sleeping!

It was unbeknownst to me to what extreme anybody else would go to in order to uphold their respect; nevertheless, I could vouch for the fact that those two girls were indeed willing to die for *theirs*.

I had to love that. If one of my niggas would've looked closely enough at me while I was lost in thought about Tan and To'Wanda, they would have seen a slight smile spread across my lips.

CHAPTER NINE
JUSTICE

"Hey stranger. Know who this is?" I was speaking into my Bluetooth.

"How can I forget the voice? I was starting to think you wasn't gonna get at me. How's my Chyna doll doin?" J.T.'s voice was even sexier over the phone than I remembered it being in person.

Since that night I had met J.T. at Nine Three Five I had wanted to contact him, but I didn't want to look too desperate or make it seem as if a sistah was too interested. So I waited a while before calling.

Sapphire and I were at my place relaxing and making plans for the weekend when I'd decided to give J.T. a call. Sapphire was milling about in my kitchen while I sat on the sofa sipping on an apple martini, enjoying a nice little buzz. It had been a couple of days since my brother and his crew had fucked up the robbery in Rock Hill; and Sapphire was still a little tight because it had been her first time on a jux and she didn't get compensated for her services. We were both regretting the fact that we hadn't stayed around long enough to clean out those chicks' closet. When Monk had told me about all of that gear we'd missed out on I wanted to kick myself in the ass! However, unlike Sapphire, I wasn't that pressed because I already knew *anything* was liable to happen in this game. Just like any other game, you were bound to take a loss every once in a while.

"You tryna see me?" J.T. asked.

I thought back to the night we'd met and I was remembering how smooth and sexy his Tyson Beckford looking ass was. How could a sistah *not* want to see all of that again? Besides, how else would I be able to get into them pockets if I wasn't going to get with him?

"We can make that happen," I stated, using my sexiest voice. "What you gettin' into tonight?"

"Hopefully *you*. And I meant that in a good way," he responded, sure of himself.

Unconsciously, my body began tingling at the mere thought of J.T. fucking my brains out, but I played it cool and chose my words carefully.

"Okay, I can see that happening. We can get into *each other* over a couple of drinks out somewhere."

I was letting him know that I was only referring to conversation. Seriously though, I already knew that sooner or later all of that chit-chatting would eventually come to an end. Then more than likely we'd end up somewhere messing somebody's sheets up. However, I'd told myself that I wouldn't get attached to this nigga and I wasn't going to let my desire for a climax hinder my quest for cash. So, I'd made up my mind to just tease him, please him and let Monk *squeeze* him.

J.T. said, "That's a bet. Just let me know when and where."

Just then, Sapphire entered the living room carrying a daiquiri she'd mixed up. She saw me smiling and glowing like a schoolgirl while twirling the ice in my glass with my index finger. She sat on the love seat in front of me and looked at me with inquisitive eyes before silently mouthing, "Who is that?"

I sucked the liquor off my finger, then raised it and spelled the letters J.T. in the air. I saw her eyes light up and I knew exactly what she was thinking. She wanted me to hook her up with the guy who'd been driving the Hummer the night I met J.T. I sighed and whispered to her, "Chill. I got choo."

Damn, I hated match making!

"J.T., my girl wanna know if you got any friends?" I reluctantly asked.

"Nah, but I got plenty enemies. Why?" J.T. laughed because he knew what I was getting at.

"Where your boy at? The one who was with you that night we met?"

"Oh, so you told her he was fine or somethin', huh?" he teased.

"No, I told her *you* were fine and that I didn't get to see him." I lied.

"That was my cousin. Matter of fact, he sittin' right here."

I heard his cousin ask who wanted to know who he was. Just then, my other line beeped. I looked down at my phone and saw Carlos's number.

Not today, I thought.

I'd made up my mind to stop messing with Carlos because nothing prosperous was coming out of sexing him but a good nut. I was tired of hustlin' backwards and I knew as long as I continued to see him I'd never be able to get over him. So, I ignored his call and continued to kick it with J.T.

J.T. asked, "So, what we doin'? Double-datin'?" He had a hint of sarcasm in his voice. I could tell the idea wasn't setting too well with him and I must admit double dating wasn't what I had in mind either.

I made it seem as if he'd suggested the idea of the double date. "Yeah, that's a good idea!"

"Nah, I was just say—"

"You were just saying it was a good suggestion also, right?" I looked at Sapphire and spoke so that he could hear me. "J.T.'s cousin wanna meet you."

I heard J.T. sigh into the phone with a hint of frustration.

I told him, "I know the perfect spot." I paused and waited for any objections. When he didn't object I continued, "You know where Skylar's café is?"

"You talkin' about that boring ass jazz club or whatever it's supposed to be?" He sounded slightly disappointed because I hadn't suggested somewhere else.

"It's a *spoken word* café, and that's where me and my girl will be tonight. If I see you, I see you. If not, I guess we'll have'ta connect some other time." I was being blunt but I definitely didn't want to run this nigga off.

J.T. thought about it for a minute, and then gave in.

"Aiight. We'll be there. What time?"

I told him that Sapphire and I would be there at eleven and would be staying until closing. He assured me that they would be there, and we ended our conversation. My plan was already coming together.

Sapphire left my condo soon after my conversation with J.T. ended so she could go and get dressed. We decided to meet at Skylar's at ten so that we could get good seats before they got crowded. Both Sapphire and I enjoyed hearing spoken word artists do their thing on stage. Seeing it on television on shows like *Lyric Cafe* and other poetry shows was nothing like being there in the same room with the artists, feeding off their energy.

It was a little past six when Sapphire had left, so I sat around and wasted a little time by playing around on the internet before getting dressed. I went to Amazon.com and ordered a few books I'd heard were "must reads." I ordered *Ghetto Resumè, Trust No Man,* and a new joint *Thug Lovin'.* Those were just a few to add to my ever-growing collection. At nine-thirty I left my condo and headed downtown towards Skylar's to meet my girl.

Located on South Tryon Street near the downtown area, Skylar's was one of Charlotte's oldest jazz clubs that had been renovated in the early 2000s and transformed into a poetry café. Wednesday nights, amateurs took the stage and did their thing. On Saturday and Sunday nights the more seasoned vets along with a few celebrity artists made appearances. The club was built like an antique theatre with tables posted all around the stage so that everyone could get a clear view of the performer. There were also a few booths just in case someone wanted a more intimate setting. This Saturday night the club was packed to capacity. When I pulled up to the entrance valet took the keys to my Chrysler and I entered the dim café to look for Sapphire. I was hoping she was already seated at a table.

As soon as I passed the hostess' station I saw Sapphire seated in a corner booth sipping on a tall, fruity-looking concoction. She looked like a chocolate Barbie doll. I could tell she was trying to make an impression because she was displaying mucho cleavage in a banging ass dress that I'd never seen her wear before. She spotted me and waved me over.

"'Sup bitch?" I spoke as we shared a sisterly embrace. "Daaamn, I see you are in rare form tonite. Lemme find out," I teased. I was referring to the new dress.

"Oh, you mean this old thing?" Sapphire mimicked a white woman as she struck a Tyra Banks pose.

"Yeah, *that* old thing. Gurl, yo' ass is tryna catch. Just don't forget that this shit is only business." I looked at the expression on her face. "Lemme find out you really lookin' for love." I laughed as I slid into the booth opposite her and waved for the waitress.

Once the waitress appeared, I ordered an apple martini and got ready to enjoy a little of the show before J.T. would arrive. It was just after ten so we had almost an hour to kill. We drank and listened to several poets do their thing onstage while we waited. A few of the poets were mediocre and one of them, Sean Ingram from Raleigh, North Carolina, was good. But when my favorite poet, Shakim, graced the stage, I was all ears because he always sent me home with something to think about.

Shakim had been my favorite poet for over a year because he always spoke about conscious topics, and things you could relate to. He was a pecan-tan brother with neat, shoulder length salt and pepper dreadlocks that accented his handsome, hairless face. By his youthful appearance and gorgeous physique one would never guess him to be in his mid-forties. The only thing that gave a hint at his age was the specks of silver that streaked his dreads.

The cafe was dim and cozy with only the smooth sounds of the live jazz band playing in the background when Shakim graced the stage and took the mike.

He looked out over the crowd and smiled his signature smile before asking, "Ladies, how much do you know about men?" He paused, then asked, "And my men, how much do you know about yourselves?"

Shakim grabbed the microphone stand and walked slowly to the back of the stage and put the stand out of sight so that he would have room to maneuver.

"This piece is titled 'Men,'" Shakim stated, then commenced to do his thing.

"*Men*...we are perceived to be a complex species, but in all actuality, we are fairly simple creatures with a very simple mission. Although we spent nine excruciating months trying to escape the womb, we end up wasting the rest of our lives attempting to get back in."

I heard a few closed-minded men whistle and nod in agreement as Shakim continued to pace the stage and make hand gestures, emphasizing his point.

"We intend to accomplish our mission by *any* means necessary. We even spit enough game to maim the lame and we prey on weak-ass minds. Women find...it hard to resist us, though they try to no avail. Egos swell—pride resides and we sometimes experience a chemical imbalance that hinders our thought process when it comes to trying to be monogamous. We cheat and they flee. Then we chase with haste, without realizing it's *their* time we waste!"

At this point I heard my sistahs agreeing and shouting "Amens."

I raised my drink as if to salute him and commented, "You go, wit' yo' bad self!"

He continued, "If we knew how to treat them, maybe we could keep them. But we don't, so we won't. We tend to use, abuse, and disilluse them while regarding them as mere puppets on a string. Realizing all too late that out of all things God ever created, the *woman* is the most precious and the most beautiful thing! Instead of encouraging our Queens to succeed, we'd rather encourage them to bend their knees and *suck seed*."

Shakim paused to allow his last verse to sink into the minds of the crowd. I was yearning to hear more because the resonance of his smooth voice along with his conscious words had me feeling like he was making love to my mind.

"*Men*...a strange breed we are! The undisputed champion in the battle of the sexes. At least that's what our guess is. We love to make love, but we hate to truly love! We make up excuses and alibis to avoid long-term closeness. Yet, we want our women to be devoted. We even overprotect and outright overshadow our women with possessiveness and mind-blowing, controlling behavior. Why?"

He looked out over the hushed crowd, and then continued without waiting for a response because he knew no one in the audience could answer his question.

"I'll tell you why! Because it is our primal instinct to assume we own whom we bed. A way of thinking that's *so* sad! But this assumption was derived from our caveman ancestors whom led us to believe women enjoy being clubbed over the dome and enjoys getting drug home. We even practice the *club* and *drag* technique to this very day, only in a more modern way.

"Instead of utilizing the club, we beat our women over the head with manipulative, deceitful, misleading nouns and verbs. Phrases so slick, women forget that they're merely just words. We still drag them also, though maybe not always in a physical way. We break them down *emotionally*, tear by tear, day after day!"

When Shakim spit this verse, me and every woman in the crowd was moved by those words. He was verbalizing what we'd been silently thinking for years.

"*Men*...Women can't live with us and they definitely can't live without us. They doubt us; they love us, and they hate us all in the same breath. Giving so much of themselves 'til there's nothing left!"

Shakim stopped pacing the stage and stood in one spot for the first time since he'd taken the mike.

He continued, "I know us Y and X chromosomes must share this universe, so we should try to meet one another halfway. But which one is going to be first? Which one of us is gonna take that first giant step towards this thing we call *trust*? Hell, knowing me and my species and how stubborn we are, I'm more than certain it won't be *us*. Why? Simple...'cause we're men!"

The crowd erupted in cheers and applause as Shakim replaced the mike stand and gave the host a brotherly hug while bumping shoulders before gracefully exiting.

I was thinking, *Any man who is that in touch with his inner-self has gotta be a bad mutha!*

"Damn, that was deep. That shit was *so* true," Sapphire commented while looking around at the faces of the men throughout the room and noticing a few grim expressions. "He called these niggas right out and they don't know how to take that shit," she giggled.

I looked around and noticed the confused expressions also.

"That's right. It's 'bout time somebody checked their asses," I replied as I felt a hand touch my shoulder. I saw Sapphire looking over my shoulder smiling. I turned to see J.T. standing there smiling that same sexy ass smile that had made me lose focus that night at Nine Three Five.

"Hey stranger," his voice boomed.

I slid out the booth and gave him a hug as his muscular arms encircled my waist. I must have held him a little too long because I heard the sound of someone clearing their throat and it dawned on me that we were not alone.

"Oh, damn, I'm sorry, J.T. This is my girl, Sapphire. Sapphire, J.T."

I made introductions and watched as they casually shook hands then J.T. introduced his cousin.

"This is Red," he said while keeping one hand on my waist. I noticed that J.T. was now wearing the jewelry that Red had been wearing the night we'd met. I thought of how corny it was for them to be sharing jewelry like that.

After introductions were made we all slid into the booth. J.T. and I were side by side and Sapphire and Red were opposite us. One look at the gleam in my girl's eye is all it took for me to know that she was digging this dude. I had even given her the raised eyebrow gesture, letting her know to tread lightly because I knew how easy it was for her to get caught out there. And the fact that this dude was cute wasn't doing anything but making matters worse. Red was light brown skinned, muscular built with hazel eyes and short, wavy hair. This guy was Sapphire's type all the way around!

We all ordered drinks and engaged in small talk while getting to know one another as the poets continued to do their thing. Soon the conversation turned to Shakim and what he'd spoken on. J.T. and Red had caught most of what Shakim had recited when they had first entered the café so they were a little up to speed with the topic.

"So, you believe all men are like that?" J.T. asked me.

His lashes were so thick I wanted to reach out and touch them. But I didn't want to seem too forward.

"I believe all men got a lot of what he was saying in them," I said, staring into J.T.'s eyes.

"I feel like if a woman stands behind her man for support and respect him then it shouldn't be no problems," Red interjected from across the booth.

I looked at him. "Yeah, a man *would* say somethin' bogus like that. But I think a woman should stand *beside* her man to be supportive, not *behind* him." I looked at Red and rolled my eyes, then continued, "'Cause if she's *behind* him he might end up blocking her vision."

Only a few minutes into the date and Red and I were already bumping heads. I saw Red look at me with a "Whatever bitch" scowl and it set me off!

"Niggas kill me with that ole 1922 mentality, thinking women don't even have the right to make a decision!"

Damn all that! I thought. *Anyone who knows Justice knows I'm a very opinionated woman and I don't give a damn who don't like it. I say what I mean and mean what I say. Because those who matter don't mind and those who mind, don't matter!*

J.T. must have sensed my frustration because he changed the subject, tuning out his cousin and Sapphire. He wanted me to tell him a little about myself, so I told him what little I wanted him to know. He seemed satisfied with it and didn't press the issue. I also found out a little about him.

His real name was Joaquin Turner, and I joked him about it because that was also my uncle's name. He told me that he was originally from D.C., but had been living in Charlotte for a few years. He also said that he was the owner of an import/export service and a trucking business.

I also found out that the jewelry and Hummer belonged to *him,* and not his cousin like I had assumed. This man had it goin' on. Fine as hell *and* paid! I was thinking that maybe I'd have a little fun with him before I released my goons on him. Because I just had to have me some of that dick!

After getting to know one another a little better over drinks, we all decided to head to Skyland's restaurant on South Boulevard for a late night bite to eat. Sapphire and I both drove, so she decided that she would park her car at her aunt's house. J.T. and Red followed us in the Hummer as we made the small trek from Skylar's café to the Wilmore neighborhood where Joy's mother's house was located. The drive only took a few short minutes because the neighborhood was only blocks from the café. Soon after leaving the café we were pulling into Sapphire's aunt's driveway. While Sapphire was parking her car I saw Joy peep her head out the front door being nosey. After securing her car, Sapphire flipped Joy the bird before hopping into the Chrysler with me.

Sapphire huffed as soon as she shut the door. "You see that nosey bitch?"

"Yeah, I saw her tired ass," I replied while pulling out of the driveway and backing out into the street.

During the ride we discussed our plans for the remainder of the night. I already knew if J.T. suggested that we go somewhere to be alone a sistah was *out!* It was understood that Sapphire would have to take my car if it came to that point.

Sure enough, J.T. asked the magical question as soon as we'd finished eating. We were in the restaurant's parking lot standing beside his truck, hugged up like school kids. He had kissed me slow and deep with those sexy ass lips and had my kitty leaking juices in anticipation.

He whispered in my ear, "You tryna stay wit' me tonite?"

His impressive erection was pressing into my mid-section due to the height difference. I ran my hand across his stomach and discreetly let it brush against his hard dick before dropping my hands to my side. With pursed lips and squinting eyes gazing out at the sparse traffic on the road, I was faking like I was giving his invitation some thought. My mind was made up hours ago. I was wondering what had taken him so long to ask.

I gently pushed him away while smiling my sexiest smile, letting him know my answer without verbally speaking it.

"Let me holla at my girl for a minute," I said in a soft tone.

I walked over to my car where Sapphire and Red were standing. They were engaged in conversation and I could tell Sapphire was all into him by the way she kept smiling and twirling her hair between her fingers like an awestruck teen. I approached them and told Red to excuse us for a minute as I steered Sapphire back towards the restaurant. On the way back inside I yelled over to J.T. that I'd be right back, I was going to use the restroom.

Once inside the restroom I began to lay out the game plan.

"Look, you gotta take my car," I handed her the keys. "I'll be by to get it in the morning. You good wit' that?"

"You ain't gettin' ready to call Monk an' nem is you?" Sapphire asked while dropping my keys into her purse.

"Nah, but I need to find out where this nigga lives. But first, I think I'ma milk this cow for all it's worth. Starting with that dick!"

I walked over to the mirror and checked to make sure I was still flawless before teasing my hair and reapplying the lip-gloss that J.T. had licked from my lips.

I asked her "What's up wit' you and ole boy?"

"He cool as hell. I like 'em," Sapphire replied

I looked at her in the mirror with a stern expression and stated, "Aiight now, you know this is only bizness. Don't mess around and get caught out there."

"Caught out there? You the one actin' like you an' that nigga finna tie the knot," Sapphire replied. As I moved aside, she took my place in the mirror.

I laughed at her remark.

"That just goes to show how good of an actress I am. Got yo' ass fooled already, huh?"

I opened my handbag to make sure my "baby" was still there. I closed it back and smiled wickedly at Sapphire.

"You know I'm 'bout to get my freak on, right?"

She laughed at me.

As an afterthought, I grinned and added, "Giiirl that nigga's dick is *huge*. You hear me?"

I was opening the door to exit the restroom when I made that comment.

Sapphire laughed again. "Bitch you is crazy!" She was still in the mirror playing in her hair, making sure her do was still tight.

Moments later, I was climbing into J.T.'s truck. Unsurprisingly, Red was getting into the passenger's side of my car with Sapphire. I was hoping that she was really aware of the fact that she was indeed playing a role because I knew how naïve she could be when it came to cute niggas.

Once I was in J.T.'s truck, I purposely sat so that my short skirt would rise high up on my thighs. As predicted, J.T. could keep neither his eyes nor his hands off of my thick legs. During the ride to his house he would momentarily reach over and caress my thighs while licking his lips as if he could already taste my silky skin. I smiled inwardly as he sat there obviously lusting for me and fantasizing about what he was going to do to me once he got me to his place. Little did J.T. know, I probably wanted him more than he wanted me. I was in so much heat. My pussy was bubbling as I anticipated the feeling of all of that dick sliding up in me from every angle. But I played it cool as I sat back and tried to focus on the television screen that was hanging from the visor in front of me.

As if my shit wasn't already wet enough, the old school movie *Love Jones* was playing and Nia Long was in the middle of getting long stroked by fine ass Lorenz Tate. I had to squeeze my thighs together to try to soothe the sudden throbbing sensation I was experiencing. I was so ready to slide over there and wrap my lips, both sets, around J.T.'s dick, but I didn't want to cause an accident so I stayed grounded.

I looked over at his fine ass and felt my clit jump.

"This big ass truck can't go no faster?" I whined.

He smiled, knowing my reason for asking, and then he put the pedal to the metal, because I knew the anticipation was killing him as well!

CHAPTER TEN
SAPPHIRE

Ssssssss…yeah, baby! That's it! Right there!" I was cooing with clenched eyes.

I was thinking, *Damn, I wish I could wake up like this every morning.*

With both hands I reached down and grabbed the head that was between my thighs licking me with expertise.

The previous night had been crazy as hell. Me and Justice had met J.T. and his cousin Red at Skylar's and we ended up separating at the Skyland restaurant. Justice had left with J.T. and Red had ended up riding with me. I had taken him by his place and decided not to join him inside. Instead, we talked for a few minutes, exchanged numbers and kisses before I'd left to head home. On my way home I'd gotten a call on my cell from a familiar voice asking if he could come over. I was already a tad bit horny from Red's kisses and caresses, so I told the caller to come on over.

I knew my girl would give me the third degree if she knew I had *this* guy lying up in my bed, so I chose to keep it a secret from her. I just couldn't help myself because his dick-game was on point and his head-game was off the meter!

He was in the process of feasting on my pussy like it was his last meal. I pulled my knees toward my chest like I was about to cannonball off a diving board, allowing him better access to the kitty as he licked me slow and deep. When I felt that tingling sensation in my toes and those tiny contractions in the pit of my stomach, my legs started involuntarily kicking like I was pedaling a bike. He had me climaxing.

"Oh, my, God…oh, my, God…oh, shit…mmmph…oh, sh…" I

screamed.

I had to let my legs go in attempt to escape the assault his tongue was making on my clit. He had sucked my nub until it was at the point of sensitivity to where I couldn't take it any longer.

He tried to continue to eat me but I had to push his head away. After finally getting the hint he slid his body up mine and kissed me, letting me taste myself on his lips. He then used his knees to nudge my legs apart and aimed his stiff dick at my opening. I felt the tip of his penis easing into my slippery hole, which was already soaking wet from his oral ministrations. This nigga felt so good penetrating me. There's nothing in the world like the feeling of that initial penetration that stretches your walls upon that first thrust.

When he had only half of his length inside me I gasped at the sudden feeling of fullness. His thick dick felt delicious, but I had to stop him and make him strap up because he was up in me *raw dog*. I placed my hand on his stomach and gently pushed him back as I scooted my hips backwards away from him until we became disconnected.

I told him, "You know it ain't even goin' down like that."

I was pointing at his enormous, unprotected dick, which was glistening with my juices. It was throbbing and looking so powerful with those thick veins protruding from the shaft.

I heard him release a frustrating sigh as he crawled off of me and reached for his Coogi shorts to retrieve a Magnum. I smiled as I watched him roll the XL over his rigid penis. Just the thought of him being seconds away from penetrating my shit again had me throbbing. I just loved big dicks, and this guy was hung like Mr. Ed!

As he neared me again, I rolled over onto my stomach and tooted my ass into the air, inviting him to hit it from the back. There was just something animalistic about getting fucked from behind that drove me wild. What really got me off was the act of having my ass slapped and my hair pulled, and every once in awhile being grabbed around my throat and choked a little was a turn on. That painful pleasure always triggered multiple orgasms deep within my core.

He pulled me by my waist, urging me to rise up on my hands and knees, doggie-style. I complied and felt him spread my ass cheeks and then he guided himself back into my wetness again. He knew this time I wouldn't make him stop.

"Ummm, shit, fuck me!" I demanded as I felt him plunge into me with such force it seemed as if I could feel him in my throat! "Oh. My. God! Oh. Yeah!" I screamed.

He grabbed a fistful of my hair and tugged with just the right amount of force to send a shiver down my spine. At this point he already had me gone, but when he started slapping my ass as he thrust deep into me I lost it! I thrust my ass backwards, matching him stroke for glorious stroke while gripping my sheets in balled up fists. I was holding on for dear life. My screams and the sound of his palm spanking my ass, coupled with the sound of our sweaty thighs slapping together was echoing off my bedroom walls.

He fucked me until we were both breathless and I would've sworn on a stack of bibles that I came at least six times during that episode. When he was about to come he pulled out, snatched off the latex, and ejaculated all over my back and ass. The feeling of his hot cum running down between my ass cheeks made my clit pulsate. I fell flat onto my stomach with exhaustion. I was purely satiated as I basked in the after-glow of so many mind-blowing orgasms. He slapped my ass once more for good measure, causing me to smile as he climbed out of bed and headed towards my bathroom to take a shower. I turned to watch him walk away and silently reflected on how this man and I had ended up screwing like we were a couple.

It had happened a few days after Justice and I had been at Nine Three Five, the night of the Embassy Suites robbery. I'd bumped into him at a gas station the following Sunday evening on Beatties Ford Road while I was on my way to Hornet's Nest Park. He'd just left from the park and was on his way to South Park to the Cheesecake Factory to eat. He was gassing up his motorcycle and had asked if I wanted to join him for dinner. I accepted his offer only because I was hungry as hell and the Cheesecake Factory was my favorite spot. Besides, I'd never been the one to turn down a free meal so I followed him to the restaurant.

We talked over dinner and I found myself becoming intrigued by how smart he was. He was very knowledgeable in certain areas some men twice his age wouldn't have the slightest clue about. I also took a good look at him and noticed for the first time how handsome he was. He had me looking at him and wondering, *What if...*

We exchanged numbers and he called me the next day to invite me out for drinks, and once again, I accepted. This time we ended up back at my place, in my bed having some of the wildest off-the-wall sex I'd ever experienced! He had put that *beast* head on a bitch and turned me out that night. Needless to say, he had a bitch fiending for his ass ever since.

I snapped out of my daze when I heard, "Ay, Phire, you comin' to wash a nigga's back or what?"

His sexy ass voice was echoing from my bathroom as I heard him turn the water on in the shower.

I yelled back, "You wore a bitch out! I'on' think I can walk right now!" I was smiling and I knew he was smiling also at the thought of having just blown my back out!

Just then my phone rang and I let it go to voicemail, thinking that I'd just return the call later. Then I thought it might have been Justice because I had her car, so I reached for the phone but it had stopped ringing. I picked it up to check the message, hoping it wasn't her saying that she was on her way to get the Chrysler because I definitely didn't want her to see *him*! I punched in my code and waited for the message to kick in.

I was surprised to hear my Cousin Joy's voice say, "Sapphire, this is Joy. I know we ain't getting along right now, but we still blood and I just wanna let you know about them niggas you and Justice was with last night. I know them niggas. Red and J.T. is snakes! Girl, just be careful around them niggas."

"Fuck you, stop hatin'!" I spoke into my phone as if Joy could hear me.

I erased the message and closed my phone before climbing out of bed to go join this sexy ass nigga in my shower for round two. I donned my shower cap to keep my hair from getting wet and entered my bathroom with a wicked grin glued to my face. He was in the shower trying to sing and I thought his off key crooning was so cute. I pulled back the shower curtain and just stared for a second at his amazing body before stepping in with him. There was no conversation.

Moments after stepping in with him I was on my knees trying my best to deep-throat what seemed like thirteen inches of dick without gagging. My eyes watered every time the head of his throbbing penis tapped my tonsils, but I held on and took him for a ride. Oral love was all he was getting this round because no matter how bad I wanted it, I surmised if there was no glove, there would be no love.

I made him come again, this time on my tongue and all around my mouth with a little dripping from my chin as I looked up at him smiling. The look in his eyes told me that he loved that nasty shit.

He finally got a chance to finish bathing and then he exited the shower while I stayed in and let the steamy water from the spraying showerhead caress my skin. My pussy was throbbing and kind of sore, but that *good* kind of sore that let's you know you've really been fucked! I opted to take a bath so that I could soak for a minute.

When I had finished bathing and finally exited the bathroom I re-entered my bedroom and heard him on the phone with a cab company, giving them my address. He was almost fully dressed as I strode past the bed where he was seated. He was tying up his brand new Prada tennis shoes. I grabbed my robe from the lounge chair and tied it at the waist before opening my walk-in closet.

"Why you call a cab? You know I'll take you wherever you need to go," I commented from the closet.

"Nah, I'm cool. I gotta take care of some binness. You know how it is," he replied while clicking on my television with the remote.

"Oh, okay I was just offering."

"I know. That's good lookin', but I'm straight," he replied while walking over to where I was at.

I was still standing in my closet searching for something to wear for the day. He walked up behind me and put his arms around my waist.

He asked, "When I'm gonna see you again?"

"You know the routine, just call me," I cooed as I put my hands atop his and slowly rocked in his arms to the beat of Beyonce's video as it blasted from the tube. We stayed like that, with him holding me in his arms for a minute.

I smiled and whispered over my shoulder, "Don't start nothin' you can't finish," because my body had begun to tingle again from the mere feel of his arms around me.

He playfully swatted me on the ass as he laughed and let me go.

"You got that. I wish I did have time for round three, but you know how it is when the streets call. A nigga gotta answer."

He walked back towards my bed to take a seat. As soon as he sat down we heard the sound of a horn blowing in front of my house.

"Damn, that was fast."

He went to peep out the window to see if it was the taxi that was blowing.

"Yo, that's my ride. You can damn sho' tell this ain't the projects, fast as his ass showed up."

We both laughed.

"I'ma hit you later, aiight."

He was grabbing his jewelry and cell phone off my dresser as he spoke. He approached me again and gave me a wet, passionate kiss before turning to leave.

"Lock my door on your way out," I said to him as he was exiting my bedroom and heading for the front door. As an afterthought, I yelled, "Be careful!"

"I'm always careful!" he yelled back just before I heard my front door open and close.

I found the outfit I'd been looking for and placed it on the lounge chair where my robe had been laying, then walked over to my bed and begun snatching off the sheets, which were stained with our juices, and headed down the hall to my laundry room. I was almost at the door to my laundry room with the sheets in my hand when I heard the unmistakable sound of gunshots coming from up the street from my house. I instinctively gasped from the shock of it all, and then purely out of habit I hit the deck! As quickly as the shooting had started, it had stopped just as abruptly. The next thing I heard was the sound of screeching tires zooming off in the distance. As I lay on my hallway floor my heart was racing a mile a minute. In the back of my mind I just knew whatever had just happened, had happened to the man who had just left my house.

CHAPTER ELEVEN
CARLOS

I was still heated from the news I'd gotten from Sabrina about Monk and D.C., but I managed to maintain my composure around everyone. For a few weeks Ali was the only one out of my crew who knew about what she had told me. Then I'd decided that it was time to move, so I subsequently put Face up on what was happening. As expected, Face was ready to put in work as soon as I told him. I had to admit, I was starting to lose my patience as well. My mind had been made up to tear these niggas some new assholes! And to make matters worse, I'd been trying to call Justice for the past few weeks and that bitch had been avoiding me.

That only confirmed what I'd been thinking: *That bitch had known about that shit all along!*

Her dodging me had infuriated me to the point in which I was ready to blow that bitch's wig back upon sight.

It was a little past 11:00 A.M. on a Sunday morning when Face and I were leaving Captain Steve's restaurant in Fort Mill, South Carolina when out of curiosity I decided to ride past Justice's condominium complex to see if she was home. I was behind the wheel of the rented Durango while Face sat silently on the passenger's side puffing on a Newport.

Once on the main road, I dialed Justice's number again and waited for an answer. As expected, she never picked up. I even called back from Face's phone and she still didn't answer.

I mumbled, "Snake ass bitch."

I hung up and texted her. After punching in my message I hung up and texted Monk just to see if he would call back.

"Justice still ain't answerin'?" Face inquired.

"Nah, that bitch still playin' it raw. But it's aiight though. 'Cause she still guilty by association," I stated while punching in the last of my message to Monk.

After I finished texting I looked over at Face to try to see if he expressed any type of remorse for having to murk a woman. I'd hated it had come to that point with me and Justice, but my mind was made up and there was no turning back. I had been giving her all the opportunities in the world to talk to me but she had chosen to avoid me.

To my knowledge, Face had never killed a female before and I wanted to know if he viewed the situation at hand any differently from any other hit.

"You got a problem wit' noddin' Justice?" I asked while stopping for a red light.

Face looked over at me with cold eyes and stated, "The only thing I *won't* kill is a baby. Fuck e'rybody else." He was stroking that grotesque scar. It was a habit of his whenever he was deep in thought.

As the light changed I pulled off and commented, "That's good, 'cause Los luh da kids," I snickered. I then changed my tone and added, "You know they say every time a person dies, a child is born somewhere in the world at that same instance."

"Fuck is you doin'? You preachin' to a nigga now?" Face laughed sarcastically. "Nigga, I know death is just as much a part of life as livin', an' I ain't got no quarrels about handlin' my binness. You just keep breakin' bread wit' a nigga. I wouldn't give a fuck if it was that bitch Sarah Palin you wanted slumped, we'll put some snow chains on this bitch and be headed to Alaska today."

He was professing his loyalty and I heard the sincerity in his words as he spoke.

I sat back in the comfortable leather and gripped the steering wheel as we got onto the highway and zoomed back up I-77. Thirty minutes after leaving the restaurant I was turning onto W.T. Harris Boulevard. While I drove towards Justice's neighborhood I was thinking of how I'd always prided myself on being a professional "sucker ducker" and how I had always steered clear of grimy muthafuckas. I should've known better than to be actually fucking one. Those muthafuckas had worked their way into my circle and had infiltrated my shit like a mole. I couldn't believe I had allowed a crab like Monk and his trifling ass sister to play me like a piano. I hadn't even suspected they had been the ones that had tried me.

My cell phone rang and brought me out of my reverie as I neared Justice's complex. I looked at the number and was surprised to see who was calling. I knitted my eyebrows in astonishment and raised the phone to show Face the number. He let out a sarcastic grunt when he saw who it was. I flipped open the phone and answered.

"What it do!"

"You tell me. *You* texted *me*," Monk answered.

I was thinking, *This lil' arrogant fucker is bold as shit!*

"Where you at, my nigga? I need to holla at ya," I replied while passing the security gate that led me into Justice's complex.

"I'm a little busy right now. I got company. Talk quick but don't talk slick." He sounded as if he was trying to rush the call.

"You heard from your sister?" I was driving through Justice's parking lot, searching for her car.

"Yeah, I heard from her. She doin' aiight. Want me to tell her to get at ya?" Monk sounded impatient.

"Yeah, yeah, you do that. Your man D.C. wit' you?" I was trying not to sound agitated, but just the sound of this nigga's voice was making my blood boil!

"Nah, I ain't seen my nigga. Look, yo' text said you needed to holla at me about somethin', so what's good? I told you I'm busy."

"I got a proposition for you. It's about some biness. You need to get back at me when you got time to talk. Matter of fact, where you at? I can come to you."

"Ain't none of yo' biness where I'm at. I am where I am. Matter of fact, I'll holla back when I finish doin' what I'm doin' while I do what I do where I'm at. Ya' dig?"

This slick talkin' ass nigga is gonna make me make him suffer when I catch his ass! I thought.

"Make sure you get back at me because it's gonna be beneficial to you."

I was trying to make it seem sweet so I could keep him sleep. Thinking it was about getting some dough and not knowing I knew he'd been involved in robbing my spot, that thirsty ass nigga would be sure to holla back.

"Alight. One."

Monk ended the call.

I closed my phone while exiting Justice's parking lot after not seeing her car or any other vehicle parked in either of her two reserved spots.

"That nigga really tryin' a mahfucka," Face stated. He was referring to Monk as he thumped ashes off the cigarette he was smoking.

Face was right about Monk. That nigga was really trying me like I was Boo-Boo The Fool or some damn body. But I felt a slight sense of contentment knowing that I had a cake baked for his ass.

I pulled out of Justice's complex and back out onto W.T. Harris Boulevard, and headed down the street towards the Hickory Grove neighborhood. I knew if anybody knew Justice's whereabouts it would be her girl Sapphire. Since I was already on her side of town I decided to drop by for an unexpected visit.

Minutes after leaving Justice's neighborhood I was turning into Sapphire's neighborhood. I drove until I reached her street, McAlpine Drive. I had intended to go by her house and speak with her for a brief moment and try to find out where her girl was at without arousing her suspicion. I knew Sapphire probably had no idea as to what was going on, so I didn't want her to get the impression that I was looking for Justice to harm her.

As I slowly cruised down Sapphire's street I couldn't believe my luck! I spotted Justice's car parked in Sapphire's driveway.

"Bingo," I stated as I pointed to the Chrysler.

Face looked over and saw the car and instinctively reached for the pistol that was tucked away in his waistband.

"Hold up for a minute."

I stopped Face as I saw him reaching for the door handle to get out.

I didn't want him to go up in there on a Rambo mission like that. I wanted to wait until Justice left Sapphire's house so I could follow her and do her somewhere more discreet. A deserted street would be more than perfect. If Sapphire were to leave the house with her, then she would have to get it too. Sapphire's destiny that morning was being determined by whether she stayed her ass home or not. I silently hoped that she'd make the right decision and stayed home because I truly believed that she knew nothing about what had been going on.

I pulled the Durango around the corner from Sapphire's house and parked in a spot where we could still see her front door. Twenty minutes or so elapsed without any movement from Sapphire's house until we saw a taxi pull up in her driveway. We watched intently as the cabdriver sat as if he were waiting for someone to emerge from the house.

When Sapphire's front door opened I had to blink twice because I thought my eyes were playing tricks on a nigga.

"What the fuck!?"

Face started, "Yo, ain't that…" but he didn't finish his question as he pointed at the dude that was walking to the cab.

"Christmas in July nigga! That's what that is," I answered Face's question as I put the Durango in drive. I was somewhat confused as to why Cross had just come out of Sapphire's house, but I must admit it was definitely a pleasant surprise.

I told Face, "You know what it is, my nigga."

He let his window down and cocked his pistol back, loading one into the chamber.

The taxi backed out of Sapphire's driveway and headed up the street as I followed, waiting for it to stop. There was a stop sign at the end of the street and I waited for the taxi's brake lights to come on, signaling that it was slowing down and getting ready to stop. I was directly behind them as they came to a complete halt. Cross was seated in the back of the taxi, directly behind the driver so I quickly steered the truck alongside them so that Face was right next to the driver's window. I watched as Cross looked up with a confused expression on his face. I leaned across Face to look down at him because I wanted him to see my face before he died. As we locked eyes I smiled when I saw him reaching beneath his T-shirt. He was reaching for his tool, but it was too late because Face was already leaning out the window with his ratchet aimed directly at him.

Without hesitation, Face commenced to let his .40 cal vomit lead into the taxi's interior. He hit both Cross and the driver. Seconds after the first shot had been fired; live nerves in the driver's lifeless body caused his foot to slip off the brake and the taxi slowly rolled a few feet away from the Durango. As if he weren't satisfied, Face opened the door, hopped out the truck and walked alongside the taxi, matching its snail-like pace. I watched as he leaned in through the broken glass and fired three shots into Cross's face and two more into the back of the driver's head.

Face jumped back into the truck and I was smiling from ear to ear as I peeled out, burning rubber away from the scene. Two lifeless bodies were left inside the blood-splattered taxi as we exited the neighborhood and hit the highway.

I thought, *Now that was some real gangsta shit! Jack me and think you're gonna get away with it? Oh, hell nah!*

My morning had started out fucked up, but when we rocked Cross's bitch ass to sleep I knew it was going to be a beautiful day. Two bodies in less than two minutes—one was deserving and the other was just in the way. I felt no remorse whatsoever for what had happened. In fact, I was feeling a sense of vindication! After leaving Hickory Grove we drove directly to Grier Town to pass off the rental to Ali's sister. On the way, I was thinking about how fate sometimes deals you a dirty hand, and then turn right around and drop opportunity right into your lap.

It was one down and four more to go. D.C., Monk, and Justice were already walking dead and now Sapphire had just been added to my hit list. I had no idea what that nigga Cross had been doing at her house, but she'd just initiated herself into the tangled web he'd woven by having him there. For all I knew, they *all* could have been in cahoots with trying me; so in turn, they were *all* going to get it. Guilty by association! Sapphire had just taken on the label as a "problem" and it was already understood how my problems were handled—I made them go away!

I was more than thankful for Sapphire having that nigga Cross in the wrong place at the right time, but in this case gratitude would have been a burden. However, the vengeance of it all had been an extreme pleasure.

I looked over at Face and saw no remorse whatsoever in his cold eyes as he casually blew smoke out the open window. My nigga was definitely about his B.I. and I loved that shit!

CHAPTER TWELVE
MONK

Yo, you'll never believe who I'm with."

I was inside the restroom at Red Lobster on Albemarle Road in East Charlotte, speaking to D.C. on my cell phone. It was a little pass 12 P.M. on a Sunday afternoon and I was about to have lunch with a beautiful woman. I was awaiting D.C.'s response because I knew he'd never guess who my lunch date was.

"That bitch Tan," he responded.

I wrinkled my eyebrows with astonishment and asked, "How the hell you know?"

"Because I'm wit' her girlfriend," he laughed and I laughed with him.

"Boy, you ain't got *no* morals, do you?" I was still laughing.

"Me? Nigga you was the one who slapped the taste outta that bitch's mouth!"

We were both cracking up. Tan had called me earlier that morning and asked if I wanted to grab a bite to eat. At first I was a little hesitant because of what I had done to her. Then I had come to the conclusion that she had no idea it had been me who had invaded her home, so I figured I had nothing to worry about.

"Man, lemme hit you back later." I was about to end the call, then I added, "Oh, yeah, that nigga Los called me 'bout an hour ago talkin' 'bout he wanna holla 'bout some binness."

"Oh, yeah?" D.C. had a hint of skepticism in his voice.

"Yeah, I'll hit you later and let you know what he talkin' about."

"You gonna fuck wit' that nigga?"

"I'on' know. I'ma see what type of game he playin' though." I was exiting the restroom and heading toward the table where Tan was seated.

"Holla back then."

"One," I ended the call as I approached the table. I was stuffing my phone back into my pocket as Tan looked up from the menu. I sat down across from her and asked "You ready to order yet?"

She was looking at me with those sexy ass eyes and responded, "Not yet. I guess I'll just have whatever you have."

I studied her face for a minute, noticing a slight bruise from where I'd slapped her a few days earlier. Because of her light complexion, the bruise was still slightly visible. I also noticed that she'd taken out the weave. Her hair was now short and naturally curly, which made her even more beautiful.

I waved for the waitress, and then commenced to order once the big-boned blonde approached the table.

"Lemme get two steak and shrimp dinners." I looked over at Tan. "That's straight with you?"

"That's fine."

"I want my steak well done, how you want yours?" I asked.

"Medium-rare, thank you."

"And two iced teas," I added.

"One check or two?" The waitress asked while taking our menus.

"One" I replied. I thought that the least I could do was pay for the bitch's meal. I did slap the shit out of her.

While we waited for our food I struck up a conversation, trying to get her to mention what had happened at her place.

"What happened right there?" I was pointing at the bruise on her cheek.

"You won't believe it if I told you," she replied with a slight sense of embarrassment.

"Try me." I was itching to hear that shit as I leaned back and prepared to listen.

Tan took a deep breath and unconsciously looked around at the nearby tables to see if anyone could hear our conversation. Satisfied that no one was in earshot, she began to convey to me everything I already knew, except who had found them bound and gagged.

"Thank God it was the day my two brothers were supposed to come by with the receipts from the payroll and the rest of th—"

"Receipts?" I interrupted with confusion.

"Yeah, *receipts*. We own three construction companies that were left to us by our father a few years ago. He passed away from a heart attack. I run one and my brothers run the other two. To'Wanda is our accountant; she handles all of the receipts, taxes and things like that. My brothers come twice a week with the receipts from the supplies and the payrolls, and drops them off for To'Wanda to sort through and put on file."

I was sitting there listening to her while feeling like a damn fool.

Construction!? Hell nah!

"What's wrong? I'm boring you, aren't I? See, that's why I didn't wanna tell you." She must've peeped the look on my face and the change in my demeanor.

"Nah, you ain't boring me," I tried to perk up a little. "I was just trying to figure out why somebody would want to try to rob *you*, a construction company owner." I lied.

"I guess they thought we had cash or something of value in the house. They even killed Ralphie."

"Ralphie?"

"Yeah, my baby pit bull."

I thought, *Baby my ass, that muthafucka looked full-grown to me.*

"And they stole the gun my brother had given me for protection." Tan paused and took a deep breath. "*Some* protection, huh?"

I started feeling a little bad for this broad. She almost had me ready to call D.C. and tell him to bring me her gun so I could give it back to her.

Damn, we'd went on a dummy mission, I thought. *A fuckin' construction company owner!?* I couldn't get over that shit.

"And those two bitches who knocked at my door…I'll never forget those faces," Tan stated with hatred in her voice.

"I know, right," I agreed while making a mental note to never let her see even a photo of my sister or Phire.

Tan added to her previous statements, "And that voice, that raspy voice of one of the robbers, I'll never forget that either." As an after-thought, she said, "Whoever these guys were had expensive taste. I can say that much."

Out of curiosity, I asked, "Why you say that?"

"Because one of them had on a pair of all black Bapes. Those sneakers cost at least $250 a pair, at least all the ones I've seen in Jersey cost that much," she reported.

Just then, our food arrived and I dove right in with hopes of Tan changing the subject from the robbery. I discreetly slid my right foot from beneath the table so I could look at my sneakers. I was silently praying that I didn't have on my Bathing Apes. Seeing my Jordans, I exhaled a sigh of relief.

The atmosphere was kind of weird because I was feeling a little remorseful for running up in this bitch's house and slapping her around. And now here I was sitting directly across from her, having lunch with her. If this broad was in the game I wouldn't have felt any kind of guilt for what I'd done. And nine times out of ten I would have more than likely been making plans to jack her ass again! But this girl was nothing more than a successful, bi-sexual construction company owner.

During the meal, Tan had mentioned that the police had arrived shortly after her brothers in response to the alarm being tripped. The only evidence the police gathered were two bullets from Ralphie's skull and the shell casings from the gun that had been fired. At this point my mind started reeling. I was trying to remember who had loaded the gun I'd used that night. I was hoping whoever it had been had at least enough sense not to leave prints.

"Chink, you sure you're okay? You seem a little distant," Tan commented.

"Yeah, yeah, I'm cool," I replied while still trying to remember who had loaded the pistol I'd killed Ralphie with.

After a minute or two of wracking my brain I finally remembered that I had been the one who had loaded the gun that night. I could also remember using a handkerchief. Tan went on to tell me how she had tricked the robber into going to the tool shed where the alarm had been tripped. She was laughing at her brilliance and at the same time she was laughing at our stupidity. I was thinking about how lucky this girl had been that I'd pulled Cross away from the house after that incident. That nigga had really wanted to fuck her up because of that stunt she had pulled. That thought caused me to laugh a little harder. She thought I was laughing with her, but little did she know, I was laughing *at* her simple ass!

After we finished our meal, we stood out in the parking lot conversing and making plans to see one another again. While we were talking I saw several police cars, an ambulance, and a fire truck race past the restaurant and zoom up the street with sirens blaring and lights flashing.

Damn, somebody must be fucked up, I thought as I watched the ambulance run through the light.

My belly was full and I was nickin' like crazy so I dug into the pocket of my shorts for a Newport. After the sirens had passed I walked Tan to her Range Rover and noticed how jiggly her ass cheeks were in the thin sundress she was wearing. When she climbed into the truck the dress rose high up on her thick thighs and she saw me staring with lustful eyes. I held her door open and leaned against it while flicking ashes to the pavement.

"So, I still can't get your number?" I asked.

I knew she was at a vulnerable stage at this point after being scared by a home invasion. I figured she'd want a nigga like me on her team to have her back in situations like that, if it were to happen again.

Tan thought about it for a minute, and then she held out her palm for my cell. I dug it out of my pocket and handed it to her. She commenced to punch in her digits just as I'd figured she'd do.

I smiled and commented, "Your man must be in the dog house, huh?"

She didn't respond. She only smiled slightly while continuing to program her info into my phone.

When she was done she handed it back to me and stated, "On weekdays call after five, and anytime on weekends."

I moved away from her door, allowing her to close it while she started the truck and rolled down the window. I was walking towards my bike which was parked a few spaces down from where her truck was parked.

I told her, "I'll holla at you later, aiight. And be careful ma, 'cause it's all types of criminals and thugs on the loose out here."

I was smiling inwardly. I looked at her and noticed a slight smile on her face as well.

When I reached my bike I unlocked my helmet from the side of the seat and saw Tan pulling out of her parking space. She rolled past me slowly and approached the exit.

When she stopped at the exit, she leaned out the window, "And just for the record, I don't have a man." She was smiling as she rolled her window back up and disappeared behind the tint.

I watched as she pulled out onto Albermarle Road and blended in with the mid-afternoon traffic while thinking to myself, *I know you ain't got a man, because you got a BITCH!*

I smiled because there's nothing like knowing someone's most inner-most secrets unbeknownst to them. Knowledge is power, especially if you have knowledge of things people have no idea you are aware of.

I slipped my shoe cover over my Jordans to prevent scuffing, then hopped onto my bike with plans of heading to my apartment for a little rest and relaxation before hooking up with Cross and D.C. later for a lick we'd setup. A girl who Cross was fucking had put us up on some out of town niggas and we had planned to touch them later that night. However, curiosity ended up getting the best of me and instead of going straight home I followed the sounds of the sirens to see what had happened up the street from the restaurant since it was so close to my sister's neighborhood.

I rode up Albemarle Road until it intersected with W.T. Harris Boulevard, then I made a left going towards my sister's place. When

I passed Ice's complex I kept riding until I reached the Hickory Grove neighborhood, Phire's neighborhood. I followed the sirens and blinking lights to McAlpine Drive, Phire's street. My antennas immediately went up when I saw that they had her street blocked off. When I looked down the street and saw Ice's car parked in Phire's driveway my heart dropped!

I pulled off to the side of the road and killed the engine. After putting my kickstand down I removed my helmet and watched as police tried to control the small crowd that was milling about. I dug into my pocket for my phone and dialed my sister's number. When her phone went straight to voicemail three times in a row I started my bike and drove straight through the crime scene tape!

CHAPTER THIRTEEN
JUSTICE

Wait a minute. Wait a minute. Slow down, I can't understand a word you sayin'."

I had a finger in my right ear, trying to drown out the loud noise those big ass tires on J.T.'s Hummer was making as we zoomed down 1-85. My cell was pressed against my left ear as I tried to make out what Sapphire was saying on the other end.

I tried to calm her down, "Take a deep breath gurl and calm down."

"They shot him, Justice! They shot him!" she was crying.

"*They* Who? And who got shot?" I asked with concern because she was crying hysterically.

"He'd just left my house. I mean, he hadn't been gone five minutes. Somebody was waiting for him. Oh my, God."

"*He* who?" I asked again because I had no idea of whom she was referring to. At first I thought it was Red because he'd been the last person I'd seen her with. Then I thought that maybe it was that dog ass Travis.

But she shocked the hell out of me when she said, "Cross! They killed Cross!"

"*Who*? What the hell?"

Now, I was really confused. I started to say something but I heard her speaking with someone in the background.

"Justice, the police wanna talk to me. Please come over here. Please!"

"I'm on my way. I'll be there in a minute," I assured her. "J.T., speed up. Damn!"

It seemed as if the truck was traveling at a snail's pace. I looked over and noticed J.T. looking at me with inquisitive eyes as I ended my call with Sapphire. I knew he wanted to know what was going on.

Just to curb his curiosity I told him, "Something just happened at Sapphire's house."

"No shit, Sherlock," he stated sarcastically.

I looked at him and wanted to say something smart but I held my tongue.

"Who was it?" he asked.

I took a deep breath and let out a long sigh. "You probably don't know him."

I was looking out the window. He was still periodically glaring at me so I told him, "It was a guy who used to run wit' my brother. A guy named Cross."

As soon as I said the name I felt the truck swerve. I looked over at J.T. and noticed his eyes had gotten wide as hell and the blood seemed to have drained from his chocolate face.

"Damn, you aiight? You knew him or something?" I asked curiously.

"I got a cousin named Ross, he out here wildin'. I hope it wasn't him," he replied while regaining his composure.

"I said *Cross*, not Ross," I corrected him.

"Oh, okay. I thought you said Ross," he breathed a sigh of relief.

When we finally reached Sapphire's neighborhood I saw that two police cars blocked off her street. I could see a taxi cordoned off by Crime Scene Investigators along with a slew of other officials that were checking out the scene. I assumed whatever had happened, happened inside that taxi. I could also see Sapphire's house from where we were parked and I noticed my brother's motorcycle parked next to my car in her driveway.

"I'ma get out right here," I told J.T.

I gathered my handbag and bent down to slide my sandals back on. I was getting ready to exit the truck when J.T. asked if I was gonna be okay. The genuine concern in his voice made me smile. Unlike most men, J.T. seemed to be sensitive to a woman's feelings and that was one of the reasons why I liked him and why I wasn't in a rush to let Monk lay him down.

"I'm good, thanks."

I leaned over and kissed those luscious lips, which were giving LL's a run for his money. As soon as our lips met, I began to have flashbacks of the previous night. J.T. had done me oh so right! I could've sworn that his room had rotated when he'd made me cum. I had to break our lip lock before our hormones got out of control again.

"I'll call you later, okay."

I was still rubbing his chest while gazing into his eyes, not really wanting him to leave. But I knew I couldn't let him stay because he'd probably end up finding out more about me than I wanted him to due to the tragedy that had just taken place.

"Make sure you call me and let me know you're okay," he stated as I was exiting the truck.

I closed the door behind me, waved goodbye as I walked down the sidewalk towards Sapphire's house. I watched curiously as the police did their jobs. They were taking photos of the taxi and the area of the ground surrounding it. At several yards away I could clearly see blood on the windshield and what looked like the driver's head slumped onto the steering wheel. I felt a shiver run through me as I watched this scene that looked like something straight out of a movie. I looked back and saw that J.T. was still parked in the same spot. He was looking at the taxi as well. When he saw me looking at him he waved at me once more and slowly pulled off.

"Ice!" I heard my name being called.

Looking up, I saw my brother walking towards me looking vexed.

"Why you didn't answer ya damn phone when I called you? Had a nigga worried about your ass." He looked at J.T.'s Hummer pulling off and added, "Neva mind, I see why. Let me find out you feelin' dat nigga." He looked at me curiously. "Don't let the dick make you slip."

I ignored him and thought back to when I'd missed his call. He had called while I was in the middle of having my fourth orgasm that afternoon. I'd planned to call him back later because I didn't think it was anything important. As I looked around at the scene I was finally seeing what his call had been about.

"My phone was dead." I lied while approaching Sapphire's front yard.

I saw her standing on her front porch in a pair of gym shorts, a baggy T-shirt and a pair of flip-flops. Her hair was wrapped in a scarf and her eyes were blood-shot red and very puffy, obviously from crying. She had her arms folded across her chest while talking to an officer who was listening and taking notes on a small tablet.

My brother was at my side and I could tell he was heated. He just kept staring at the taxi and shaking his head. One of his crime partners had just gotten slain and I couldn't even imagine what was probably going through his mind at that instance. I was somewhat confused and still didn't know what the hell was going on. As Monk and I stood in the driveway near my car I was trying to piece that crazy ass puzzle together.

"What was you and Cross doin' over here?" I asked curiously.

"I just got here right before you did. I 'on' know what Cross was doin' over here. But fuck what he was doin' over here, that don't even matter. Somebody slumped that nigga!" Monk was leaning up against my car. He dug into his pocket for a cigarette and lit one up. I could tell he wanted some answers.

The atmosphere was solemn and the ambience of death was in the air. I'd never been afraid of death, but when it hits close to home it makes you think, *Damn, that could have been me!*

I stood there and watched my girl answer the officer's questions while periodically glancing at me with a peculiar look in her eyes. The more I watched her, the more familiar that look became. When you wear your heart on your sleeve the look in your eye tells a tale.

"Oh, hell no. I know she wasn't..." I mumbled as realization dawned on me.

"She wasn't what?" Monk asked in between puffs of his cigarette.

"She was fuckin' that boy," I stated. The look in Sapphire's eyes told it all and I picked up on it. "That's why she said he had just left her house. And that's why she so upset. No wonder she was so hysterical. She was screwing that nigga," I stated while eyeing her with a knowing look.

"Cross and Phire?" Monk was pointing over his shoulder at Sapphire. "Hell, nah," he said in disbelief.

"Hell nah" was exactly what I'd thought as well, but my girl's eyes told a totally different story.

Just then, I saw Sapphire and the officer shake hands, which indicated that their conversation had ended. I walked over to the porch where she was standing and Monk was directly on my heels. I held open my arms and embraced Sapphire with a sisterly hug while she sniffled and let the last of her tears roll down her chocolate cheeks.

Patting her on the back, I whispered, "It's okay, ma-ma, let it out."

We held one another for a moment before breaking our hug, then we all went inside. Monk took a seat in the living room while Sapphire and I went into her bedroom. As soon as we entered the room I started with her.

"How long?" I asked.

"How long what?" she asked back while entering her bathroom to wash her face.

I looked around her room and noticed that her bed was sheetless. The unmade bed had confirmed the suspicions that had been swirling through my head.

"How long you been fuckin' wit' that boy?" I asked matter of factly.

Sapphire replied from the bathroom.

"Gurl, you know I ain't did nuthin' like th—"

"So he just stopped by to say hi?" I asked, cutting here off, yelling into the bathroom. Sapphire knew she couldn't lie to me without me seeing straight through her game like it was glass. We'd been friends *way* too long.

She re-entered the bedroom, plopped down onto her bed, and looked at me with that look a person has when they know they've been busted.

She let out a deep sigh, then stated, "About a week after we met them that night of the Embassy Suites thing."

For a slight moment I was in disbelief, but then I had to acknowledge whom I was dealing with. Sapphire's men magnet *always* attracted niggas like that so I shouldn't have been so surprised. She conveyed to me about how she had hooked up with Cross the previous night and how he had called a cab that morning and then was gunned down as soon as the cab left her driveway. I began to become concerned because it was evident that whomever had been responsible for Cross's death had obviously watched him leave her house. They may have also been watching Sapphire as well. I told her my concerns.

"Oh shit! You think they want me too 'cause he was at my house?" Sapphire was getting scared.

"I hope not. Just stay on your Ps and Qs and if you see anything that don't look right call the police."

We went back into the living room where my brother was still seated and I told him what Sapphire and I had discussed. Monk had even more reasons to be concerned about Cross's murder because he had been hanging with him and had even robbed with him on a few occasions.

Maybe *his* life was in danger as well.

Monk decided that he would have to be even more on point now than ever before, at least until he could find out the circumstances surrounding Cross's demise. He even called D.C. and told him everything he'd heard from me and Sapphire. Even I was in a state of apprehension because the two people I cared about more than anything in this world could have possibly been in danger.

Monk left after about an hour or so after our conversation, leaving Sapphire and I alone. We had a few drinks and tried to relax so we could get our minds off of what had just happened. She told me about her cousin's phone call.

"Joy called and left a message on my voicemail this morning."

She told me what Joy had said about J.T. and his cousin and my response to this was, "Fuck Joy! Her hatin' ass needs to get some damn bizness."

I thought, *That damn girl is always hatin. It never stops with that silly heifer.*

Joy was jealous as hell and enjoyed keeping that thing called *misery* company. But I wasn't getting ready to feed into her childish drama.

Sapphire and I chatted for a while before I decided it was time for me to head on home.

"You gonna be okay here by yourself? You sure you don't wanna come to my place for the night?"

I was concerned about her. She assured me that she would be fine, so I left and headed home to relax. As soon as I stepped inside my condo I kicked off my sandals and began removing my clothes, going straight to the bathroom to run some bath water. I was in dire need of a hot bubble bath because J.T. had left me with aching limbs due to all of the acrobatic positions he had put me through the previous night.

Apricot scented oils from Victoria's Secret had my bathroom smelling delectable as I climbed into the tub with a tall frosted glass of Nuvo. All lights were out and the dim room was illuminated by candles as I relaxed and treated my body to a much-needed soak.

The rest of my night consisted of me drinking and watching television until my eyelids got heavy. I finally passed out after the eleven o'clock news went off. The last report I remembered seeing was about Cross's murder. They reported that the police were on the lookout for a navy blue SUV. Neither make nor model was mentioned.

I slept the night away peacefully until my phone rang early the next morning, bringing me out of my alcohol-induced slumber. I rubbed my eyes and looked over at the clock and noticed the time.

"Who da hell callin' here this goddamn early?" I hissed as I squinted at the sunlight that had peeked its way through my venetian blinds. I rolled over and snatched up the phone from my nightstand.

"Yeah?" I answered in a tired and agitated voice, ready to go off on whoever it was. However, what I heard the person on the other end of the phone relay to me snapped me wide-awake, and had me gasping for air!

CHAPTER FOURTEEN
SAPPHIRE

After Justice had left my house, I tried to no avail to go about my day as normally as possible. But I couldn't stay focused. Visions of Cross's smiling face and the sound of his raspy voice kept invading my mind. The last words I'd told him before he had left my house were, "Be careful." Damn, I guessed he just hadn't been careful enough and it had ended up costing him his life.

I sat around and thought long and hard about what I'd gotten myself into. The game I had initiated myself into was *no* joke. I really started having major regrets for asking Justice to put me on with her hustle because it was just too dangerous. Whoever had gunned Cross down was more than likely someone who he'd robbed and the retribution he'd paid was something you can not give back. There were so many things I wished I could say to him. So many feelings and emotions I wished I could've expressed to him to let him know that he had someone in this cruel world that truly cared about him. The more I thought about him the more my heart ached. I felt as if I'd dissected the bitter ending of his life from what little I actually knew about him, and I ended up keeping the wrong piece.

I thought back to when I'd helped Justice gain entry to the house in Rock Hill and wondered if this incident with Cross had been a repercussion from that. If so, I knew those girls definitely knew what me and Justice's faces looked like. So many thoughts swirled through my head, to the point in which I'd ended up with a brain-throbbing migraine. This night definitely called for a couple of Valiums.

I'd needed a few hours of solitude, so my house was eerily silent. There was neither television nor radio playing. My cell had been turned off so I couldn't be disturbed as I brooded and waddled in my self-misery. Lying in my freshly made bed, I stared up at the ceiling and tried to push myself to get up. As soon as I'd mustered up the strength to move I arose from my bed and headed for the bathroom. My bare feet disappeared into the carpet as I drug myself to the bathroom and flipped on the light switch. When my eyes adjusted to the sudden brightness I looked into the mirror and saw how red and puffy they were from crying for Cross. I reached up and opened my medicine cabinet and retrieved my much-needed bottle of Valium. I popped two of the small pills and put the bottle back.

"Fuck that," I said aloud as I grabbed the bottle once more and poured yet another pill into my palm. I threw all three into the back of my throat followed by a glass of tap water.

"That oughtta do it," I mumbled. "Three of them should do the job, 'cause I really don't feel like dreaming about no damn bodies tonight."

After rewrapping my scarf, I turned off the light and made my way back to my bed praying for some peaceful sleep. My satin sheets felt so damn good as I curled up beneath them and let the Vs do their thing. The comfort of my soft, warm bed coupled with the effects of the pills was powerfully soothing. The feeling reminded me of a gentle cascade of warm water as I closed my eyes and let sleep consume me. It seemed as if I had passed out as soon as my head hit the pillow.

"Sssssssss, ummmm," I purred, because I felt Cross's hands caressing my inner thighs as I licked my lips with a sensuous smile plastered on my face.

He moved from my thighs to my crotch area and I felt myself getting wet with anticipation. My hips started involuntarily rotating in tune to his caressing fingers as I attempted to open my eyes so I could look at him. The Valium had my eyelids feeling as if they weighed a ton as I felt Cross's hands all over my body. Then there were more hands. Travis's hands. Then there were yet another set of hands that belonged to Red. It felt as if an octopus was caressing me with eight different hands that gradually began getting rougher and rougher. They were so rough that they became torturous. I attempted to escape these brutal hands as they squeezed, kneaded, and plowed along my body with vigor, but I couldn't seem to get away from them. No matter how hard I tried, my eyes would not open so I could snap out of this crazy dream.

Suddenly, I felt a hand slap me with so much force that I could taste blood pooling up in my mouth and at this point my eyes immediately sprang open. I was somewhat lost in a haze and my vision was cloudy for a moment. But when the fog in my head cleared and I could finally focus, what I saw almost made me piss on myself!

Three figures in all black with the faces of Satan were looming over me. I saw their horns and I just knew I'd overdosed, died, and gone to the life beyond.

"Welcome to hell bitch!" I heard one of the figures say just before a powerful fist to my left cheek made my vision blurry again. I felt the bone in my jaw shatter beneath the madman's fist as he struck me repeatedly.

This was definitely *not* a dream as I tried to scream but one of the assailants put his hand over my bloody mouth and muffled my cries while applying pressure to my freshly broken jaw. My scarf was pulled from my head just before a hand grabbed a fistful of my hair and drug me from my bed and slammed me onto the floor so hard it seemed like I could feel my ribs cave in. All the breath had been knocked out of me as I began gasping for air.

I tried to plead for my life but I was rewarded with a kick to my face so hard it made me see stars.

Oh my God, why hadn't I gone with Justice?

One of them hissed with a deadly tone.

"Bitch, didn't nobody pull yo' chain, so stop fuckin' barkin'!"

I recognized this voice just before he kicked me in the stomach, causing me to throw up all over his shoes.

I screamed out in pain, "Please. Stop! Oh, God. Noooooo!"

"Didn't we say shut the fuck up?"

Another kick to my face. I felt my nose crack. Blood spurted from my nose and mouth, causing me to get choked as I crawled on weak, wobbly knees. I was in so much pain that I prayed for death to come as viscous blows rained down on my head and body until I faded to black.

In my state of unconsciousness, I heard a sound that mirrored that of a wounded and dying animal. I was so numb and delirious that I hadn't even realized that the sound was coming from *me*.

I prayed again for God to come and claim my soul just before total darkness swept me away.

CHAPTER FIFTEEN
CARLOS

So you gonna keep frontin' on a nigga like that, huh?"

I was walking towards the bar area in my condo with my phone up to my ear. The woman on the other end was someone whom I'd been wanting to fuck for months, but we'd been playing phone tag. She would hit me on my cell and I'd miss her call, then I would hit her back and she would miss my call. It had been going down like that for a while but I'd finally caught her. I was standing there listening to Janeka tease a nigga with a seductive tone in that baby-like voice I'd become obsessed with since I'd first laid eyes on her.

"You know I'm tryna see you, Daddy. But you never seem to have time for a sistah," Janeka whined. Just the thought of how fine this bitch was had my dick tapping my zipper, trying to escape the confines of my shorts. Standing right at an even five feet and weighing in at 135 pounds, this girl was stacked like a brick shit house. She was light skinned with shoulder-length jet-black hair and I fantasized about eating her fine ass alive. This bitch was nothing but the truth.

"Let's stop cuttin' corners, I'm tryna see you ASAP. So, what's good?" I was pouring a shot of vodka into a glass and balancing the phone against my shoulder and ear.

"Well, you know I gotta be at work at six in the morning and after I get off I got a few clients at the salon tomorrow evening. So, what about tomorrow night? I can call you when I'm about to leave the shop."

"No doubt," I responded. We talked for a few more minutes before the call ended. I was already anticipating seeing her the following night. But what I really wanted to do was to call her back and tell her to meet

141

me somewhere right then. But it was late and I knew she had to get up early the following morning so I just satisfied myself with the thought of seeing her later.

Janeka was definitely my kind of girl. Intelligent *and* fine? That was a combination a nigga could rarely find. I was kind of impressed by the fact that she was independent and working two jobs. She was an accountant with Wells Fargo by day and a beautician by night. I loved the fact that she was trying to pave her own way without riding on the coattails of a man. Independence in a female is always a plus and without a doubt, a definite turn-on. I was digging this chick!

"You finally got her, huh?" Dave asked from the sofa, while puffing on a chronic- filled leaf.

"Yeah, it's about damn time. We been missin' each other like two ships in the night, but I got her ass now."

I took a seat on the sofa also.

"You know I gotta cop some of them 'blue diamonds' and fuck that bitch for hours! She gonna remember Los for a loooooong time to come!"

We both laughed at my idea of using Viagra to keep my dick hard for hours.

"I'ma have that bitch Jonesin' for this wood like a junkie needin' a fix!" I grabbed my crotch as Dave laughed.

"Nigga, you a fool," Dave commented.

Dave and I had been lounging around the condo all evening counting money and weighing out dope. As soon as the last ounce of coke had been weighed and the last bill had been spit out of the money counting machine we'd started smoking and drinking. It was somewhat an unwritten rule for me that while handling business no smoking or drinking was allowed. Too many mistakes were imminent when a person doesn't have a clear and sober mind.

Dave passed me the weed he'd been puffing. I took it and inhaled it like I was taking my last breath. I got choked immediately.

"Lemme find out," Dave said as he laughed at me.

My eyes were burning and I was still coughing as I handed him back the weed. He kicked his feet up on my coffee table and clicked on my 63-inch plasma TV with the remote. He was smoking that strong ass weed like it was a cigarette. It was said that this little nigga had an "iron lung" and now I was starting to believe that it was true.

I continued to drink my vodka as I sat back on the plush sofa and let my mind drift to the events that had taken place over the past several weeks. Money had been coming so fast I'd began to think that me and my niggas were the only ones in Charlotte selling dope. Money was becoming so plentiful that my dream car, the Rolls Royce Phantom, was right at my fingertips. Now that I could afford to cop two or three without it putting a dent in my pockets I didn't even want it anymore. I had graduated past that phase of blowing guap, and now stacking it had become my new obsession.

Money had become my aphrodisiac. I loved everything about it, the feel of it, the smell of it, It had gotten to the point where money could turn me on like no woman ever could. With every hundred grand I counted, my dick would get rock hard. Even stash spots had become few and far between lately after the incident that had happened at Mark's place. Because of that situation, I had begun take extra precautions.

Thinking about Mark made my mind wonder to Cross and the way Face had handled him. It still made me smile when I remembered the look in Cross's eyes when he had seen me sitting in that truck. I should have taken a snapshot of that shit with my phone to send it to all of my niggas. Telling them about it was one thing, but there is absolutely nothing like a frozen moment. Feeling remorseful was not an option because I knew that those who seek to achieve things should never show mercy. And that's the philosophy that I lived by. No mercy!

"Fuck's on yo' mind, nigga?" Dave asked as he exhaled a cloud of smoke through his burnt lips.

I looked over at my lil'nigga and took a deep breath.

"Ain't shit. Just thinking," I replied as I picked up my drink from the coffee table and gulped down what was left of it.

The television was on the Hip-Hop satellite video channel and *Raw Vids*, a down south version of *Uncut* was just coming on. For the next hour and a half it would be nothing but ass and titties bouncing on the flat screen. The first video came on and I saw a familiar face.

"Yo, you see that bitch right there?"

I was pointing at the screen at one of the females in the video.

"Right there!" I repeated as the girl flashed onto the screen again.

"The bitch in the pink?" Dave asked while slouched down in the chair.

"Yeah. That's Kat."

"Kat? The bitch from ATL?" Dave asked with knitted eyebrows.

"Yeah, the bitch who be lightweight stalkin' a nigga." I laughed.

"Damn! She phat as a muthafucka!"

"And that's *all* that crazy ass bitch got goin' for herself. She's as dumb as a box of rocks and looney as hell!" I stated as I watched Kat do her thing on the video.

Dave was right, she *was* phat as hell and I must admit that she did have a bomb shot of pussy. And the head was off the Richter scale! Superhead Steffans didn't have shit on her. Kat should've been the one to coin the phrase *"slow neck."* I'd blown her back out a few times while on those blue diamonds while I was in Atlanta. But since I'd stopped fucking with her she'd been blowing a nigga's phone up. She had even showed up at Club Stir one night when I was there with another broad and she ended up showing her natural ass that night. That had been the first time I'd beaten a bitch's ass in public and I ended up regretting doing it. It wasn't because she had called the police or anything like that, but it was because she had said that the ass whuppin' had turned her on. Crazy bitch!

"I done seen that bitch in a lotta videos. I ain't know she was the same bitch from ATL," Dave stated while watching Kat shake her ass with lustful eyes. "A paranoid schizophrenic or not, she can still get it," he added, and then thumped ashes off the blunt into the glass ashtray that was on the table.

I thought for a moment, then looked at Dave and said, "Bitches... beat 'em and they'll forgive you. Flatter 'em and they may or may not see through you. But if you fuck around and start ignoring 'em, watch 'em lose they muthafuckin' minds! Be careful what you wish for, my nigga." I shook my head at the logic I'd just dropped on Dave and added, "You just might get that shit."

Dave looked up with bloodshot eyes and pointed to the television at Kat.

"Hell, I'll fuck her and beat her fine ass if that's all she want a nigga to do." His comment made us both laugh as I arose from the sofa to refill my glass. When I reached the bar area I heard a knock on the door. I knew exactly who it was from the series of taps so I told Dave to open it. In waltzed Ali, Supreme, and Scarface.

"What's good? What up? What up?" Dave greeted the three men one by one with a pound as they entered my condo.

"Los, what up baby?" Ali spoke as he closed the door behind himself.

"What it do? What up Face? Preme, what's good, nigga?" I spoke to my three niggas who'd all taken seats in my living room and were bobbing their heads to the music from the videos.

I walked over and joined them while kicking Preme's feet off the table so I could pass. I squeezed between him and the table and sat back down on the sofa. Face had sparked up some weed and was seated on the love seat, being his usual withdrawn self while Ali was on the lounge chair dialing a number on his cell phone.

Preme kicked his feet back up on the table and I unconsciously glanced over at his shoes. His black Timbs had what looked like dried up blood and vomit on one of the toes.

"Why you ain't change them damn shoes? Matter of fact, get that nasty shit off my table."

I knocked his feet off the table and onto the floor.

Preme got up and headed towards the kitchen area. He stated, "If them niggas wouldn't have been rushing a muthafucka I *would've* changed. Thank them two niggas right there." He pointed at Ali and Scarface.

As he walked away I looked at the back pocket of his black jeans.

I told him, "I guess you didn't have time to get rid of *that* either, huh?" I was pointing at the red mask with horns that was hanging out of his back pocket.

Face commented, "I told him to throw that shit away an hour ago."

"Nah, I think I'ma hold on to this." Preme pulled the mask from his back pocket and held it up. "Never know when a nigga might have to send a bitch to hell again."

He was smiling. He looked like a wild Jamaican with his dreads all over the place.

I lay back on the comfortable leather and closed my eyes while thinking, *Hell hath no fury!*

I smiled to myself with my eyes closed and began bobbing my head to the beat that was still blaring from the television.

I began thinking, *Revenge is oh so fuckin' sweet!*

CHAPTER SIXTEEN
MONK

Life sure has a strange way of twisting your arm! Just when you think you've got it all figured out it throws your ass a curve ball.

It was late in the evening. D.C. and I were sitting in my old school Ford Galaxy in Applebee's parking lot on Independence Boulevard, getting lost in a cloud of Kush as we tried to analyze the chain of events that had taken place over the recent few days. I reached down and turned the volume of my sound system down a few levels so I could try to think. It was warm and the sun hadn't sat yet, so I had the AC on full blast and we were enjoying the coolness. Originally, we had planned to go inside to eat, but suddenly I wasn't hungry anymore.

"You tryna go in?" D.C. asked from the passenger's side.

I sighed deeply before responding. "Nah, I'm good. I was thinking about that shit at the hospital and it took a nigga's appetite."

I took off my fitted cap and rubbed my head for a moment.

"Fuck! Somebody beat that girl like, like…"

Words couldn't even begin to describe what I'd witnessed a few days earlier in that hospital room.

I remembered what I was feeling when Justice had called me and told me to meet her at Carolina's Medical Center because something had happened to Sapphire. My first reaction was anger because the way Justice was crying and bawling on the phone had already let me know that the situation was fucked up. But nothing could prepare me for what I'd seen when I had entered Phire's hospital room. Her mother was standing to one side of her bed while my sister stood at the other side holding Sapphire's limp hand. Both women were sobbing with trembling lips as Sapphire lay there motionless.

Sapphire's mother and Justice both looked up with wet eyes when they'd heard me enter the room. I approached the bed slowly, not knowing what to expect. When I looked down at the unrecognizable figure lying in that bed it made my heart sank. Sapphire's head had swollen up to the size of a pumpkin and her body was bandaged from her neck down. Whoever was responsible for beating her like that had undoubtedly intended for her to die. But God must have had other plans for her because she was still breathing. She was in a coma, but *alive* nonetheless.

Sapphire's mailman had been the one to discover her while attempting to deliver her mail on the morning after the attack. He had seen dried up, bloody footprints on her front porch and also noticed that her front door was slightly ajar; splinters of wood were visible from where it had apparently been kicked in. The police were called immediately. When they had arrived and searched the house they found Phire on her bedroom floor in a puddle of blood, unconscious and barely clinging to life. It was Phire's mother who had called Justice and in turn Justice had called me.

I thought back to Cross's death and how it had given me a reality check but it hadn't affected me that much because we hadn't really been that close. Although it did make me more conscious of my surroundings and made me be even more on point. However, Sapphire had always been like a sister to me and to see her lying up in that hospital bed straddling the thin line between life and death really had a nigga fucked up.

"So what's poppin'? Who you think did that shit?" D.C. questioned. He was referring to Sapphire. His eyes were tight and bloodshot red from the weed.

"I wish I knew," I replied while exhaling a thick cloud of smoke.

I looked around the parking lot and saw a few patrons entering and exiting the restaurant as if they didn't have a care in the world. I knew Sapphire's unfortunate circumstance was a result of her involvement with Cross, but no matter how hard I tried, I just couldn't seem to narrow down the possibilities of who these vengeful niggas could be. Like me and D.C., Cross had touched so many niggas and had so many enemies it would've been damn near impossible to narrow it down to just one person or one clique. I even thought about my own safety as well because I had robbed a nigga with Cross just before the Embassy Suites lick.

I asked D.C., "You remember that first lick we did wit' Cross?"

"What of it?" D.C. responded nonchalantly as two thick-built redbones caught our eyes as they walked past my car and entered the restaurant.

"Damn, them hoes phat!" D.C. stated, referring to the two women as they strolled out of view.

I looked away from the girls and over at my partner. "You think them niggas know that was us? You think that's what this shit is all about?"

"Fuck they gonna know it was us? We had masks on, remember?"

True enough, we had worn masks but what if someone still knew it had been us somehow? My mind reeled with unasked questions that I knew D.C. had no answer for. But then again, maybe the Kush just had a nigga paranoid.

"Quit trippin', nigga. Them niggas ain't know it was us. We woulda *been* heard somethin' about that."

D.C. tried to rationalize my paranoid thoughts. Maybe I was just trippin', or maybe I was just reading too much into the situation. Either way, my concern would not waiver. I put my fitted back on and sat back in the bucket seat, lost in thought. When I couldn't come to a feasible conclusion about the situation I decided to just let sleeping dogs lie. Just then, I saw the same two redbones exit the restaurant. They glanced our way and I smiled at them. The shorter of the two smiled back, giving me the green light so I waved her over to the car. She approached without hesitation while her girlfriend stayed grounded with her phone up to her ear, engaged in conversation.

"What up ma?" I spoke as I let my window down.

"Hey," she spoke sweetly, then turned her nose up and fanned her face as soon as the cloud of weed invaded her nostrils. "Damn, y'all blazin' up right here in the parking lot? Y'all *do* know that shit ain't legal?"

She took a step back away from the car as if she was trying to avoid getting the smell in her hair and clothes.

"We got cataracts and shit. We just havin' our daily medication, ya dig?" I responded with a chuckle.

"What's up wit' ya girl? She anti-social or something?" D.C. asked her.

The girl looked back at her friend and yelled, "Sabrina! Come 'ere!"

She was waving for her friend to come join us but her friend didn't budge right away. She put a finger up as if to say, "Wait a minute."

I commenced to kick it with this chick for a few minutes while her girl wrapped up her call.

I asked, "Why y'all ain't eat? I just saw y'all go in and come right back out."

"The waiting list was a little too long for my taste. We goin' to T.G.I. Fridays."

I casually leaned out the window to get a closer look at her. She was wearing a pair of capris that hugged her wide hips and it looked like she needed a wedge to get out of those joints. Her toes were peeking out of her sandals, looking enticing and inviting a nigga to take a lick.

"Y'all want some company?" I asked while observing her luscious lips, which were shining from a thick coat of gloss.

"Hell yeah, if y'all payin'," she replied as her girl finally walked over.

D.C. waved the girl around to his side of the car and my eyes unconsciously followed her shapely ass cheeks as she walked past the front of the car. After a few minutes of exchanging pleasantries and lies we were on the road following Sabrina's X5 to Fridays. I looked at her custom plate as we stopped for a red light. I read the plate aloud, "Queen B".

I thought for a second, then told D.C., "That bitch Sabrina look *real* familiar." I was trying to remember where I'd seen her before but I couldn't place her in my memory bank.

"Nah, I'on' think I ever seen her before. Besides, a bitch that fine, how the hell could a nigga forget?" D.C. was in the process of rolling another blunt as he spoke.

I brushed it off and thought nothing more of it as the light changed. Moments later, we were pulling into T.G.I. Fridays parking lot. We told the girls to go in and get a table while we sat and sparked some more weed. The weed had brought my appetite back with a vengeance. I had the munchies like crazy.

When we finally entered the restaurant, we spotted the girls seated in a corner booth looking at menus. We joined them and ordered drinks while the girls pondered over what they wanted to eat. When our drinks arrived, I ordered enough food for three people while the girls were still undecided. The waiter looked at me and smirked because I was sure he could smell the weed in my clothes and he knew I had the munchies.

The girls and D.C. finally ordered. When the food was brought out, me and D.C. attacked it like starving vultures. We had elbows on the table, smacking our lips and licking our fingers. The girls didn't give a damn about our lack of mannerisms, they were just happy to be enjoying a free meal. During the meal I found out why Sabrina's face was so familiar-looking. She had mentioned that she knew my sister and had seen me and D.C. on a few occasions.

Toward the end of the meal Sabrina excused herself to make a phone call. "I gotta call my babysitter," she said as she licked her fingers, then wiped her hands with a wet-nap before sliding out of the booth.

Sabrina's friend, whose name turned out to be Sophia, excused herself as well. I watched as they sashayed their way toward the exit, both holding their cell phones to their ears. Every man in the restaurant did a double take as the girls glided through the room like supermodels. They both had that "nasty walk"; the kind of walk that causes an instant erection when she walks by. That walk when a woman struts like her pussy is dripping platinum.

D.C. and I finished our meals and ordered another round of drinks as we waited for Sabrina and Sophia to return.

D.C. looked across the booth at me and asked, "You thought anymore about who might be behind that shit with Cross and Sapphire?"

"I can't *stop* thinking about that shit. Phire's like a sister to me and seeing her laid up in that bed like that brought tears to a gangsta's eyes. I'ma clap somebody behind that shit. Watch and see."

"I can dig it. I'm wit' cha my nigga," D.C. reached across the table and gave me a pound.

After about ten minutes with no signs of the girls, I begin to wonder what could be keeping them.

I looked towards the entrance and blurted out, "Where them hoes at?"

It was a statement more so than a question because I knew D.C. was just as clueless as I was.

"I'on' know," D.C. responded while wrinkling up his eyebrows as if he'd just noticed that they hadn't yet returned. He sat his drink on the table and slid out of the booth. "Lemme go see where these bitches at."

I continued to drink while D.C. exited the booth and walked out of restaurant in search of the girls. My stomach was full and I felt totally relaxed. A lit Newport was between my lips as I settled back into the booth with my right leg stretched out along the seat and my back was against the wall.

Three minutes later, D.C. was reentering the restaurant with an ill look on his face. He walked back over to the booth and smiled.

"Them bitches dipped. Them triflin' hoes played a nigga for a free meal. Damn, I thought I was beatin' that up later. Thirsty ass bitches!"

He was laughing as he sat back down.

"Straight up?" I said in disbelief.

But at the same time I was somewhat amused. I looked around the table and tried to find any signs that may have indicated a possible return for them. There weren't any. They hadn't even brought their purses in with them. They'd played us! All we had were two names, which were probably bogus, a vehicle description, and that name plate

Queen B. If my sister knew them, I'd be sure to see their asses again somewhere and I was going to make it my duty to embarrass their asses.

D.C. and I both laughed at the thought of getting played for some steaks. Money? I could see that happening, but food? Now that was low!

My bladder began to expand a little so I told D.C., "Tell ole boy to bring the check. I gotta go piss."

I was sliding out of the booth as I spoke. My .40 cal dug into my ribs as I scooted out of the tight area, so I had to discreetly slide it out of my waistband and slip it into my back pocket once I was onto my feet. I walked through the crowded restaurant and entered the bathroom. All the stalls were empty so I walked over to the nearest one and emptied my aching bladder. I stood there for a second relishing in the after waves that always comes at the end of a long-needed piss.

After washing and drying my hands I stood before the mirror, staring at my reflection. My eyes looked like tiny slits and they were red as hell. I was definitely fucked up. But what happened next undoubtedly blew my high!

CHAPTER SEVENTEEN

As I started to exit the restroom I heard the unmistakable clap of automatic gunfire coming from the dining area.

"What da fuck!?"

I instinctively took cover behind the door. Then as soon as the initial shock had worn off, impulse had me snatching my ratchet from my back pocket. Beads of sweat popped up on my forehead and my adrenaline began pumping hard as shit. I was thinking that I'd gotten caught up in some terrorist shit or some Virginia Tech massacre type situation! I didn't know whether to stay where I was at or if I should've gone to check on my man. I knew D.C. had his pistol and I was wondering if he was out there blasting also.

I was still clutching my pistol and pressing my back against the wall near the door so I could blast on the first thing that sat foot inside that restroom. As I stood there my mind reverted back to the image of that blood-splattered taxi that had become Cross's burial box. And right then I'd decided I would rather be a moving target than a sitting duck. So I moved!

As I eased the restroom door open with caution I heard screams and more automatic gunfire coming from the dining area. After a few short minutes the shots finally stopped and the screams got louder. I cautiously exited the restroom and entered the dining area with my pistol in my hand, ready to squeeze.

"OH SHIT!" I muttered in disbelief as I saw two niggas dressed in black wearing Halloween masks, clutching AK-47s. They were retreating from the booth where I had been seated only minutes earlier and heading for the exit. The two gunmen were jumping over crying, petrified patrons who had apparently thrown themselves to the floor in an attempt to shun the gunfire.

For a split second, I looked towards our booth where D.C. once sat and saw him slumped over in the seat. My nigga had been hit! My vision blurred with shades of red as I raised my pistol and started busting off shots at the two assassins as they exited the restaurant. I ran towards the exit, following them out into the night while still busting shots. Just as I made it to the parking lot I saw a green Ford Excursion screeching off. I squeezed my .40 at the truck and let it blow hot kisses until I ran out of bullets.

"FUCK! FUCK! FUCK!" I spat as I watched the truck speed up the Avenue while running red lights and swerving around other cars.

My breathing was heavy and my adrenaline was still pumping like crazy as I started to go back inside the restaurant to check on my nigga. Just as I turned to head back inside, I looked across the street from the restaurant and saw a familiar looking 600 S-class slowly pulling out of the Circle K's parking lot. The driver's side window slowly lowered and the driver and I locked eyes for a brief moment. Then I saw that nigga smile at me with a knowing look plastered on his face. At that instance, everything started to fall into place like a Tetris game. It all started to make sense. My mind whirled as I dashed back towards the entrance of the restaurant.

A few patrons screamed and dove back to the floor when they saw me reenter the restaurant brandishing my empty pistol. I had fire in my eyes and my heart burned with pain as I neared the booth in which my partner lay motionless. When I reached the booth, the first thing I noticed were the nickel-sized holes in the wall behind the booth where apparently a few stray bullets had apparently gotten lodged. When I saw D.C.'s body I almost vomited. I had to hold my stomach because its contents tried to come rushing out of my mouth.

The top half of D.C.'s torso was almost severed from the lower portion of his body and internal organs were exposed. He was clutching his pistol in his right hand and his eyes were open. Just then, the realization of why AKs were called "choppers" hit me like a bolt of lightening, because those niggas had all but chopped my partner's body in half with those assault rifles.

I knew the only thing I could do was bail up out of there and try to put as much distance between myself and the restaurant as I could before the police arrived. So I grabbed D.C.'s gun and emptied his blood soaked pockets before heading to my hooptie out in the parking lot. I hopped inside my ride and tossed my empty gun on to the passenger's seat while holding D.C.'s pistol tightly in my grasp as I fled the scene. I continuously peeped into my rearview as I sped down the avenue.

So many visions and scenarios cycloned through my head as I sped away from the restaurant. But the most vivid and most disturbing image was that of Carlos and the sinister smile he had on his face as we'd locked eyes when he was pulling out of the Circle K. I thought back to when Sabrina and Sophia had gone outside and supposedly had called babysitters and whatnot. It dawned on me that those two snake bitches had called Carlos instead. Those two hoes had been the ones that were responsible for my nigga's death. I thought back to when we were at Applebee's and how Sabrina kept looking at me and D.C. when she was on the phone while I was talking to Sophia. It was my guess that she had probably called those niggas right then and was setting a nigga up the entire time. Now I had even more of a reason to want to find those trifling bitches!

Now there was *no* doubt as to whom was behind everything. Cross, Sapphire, and D.C.? Fuck that! If it's war them muthafuckas wanted, it was war they was going to get. I lost all rationality because I knew that hit was intended for me as well. Now it was no holds barred! It was time to step the game all the way up.

CHAPTER EIGHTEEN
JUSTICE

Are you sure!? I mean, it could've just been a coincidence or something." I was trying to make sense out of what my brother was telling me about my ex, Carlos.

"Fuck yeah, I'm fa sho'!" Monk's anger-filled voice blared through my Bluetooth as I listened to him describe what had happened at the restaurant.

From what I was gathering, he was telling me that Carlos had been behind it. If what he was saying had any validity to it, then it meant that Carlos had been responsible for what had happened to Cross and Sapphire as well.

I was in my car heading to my condo. I had been at the hospital with Sapphire for the past few nights eating that nasty ass food, showering in that small ass bathroom, and sleeping in that tiny ass chair. Each day I'd prayed harder than the day before for Sapphire to come around or to at least attempt to open her eyes to show some signs of life, but it was all to no avail. My own eyes were so swollen and bloodshot from shedding tears for her; I looked like I'd been up for two weeks straight.

Now, Monk was on the other end of my phone telling me *this* mess and I couldn't take anymore. I was on the verge of losing it.

Anger crept into my system for a brief moment.

"Fuck y'all do to him, Monk? Don't lie to me gottdammit!" I knew Carlos wasn't just reacting for nothing. It had to be a reason.

"I ain't did shit to that nigga....*yet!* He just got the game fucked up! He got *me* fucked up!"

He sighed deeply. I could tell he was heated.

"It's gotta be behind that shit that happened to Mark."

"Mark!?" I asked with confusion, and then my mind flashed back to the last time I'd been with Carlos and I remembered him telling me about Mark getting robbed.

"Justice, I didn't do it. But evidently he think I did 'cause I was fuckin' with Cross," Monk stated.

"Cross!? Cross robbed Mark?"

"Yeah, him and some mo' muthafuckas. Justice, I swear I didn't find out until a few weeks back. Hell, I still don't know who went up in there with him."

"Why didn't you…. I mean, why…" I was at a lost for words.

"Cross, two more niggas and a female did it. Justice, it wasn't me. I seen that nigga Los at the park after that shit had happened. You think I would've sat there and talked to that nigga if I had been the one that had jacked Mark? Cross did that shit with somebody else, it wasn't me and D.C."

"Don't try to sit up there and act like you ain't never robbed some-body then turned around and act like you ain't did nothin' wrong to them the next day. Look at you and that damn Mexican girl Tan. You takin' her out to eat and shit like you ain't go up in her house."

"Justice, I put that on mama's grave. I swear I didn't rob Mark."

I wanted to trust his words but I didn't know *what* to think at this point. I knew my brother was a dirty nigga out there in those streets, but he was far from being a fool. He knew that robbing Carlos's people was just too close to home. If Carlos would've found out it would have been a straight up Kamikaze suicidal mission.

"Ice, I want you to listen to me. These niggas ain't fakin' out here. These muthafuckas is fa real! D.C., Cross, and Phire is testimony to that. They want me dead and I'm pretty sho' if they think it was me then you already know they think you had something to do with it too 'cause th—"

"Hold up", I said cutting him off. "Fuck you mean they think I had something to do with it too? I ain't did shit to Carlos!" My voice had risen and my head had begun to throb.

"These niggas ain't playin' no games, Justice. Carlos know how me and you get down. You do the math on that shit." He paused, then continued, "Tell me, when was the last time you hollered at Carlos?"

I tried to think back to the last time I had spoken with Los, and remembered that it had been a minute. He had been calling but I hadn't answered any of his calls nor had I returned any of his messages. Shit!

"It's been a minute. He been callin', tryna get at me but—"

"Lemme guess, you been dodging that nigga, right?" He was speaking matter-of-factly as if he already knew my answer before I gave it.

I took a deep breath and let out a long exasperated sigh as I stopped for a red light. I thought my avoiding Carlos's calls had probably made him think that I had definitely been in on that nonsense or at least I had knowledge of it. I knew I had done some grimy stuff in my days but I had nothing to do with Mark getting robbed. Now at this point it was probably too late for me to try and smooth things over with Carlos and convince him that I was innocent. But knowing Carlos and his method of madness, his mind would be made up to go all out.

"Ice? Ice?" Monk's voice blared through my earpiece and at the same time a car was behind me blowing the horn. I snapped out of my daze and looked up and saw that the light had turned green. I pulled off and turned into the parking lot of KFC, which was only blocks away from my condo. There was an empty space so I pulled into it and parked because my emotions wouldn't allow me to drive any further. My mind started reeling a mile a minute because all of this was just too much for me to bear at one time. Then came the tears.

"Justice!" Monk screamed. "I know yo' lil' gangsta ass ain't sheddin' tears! Don't get soft on me, sis. We gotta get the shit strai—"

"I'll call you back."

I took my earpiece out as Monk continued to call my name. After ending the call, I let my head fall to the steering wheel as I tried to figure out what the hell I'd gotten myself into. I lost track of how long I sat there sobbing with my head buried in my steering wheel, but it seemed like an eternity.

After what seemed like ages, I heard a tapping noise on my window. I jumped from the sound and then turned my head to see who it was. My heart was beating like bass drums; my nerves were shot and the figure standing at my window made matters even that much worse.

CHAPTER NINETEEN

With a trembling hand, I hesitantly pressed the button to let my window down and asked, "Yes, officer, is there a problem?"

I was still sniffling and I could've imagined what I must've looked like at that moment.

The police officer standing next to my window was a tall, thin black guy with graying sideburns. His eyes were surveying the interior of my car as he opened his mouth to speak.

"Are you okay? I got a call from a concerned citizen saying that you've been sitting in this same spot for quite some time without any movement. You looked quite...what's a good word?"

He looked towards the sky as if he were searching for the right word.

He looked back at me and continued, "You looked sort of lifeless in the position you were in. Catch my drift?"

He was looking at me suspiciously.

"You haven't been drinking have you?"

He was staring into my bloodshot eyes.

What I wanted to say was, "No, I haven't been drinking. I'm drunk with fear! Scared of a nigga who has killed two people I know and attempted to kill my brother and best friend because he thinks we had something to do with his drug money being taken!"

But what actually came out was, "Crying? Yes. Drinking? No. Look, I'm okay. Thanks for the concern. I'll be gone in a minute; I just need to pull myself together. Long night, ya know? Had a fight with the boyfriend."

I saw it in his eyes that he believed me and was now looking at me with a little pity.

The scorned girlfriend.

"You sure you're gonna be okay?" he asked. Concern was evident in his voice.

I wiped my eyes and sniffled again, "Yeah, I'm sure. I just need a minute."

"Okay, just take all the time you need, maam. Drive safe." He tipped his hat and strolled back to his squad car. I watched as he pulled off.

I left a few minutes after the police officer. During the ride home I tried to somewhat calm my nerves with the wishful thought that maybe Carlos didn't blame me or he didn't think I had anything to do with this mess. I knew I needed to call him to see where his head was at and to let him know that he was after the wrong people, but I had no idea of what to say.

A few minutes after leaving KFC I was pulling into my condominium complex. For such a beautiful day, the complex was quite quiet. A few of the neighborhood kids splashed around in the complex pool and a few of my neighbors were walking their dogs so nothing seemed out of the ordinary....until I reached my condo!

As soon as I walked up the steps I noticed that my door was slightly ajar.

"Oh shit!" I mumbled as I looked around with my heart beating a mile a minute.

Although I had never actually had to use my "baby" before, I snatched it out of my handbag and cocked it back just the way Monk had taught me. It was broad daylight and there was activity going on all around me, but I was still scared shitless. I hesitantly pushed the door all the way open and prayed that no one was inside. For a moment I stood there, afraid to enter my own home.

When I finally mustered up enough courage to venture inside, the first thing I noticed was that both my living room and my kitchen was just as I'd left it days earlier. I walked over to the keypad on the wall and saw that my alarm had been turned off but not reset. At that instance I knew Carlos had been in my condo. The code to deactivate my alarm had been the same ever since before Carlos and I had started seeing one another. He was the *only* person other than myself who knew what it was.

How the hell did they get past security? I silently questioned as I checked every room for occupants. No one was present and nothing was missing. That let me know that he had come for one reason and one reason only...ME!

When I was satisfied that no one was in my space, I immediately began packing bags. I packed as many bags as I thought could fit into my trunk and carried them down to my Chrysler. It took three trips but once the last bag was secured I hopped in my car and left my condo for what would probably be the last time. I didn't know where I was headed but I was certain that I would not be returning to this condo anytime in the near future. I refused to literally get caught sleeping like Sapphire had done.

I pulled out onto W.T. Harris Boulevard and headed towards the highway, thinking that maybe I'd go to South Carolina and get a hotel room until I could calculate my next move. As I drove I broke down crying again while thinking about how fucked up my life had become in such a short period of time. I was on the run from a man who once held my heart in the palm of his hand, my girl was laid up in a hospital bed clinging to life and now my brother was about to go to war. All because of a damn misunderstanding.

I thought that maybe if I tried to talk to Carlos he'd see just how out of control the situation had gotten. I definitely didn't have anything to lose at that point and I thought it wouldn't have hurted to try and contact him. I was truly trying to give myself hope. I turned down the volume on my radio and reached for my cell so I could call Carlos and try to plead my case. I dialed his number and waited for him to pick up. It rang three times before it was answered.

"What it do." I heard Carlos's calm voice.

My throat became dry and my palms began sweating profusely from extreme nervousness as I held the phone in silence.

"Hello?" he spoke again.

"Carlos, it's me...Justice." I was still sobbing and wiping my nose as I spoke.

Silence.

"H-h-hello?" I thought maybe he'd hung up on me.

After a long silence Carlos calmly asked, "Justice, do you believe in miracles?"

"Huh?" I asked. He had me confused.

"I said do you believe in miracles?" he asked again.

I had no idea of where he was going with this, so I went along with him. I was thinking that I'd be able to plead my case after he'd had his words.

I sniffled, "Ye-yeah, I believe in miracles Los."

"Me too. 'Cause that's the *only* way I can justify talkin' to a dead bitch on the other end of this phone!"

"Nooo! Los! Los! Hello! Carlos!" I screamed into my phone but it was to no avail because he'd already hung up on me.

I redialed his number and as expected he didn't answer. Tears streamed down my cheeks and my vision was momentarily blurred as my car swerved slightly. I could not drive any further so I pulled onto the shoulder of the road and tried his number again and got the same results—no answer. This time I waited for his voicemail to kick in. At the sound of the beep I tried my best to speak with as much clarity as my trembling voice would allow. I then commenced to explain to his machine how the whole ordeal was nothing but a misunderstanding.

After hanging up I called my brother back and told him what had happened at my place and also about my conversation with Carlos. As anticipated, Monk was concerned about my safety and wanted to know where I was headed. I told him I wasn't sure where I'd end up but I would call him as soon as I had gotten situated.

Once I had pulled myself together enough to continue driving I proceeded back onto the road and hit I-77, driving blindly. I was headed down the highway with no definite destination. On the run for my life.

On impulse, I opened my phone again, this time I dialed J.T.'s number and prayed he would pick up. After four rings I heard, "Yo!"

I knew he was in his truck because I could hear those loud ass tires.

"Hey you," I spoke, trying my best to sound calm.

"Hey, Chyna Doll. How you doin' ma?"

I tried to hold back the tears and all of the emotions that were at a boiling point, but I lost the battle and broke down again.

Hearing me crying, J.T. became concerned, "Justice, baby what's wrong? You alright?"

I couldn't even answer him. I just continued to cry into the phone like a lost child.

"Baby, where you at? Look, I want you to meet me at my house *right now*! You hear me?" His deep voice boomed with sympathy. "If you beat me there, you wait on me 'cause I'm on my way. We'll talk when you get there."

I was still sobbing as I listened to his commanding voice giving me orders. Under normal circumstances, bossing me around like that would have been a no-no, but at that moment that was exactly what a sistah needed. I needed someone to tell me not to worry because they'd take care of me and make sure I would be safe. At that moment I was a chick with no direction. I was misguided, undecided, and on the verge of self-destruction. I needed some sort of balance and I needed it fast.

Hoping I'd find what I was looking for in the comfort of J.T.'s strong arms, I told him "I'm on my way," and then I closed my phone.

I got off on the next exit, then changed directions and headed to J.T.'s place.

CHAPTER TWENTY
MONK

A moving target is hard to hit. That's why I'd been constantly on the move ever since that incident at T.G.I. Fridays. I was determined not to go out like my niggas had gone out so I decided to flip the game on Carlos and his people. I was about to give them a taste of their own shit.

My only concern at this point was my sister's safety because my life didn't even matter anymore. After Justice had told me about what that nigga Los had said to her, I knew a war with them muthafuckas was inevitable. I knew it was time to put in work.

Since I had the keys to D.C.'s apartment and his vehicles, I'd decided to utilize it to my advantage. I knew no one would double back and try to run up in a dead man's house so I'd been staying at his spot for the past couple of weeks, keeping a low profile. Once Justice had called me to let me know that she was okay, I had made up my mind to stir up calm waters.

Just after 8 P.M. on a Tuesday night, I hopped on D.C.'s Kawasaki and rode across town to Idelwild Road where Carlos's lieutenant Ali's house was located. As I rode through the neighborhood I noticed how quiet it was. When I neared his house, I spotted his chromed-out, cream colored Mercedes SL 55 along with his Escalade parked in the driveway, so I knew he was inside. What I wanted to do was run up in that bitch and blaze everybody in the house. However, I went with my better judgement and just laid low and waited for him to come out.

I sat and watched his house for exactly an hour before there was any movement. On that sixty first minute his front door opened and out he stepped. I immediately perked up when I saw him head toward his truck, carrying what looked like a back pack in one hand. When he opened the driver's side and got in he started the truck but didn't close the door. I was wondering what he was doing, but my question was answered when I saw a little girl whom appeared to be no older than three or four years old come running out the house towards the truck. I was silently praying that she would *not* get in, but to my dismay, she did just that. Ali reached down and scooped the little girl up in his arms, then pulled her in through the driver's side.

Once the child was inside, I watched him wave at a female who was now standing in the doorway.

"Yeah, you better wave goodbye. 'Cause this is the last time that bitch'll see you breathing," I mumbled beneath the helmet.

I was undecided as to whom I wanted to rock to sleep, him or his bitch. Slumping this nigga with the little girl in the truck with him had not been part of the plan, but at this point my understanding was ZERO! Slumping the bitch would hurt him deeply but I wanted this nigga to suffer.

As Ali pulled out of the driveway I was looking back and forth from the truck to the house, trying to decide which one I was going to lay to rest. Then I decided Ali would be the one to get it because I could come back and slump the bitch at any given time if for some reason he ended up getting away from me.

I crunk up D.C.'s bike and waited for the truck to get a block or two away from the house before following him. When I felt like he had gotten a far enough distance away from me I moved. I tailed him a few blocks to another house where he dropped the little girl off. After dropping off the child he proceeded to head down Independence Boulevard, oblivious to his surroundings. I wanted to pull alongside that nigga and let my .40 cal holla at his ass, but I knew I couldn't rush it. So I bided my time and continued to follow him, hoping he would stop somewhere.

Opportunity presented itself when he got off on Arena Drive and headed to the Mart Inn and Suites, the small motel located behind what used to be the old coliseum. This was one of those hidden spots not too many people knew about. It was a spot that was perfect for creeping.

Evidently Ali had already had a room or he was meeting someone there because he bypassed the front office and headed directly around back.

I pulled up to the entrance and gave him a twenty second window before following him to the back of the hotel. As soon as I pulled around to where he was parked I noticed the truck was still running and he was still sitting inside with his phone up to his ear. This nigga was slippin'!

"Caught yo' bitch ass sleepin'," I mumbled as I pulled alongside the truck.

Ali turned his head to look in my direction. As if he suddenly recognized D.C.'s bike and realized what was about to happen, I saw him duck. But my ratchet was already spitting hot lead inside the truck!

The driver's side window shattered and paint chipped off the door as the bullets struck it. The dums-dums were penetrating straight through the door because I could see directly inside the truck through the holes. As I continued to squeeze, I heard the clap of gunfire coming from *inside* the truck and saw flames jumping from Ali's pistol as he fired back. It was like the showdown at the OK Corral as bullets whizzed past my head. A bullet struck the left side of D.C.'s rearview mirror, shattering it into pieces.

Not being deterred from my mission, I aimed in the direction of where the sparks were coming from, and squeezed. Just then, the gunfire from inside the truck stopped and I put the kickstand down and hopped off the bike.

Slowly, I approached the driver's side door with caution, not knowing what awaited me on the other side. The silence was heart-stopping as I snatched open the door, ready to blast. Once the door was ajar, what I saw inside was almost enough to make me nut in my pants. Bad ass Ali was sprawled out on the front seat in a pile of shattered glass. His head was hanging off the seat and his pistol was lying on the floorboard where he had dropped it. His left leg was bleeding profusely and his once white T-shirt was now decorated with blotches of crimson. He'd taken two to the chest and was struggling to breathe.

Although I was still wearing the helmet the look in his eyes told me that he still recognized me. I looked down at Ali and watched as his life was slowly slipping away from him. At that instance I had flashbacks: I saw images of Sapphire lying in that hospital bed; I saw that blood-splattered taxi with Cross's body in it and I saw my nigga D.C. slumped over in that booth in Fridays. I knew there was no way in hell I could leave this nigga breathing. I raised my pistol and aimed between Ali's pleading eyes. He looked up at me and his mouth moved to say something, probably an expletive. However, before the words could come out I emptied what was left of my clip into him. I watched as he bled and took his last exasperated breath.

The backpack he had been carrying when he had left the house was now lying beneath his left leg covered with his blood. I grabbed it, snatched it open and saw that it was full of dead presidents. A bonus!

"You won't be giving *this* to God. I'll take it off ya hands for ya." I spoke to the corpse as I strapped the bloody backpack onto my back.

Moments later, I was back on D.C.'s bike and hauling ass away from the motel. A few nosey patrons were now peeping out of their windows and I saw the manager standing out in front of the office as I passed. I aimed the empty gun in his direction and saw him dash back inside as I zoomed out of the parking lot, burning rubber!

As I rode through a few back streets I thought about what I'd just done. I knew I had just added fuel to the fire in the situation but at that point I didn't give a fuck. Just like Carlos had done, it was now my turn to send a message. I was wondering about when the hunter became the hunted. What would he do? How would he carry it?

By slaying Carlos's right hand man I knew I'd be throwing those niggas off balance and they would be walking on egg shells, not knowing *what* to expect. I was always told by OGs that the easiest mark is an off-balance mark, who doesn't know how or when you may come at him. I had to keep those niggas guessing.

CHAPTER TWENTY-ONE
JUSTICE

The days I'd been at J.T.'s was the most peaceful days I'd had in months. No one but Monk knew who I was with and not even *he* knew the location. The tranquility was something I definitely needed and the peace and quiet was becoming somewhat addictive. Lounging around the spacious two story home in my pajamas during the day while J.T. was out taking care of business and making love all night had become my daily routine. As much as I hated to admit it, I was becoming domesticated and was actually enjoying it. I was cooking J.T.'s favorite meals, cleaning house, and basically playing "wifey." I was starting to regret the fact that I had initially planned to have him robbed because J.T. was a good guy and had a good heart.

Since I'd been in his home, J.T. had been treating me with nothing but pure respect. True enough, there was the occasional "friend" calling ever once in a while but he made it clear to each of them that he was "occupied." I had to respect it and I had no problem with it as long as he kept his "friends" in check, and none of those hookers came out of their mouths the wrong way with a bitch!

Although I moved about his home freely as if it were my own, I still acknowledged the fact that I was in his space. The only place that he said was off limits was his personal office on the second level where I imagined he kept something very personal, like his money. How adamant he'd been about keeping me out of there only piqued my curiosity that much more; had a bitch wanting to go right up in there to see what was so secretive. But as of yet, I'd stayed clear of that office.

That day when I had shown up at J.T.'s home with a trunk full of clothes, looking like I'd been up for forty days and forty nights, he never pressured me to tell him what had been wrong with me. He'd invited me into his home with no questions asked and I felt indebted to him for that. He had simply taken me into his arms and held me as if he didn't want to ever let me go, and told me that everything would be fine. He said he'd make sure of it, even if it meant putting himself in danger by protecting me. He never even questioned my reason for distraught. I think he was allowing me to exhale, knowing that I would talk to him about it whenever I was ready.

The second day at his house was when I explained to him what was going on, or at least he thought I was explaining. I concocted a story about my brother being in some kind of trouble and he had ended up bringing that trouble to my place. Therefore, I couldn't stay at my condo for fear of someone coming there looking for him. It was only partially true, but J.T. ate it up like it was his favorite meal. He assured me that I could stay as long as I liked, and for the time being, I was definitely enjoying my welcome.

We'd gotten to know one another a little better because of the pillow talk we had been having. I already knew that he was originally from Washington, D.C., which was where most of his family was located except for his father. He had only seen him twice in his life and had no idea where he was at. All that he knew about his father was that he was somewhere in the Midwest. This had made me think about my father, Tyson's no good ass, who was back home in Chicago probably still doing what he was best at—being a straight up dog! In my father's case, Tyson was truly a "rollin' stone," and I didn't miss him one bit.

One night while lying in bed basking in the afterglow of so many multiple orgasms, I rolled over and looked at J.T.'s sleeping figure next to me and I heard a slight snore. I smiled at the thought of this punanny putting him to sleep.

I couldn't sleep, so I clicked on the television and flipped through channels until I came across the news. I sat the remote down and watched a report about the increasing violence in Charlotte due to gang activity. Homicide rates had doubled in the past few years and were at an all-time high. Most of the victims were said to be black males between the ages of eighteen and twenty-five.

They were reporting that the latest homicide had taken place in a motel's parking lot on Independence Boulevard where the victim had been found inside his truck, shot gangland style. When I heard the reporter name Ali as the victim, my ears perked up and a sense of nervousness took control of my body for a brief moment. I knew without a shadow of a doubt who the shooter had been. It had to have been my brother!

Sitting up in the bed with my knees pulled up to my chest, I listened intently, hoping that they didn't have anyone in custody. As I listened a little longer my nerves began to calm when they said that the gunman had fled the scene on a motorcycle and was still at large. The only description the authorities had at the time was that of a black male wearing dark colored shorts, a white T-shirt, and dark colored shoes. No facial description had been given because the suspect was wearing a helmet. They went on to say that they believed the motive behind the slaying had been robbery.

I had to call to make sure my brother was okay. I eased out of the bed and picked up J.T.'s cordless, which was on the table beside the bed, and I dialed Monk's number. I went into the bathroom and was closing the door behind me when I heard Monk answer.

"Yeah. Who dis?"

"It's me, boy you okay?" I whispered with concern in my voice.

"Yeah. I'm good, why?"

I got right to the point.

"That thing on Independence, tell me that wasn't y—"

"Oh, you saw that, huh?" Monk asked cutting me off. He was laughing as if this whole ordeal was a joke.

"Yeah, I saw it. You laughing like this a game or somethin'."

"Nah. I *know* it ain't no game. But I can't just find me a muthafucka to go lay up with and act like ain't shit happenin' out here. I gotta do what I gotta do to make sure me *and* you stay alive out here, ya dig?"

He had great amounts of sarcasm in his venomous voice.

"By the way sis, I caught that hoe sleepin," he added, like he was proud of what he'd done.

I sighed and rubbed my temples at the thought of my brother being at war with Carlos and his goons. Then I started thinking, trying to figure out a way we could get out of the mess we were in and leave the entire situation behind us.

"Monk, why don't we just say forget it and go back home?" I suggested. I was tired of the life I was living.

"Home? Chicago?" Monk asked.

"Yeah. I mean, we could just start over and forget about all of this."

Monk was quiet on the other end, which let me know that he was thinking about what I had just suggested.

I spoke again, "I got some money saved up. We can go out there and find a nice lil' spot and just chill 'til we figure out what we wanna do."

"Speakin' of money, I came up off that nigga Ali. He had some stacks on him when I went at him," Monk stated, then added, "I'ma think 'bout what you said. Lemme get back at you on that. That might be a good idea, sis."

"Lemme know soon 'cause if you don't, I just may leave without you. I'm serious. I'm tired of this shit Monk."

"I just said I'ma let you know, didn't I? Just chill for a minute, I need to handle a few more things."

I told my brother to check in with me every once in a while to let me know that he was okay so I wouldn't be worrying myself sick about him. He promised me he would. We ended the call and I was thinking about what I'd just suggested to my brother and began to realize just how much of a good idea it was. I didn't really want to leave while Sapphire was still in the hospital in a coma, but I really wanted to put Charlotte as far behind me as I possibly could.

I also knew that all good things had to come to an end and was contemplating on what to do with J.T. My initial intentions were to have him robbed by Monk, but after spending so much time with him I had start feeling him a little more than I should have been. I thought

Sapphire would have been the one to get caught out there but as it was turning out, it seemed as if I was the one who had fallen weak. Maybe it was the predicament I was in with Carlos that had me in such a vulnerable state; or maybe I was just tired of the streets and the drama that came along with it. Either way, I was really digging J.T. and the more time I spent with him the harder I felt myself falling.

Never had I felt such an instant connection with a man like the one J.T. and I shared. We had so much in common, we liked so many of the same things and I felt completely safe and comfortable with this man. The vibe we shared was so strong to the point it was almost scary. It was as if we had known each other for years.

After my conversation with Monk I walked back into the bedroom and saw that J.T. was still sound asleep. I watched him admiringly for a moment, then walked over and planted tiny kisses on his forehead. I was thinking about how much I'd miss him if I was to leave and wondered if he would come visit me in Chicago. I also wondered if he would miss me as much as I would miss him.

I took a deep breath, let out a long sigh, and came to the conclusion that I would have to cross those bridges when I came to them. But for the time being, I was just going to enjoy the time we had together. I leaned over and eased the comforter down J.T.'s naked waist and smiled devilishly just before lowering my head to the treasure I had become obsessed with. I was getting wet just by the thought of pleasing him because I knew this was his favorite way to wake up.

CHAPTER TWENTY-TWO

CARLOS

It was the day after Ali's closed-casket funeral. My head was still throbbing with the anger I was feeling because of the fact that I'd just lost my man. He wasn't just my man, he was also my brother from another mother. Because of Face and Preme's slip up at the restaurant my nigga was gone. Initially, I hadn't even wanted that hit to go down inside the restaurant like that. But after much debate and consultation with someone who wanted those niggas dead just as bad as I did, I had no choice but to make the call. Not only had those niggas pissed *me* off, but my connect was just as heated with them for personal reasons in which I had initially known nothing about. Those niggas *and* Justice had gotten in way over their heads!

I knew exactly who'd slumped Ali and the fucked up part was the fact that I had lost track of that nigga. I didn't know where his trifling ass sister was hiding at either, but one thing was certain, they'd eventually have to show their faces. As soon as they would, somebody would be right there waiting on them with a rain of hot lead. They were definitely not going to get away. It was war and I refused to stop until more blood was shed—their blood!

The pathetic message that bitch Justice had left on my voicemail hadn't been anything but a smoke screen to try and throw a nigga off. If they hadn't been responsible for my spot getting jacked and wanted to dead the issue, then why had Monk blasted Ali? That didn't add up at all. I decided that we were gonna keep it all the way gangsta until the last man or woman standing took their last breath.

I had put a tag on both Justice and Monk's heads and it was understood that if either of them were sighted I should be contacted immediately with their location. I didn't order another hit because someone higher up wanted to be the one to nod those two personally.

The last lead I'd gotten had been from Sabrina, who coincidentally had been the *first* lead, informing me that Monk and D.C. had been the ones at the park with Cross. I could remember her telling me that she hadn't wanted to be involved in the ordeal. Then she had turned right around and blown my phone up to let me know that those niggas were at the restaurant. Sabrina was a prime example of how money could make a person change their minds, morals, and beliefs. A mutha-fucka would tell God on Jesus for the right price. So, Monk and D.C. never stood a chance once a thirsty bitch was offered some cheddar.

Ali's funeral had me in kind of a solemn mood so I had been sitting around the house all day, lounging with Janeka. I had finally hooked up with her and this day was the third time we'd spent some alone time together. I still hadn't tapped that ass yet, but I was sort of enjoying the chase. I had called her to come over to keep me company for a while and she had accepted the offer. When she showed up, she came in wearing a pair of skin tight stretch/sweat pants that had the initials BCBG stitched across the ass. She also had on a matching T-shirt with the same initials stitched across the chest. This girl was fine and she knew it. Sexuality was oozing from every pore in her body.

Janeka had been catering to me all day—cooking, back rubs, tidying up the place, and basically just making me relax. I loved the attention she was giving and I was especially enjoying watching that phat ass bounce in those tight pants. Every chance I got, I made her get up and go get something for me so I could see that donkey bounce. I was trying to be a gentleman, but it was hard as hell for me to restrain myself as I watched her with lustful eyes. I was determined that this would be the last time we'd be together without the night ending with me laying between those thick ass thighs. I *had* to have this bitch, and I had to have her *soon*.

Later in the evening, we ventured down to the recreation room in my large basement for a few drinks and shot a few games of pool. I had sparked up some weed and offered it to her but she declined, stating that her job required random drug testing and she didn't want to get caught out there. I respected it and commenced to get lifted without her.

While showing her how to properly hold the pool stick, I knew she could feel my dick as it pressed against her ass while I stood behind her, giving her pointers. My semi-erect dick was only a preview of what was in store for her.

We drank, conversed, and got to know one another a little better as we lounged in the basement area listening to music.

"So, what happened to your friend?" Janeka's sexy voice was straining to be heard over the music. She was seated on my white loveseat as I lay back on the matching colored recliner near the digital speakers that pumped Anthony Hamilton's latest joint. All of the furniture in my house was pure white, unlike the furniture in my condo, which was all green. The green represented money and the white represented how I was making it.

I took a sip of the Goose and pineapple that she had made for me from my well-stocked bar, and then responded to her question.

"Some coward gunned him down while he was sittin' in his truck mindin' his bizness."

The thought of my partner being six feet under brought back that dreadful feeling again.

Janeka must have peeped my mood change because she commented, "I'm sorry. We don't have to talk about it if you don't wanna."

"Nah, it's cool," I answered. I needed to vent anyway. "Yeah, it was retaliation for some shit that jumped off awhile back."

"Retaliation?" she asked with raised eyebrows. She then gave me a puzzling look, which I interpreted as "intrigue." That gangsta shit was turning this bitch on. So, I decided to give it to her ass raw. "Oh, you like that gangsta shit, huh?" I asked, smiling.

Janeka smiled back sensuously while chewing her bottom lip. I knew that deep down inside, all good girls liked gangstas, but Janeka seemed to be getting off on that shit. She got up and turned down the stereo so she could hear me better.

"See, some muthafuckas robbed one o' my mans. And we got at them niggas. But one of 'em apparently got back at us and Ali paid for it."

While I spoke, Janeka had walked over and taken a seat on the arm of the recliner I was sitting in and began caressing my chest and shoulders.

She whispered in my ear, "Damn, baby, you're a dangerous man, huh?"

She was breathing in my ear, making my dick do the Bankhead Bounce in my shorts.

I was enjoying the feel of her small hands on my chest.

"Nah, I ain't dangerous. I'm just nothin' to fuck with."

This girl was *so* sexy. I wanted to fuck this bitch *bad*, and from the look in her smoldering eyes it seemed as if she was ready to rip off her own panties for me.

"I bet if I pissed you off, you'd put out a hit on me or something, huh?" she jokingly questioned while gazing at me with those doe-shaped eyes.

"Nah, I only strike when necessary," I returned while running my fingers through her silky hair. "All the niggas I've ever put in the dirt… it was necessary to give them a permanent nap," I added while pulling her onto my lap, kissing her soft, sweet lips. Her hand rubbed my dick as I removed her shirt and pulled up her lace bra, exposing the most perfect set of titties I'd ever seen. I caressed them as she moaned softly while continuing to massage my dick through my shorts.

Janeka purred in my ear, "Oooh, baaaaby, you making my pussy wet. My clit's *throbbin'.*"

I began sucking her nipples and in between licks I said, "My niggas… love AKs…T.G.I. Fridays was my work."

That shit had her moaning and pulling my head into her breasts urging me to suck harder. While still licking and sucking her titties, I let my hand slide down between her thighs in an attempt to see just how wet that pussy really was. Just as my hand felt the heat radiating from her hot pussy she clamped her legs shut.

She moaned softly, "Wait a minute, baby. This pussy ain't heard enough yet."

She was looking at me with lusting eyes.

"Oh, I'm talkin' to the *pussy* now?" I laughed.

Then I looked intently into her eyes and peeped a slight change in her demeanor as if she were trying to decide whether or not to let me get it. I reached for her crotch again, and again she avoided my hand. A strange feeling washed over me for a moment and just as I was about to question her actions I heard the unmistakable sound of my front door come crashing in.

I looked at the sinister smile on Janeka's face and knew at that instance that I'd been snaked! I threw that bitch off my lap and dashed for my pistol, which was stashed behind the entertainment center. If I was going out, I wasn't going out by myself and this snake bitch was gonna be the first to get it!

I looked over at Janeka as she was hastily putting her top back on and mumbling to herself.

I thought I heard her say, "*We're in the basement. He's strapped.*"

"Fuck you talkin' to?" I hissed at her and pointed the pistol in her direction, ready to squeeze.

"Carlos, you don't wanna do that. I suggest you put the gun down and we can both come out of this situation unharmed."

She was speaking with calmness that I'd never heard her speak with since I had been dating her.

"Bitch, shut the fuck up, and don't move," I demanded as I heard some niggas moving about above us like they were headed towards the basement where we were. I yelled as I walked toward her with fire in my eyes.

"Who da fuck you send at me? You fuckin' wit' Monk, ain't you?"

"Carlos, don't point that damn gun at me!" she stated, more like demanded.

"Bitch, you got me fucked up!" I hissed as I cocked my pistol back, loading one into the chamber. I was ready to blow this bitch's wig back.

I heard footsteps getting closer as Janeka stared toward the stairs with a look of apprehension in her eyes. She took a step toward the staircase and I knew she was thinking about running, so I grabbed her by the throat and put my arm around her neck. I held her in a choke hold with my pistol resting on her temple. I could feel her body trembling with fear as the footsteps got closer to the stairs. I positioned her body in front of mine so that she would catch the first piece of lead from her people's guns.

"Carlos, you hurtin' me, let me g..."

Those were the only words she was able to get out before I looked up and saw my worst fear become a reality!

CHAPTER TWENTY-THREE
MONK

Tan and I were sitting in D.C.'s living room blowing Haze and relaxing.

I blew a cloud of smoke towards the ceiling as I thought, *Sixty-two grand ain't bad for an unexpected bonus.*

After I'd slumped that nigga Ali, I went back into hibernation because I thought Carlos and his boys would be on a rampage. But word on the street was that Carlos had subsequently met an unfortunate circumstance and just as I figured, his boys were lost without him. They say if you strike the shepherd the sheep will scatter. That old proverb was so true in the situation at hand because those niggas couldn't even think without him.

Once Carlos was gone, I'd turned the game up on them. I stalked them from a distance until I'd found out where they were hanging out. They were congregating at a condo out in Ballentyne, which was on the outskirts of Charlotte. This spot was so secluded that if you weren't actually looking for it you'd probably miss it. They thought they were being discreet, but they had no idea I was laying on them. Preying on niggas was second nature to me because it becomes a habit for a true-to-heart stick up kid.

Every time I thought about what I'd done to those niggas it brought about a hearty, satisfying laugh because I had definitely made them feel me late one Friday night as they exited the condo. I emptied my clip on them niggas and saw two of them fall before I fled the scene. The element of surprise is a beautiful thing.

I sat back on D.C.'s sofa and thought about what I'd heard about Carlos and how he'd went out and it made me laugh out loud, causing me to choke on the blunt I'd been puffing on. Tan reached over to pat my back and offered, "You good?"

"Yeah, I'm aiight," I responded between coughs as I passed her the weed.

Tan and I had been lounging on the sofa listening to the quiet storm for the past hour or so in a state of total relaxation. I'd been spending quite a bit of QT time with her over the past couple of weeks and had really been enjoying her company. Since I'd been laying low, her and my sister were the only people I'd been in contact with because I didn't need anybody else in my mix at this point.

By Tan not being from Charlotte, she was clueless as to what was going on and she had no idea that I was in the middle of a fuckin' war. My predicament was foreign to her, so that alone made her the perfect person to hang out with. She'd been playing hard with the ass, but I could tell she was about to break at any minute because she'd become too comfortable around me. I was just waiting it out like a Mexican stand-off.

I turned up the volume on the stereo with the remote when I heard "Seems Like You're Ready," an old school joint by R. Kelly. Tan began singing along with the radio. It was at that minute when I actually took a good look at her and realized just how beautiful this girl was. Tan had a natural beauty that most women of her ethnicity were blessed with and her body was unbelievable!

As I stared at her through half-closed eyes, I thought about when I'd run up in her house and slapped her around. It made me feel kind of bad about the whole incident. My feeling half sorry for her was another reason I'd been spending time with her and wasn't pressing her for the pussy. I felt like I owed her, in a weird kind of way. She was cool as hell with a kindred spirit and was seemingly green to the street life. I admired that about her because I was tired of dealing with those wanna-be half ass slick bitches. And the fact that she was bi-sexual, something that she still hadn't openly admitted, was a turn on all within itself.

Being around Tan was therapeutic for me because she seemed so genuine and down to earth, and I needed that. She never questioned me about my life in the streets and she never once passed judgment. However, she did mention that I should consider slowing down once I'd told her that D.C. had gotten gunned down.

My silent thoughts on her suggestion of me slowing down were, *Thanks, but no thanks. Shit is way too thick out here for a nigga to slow down.*

As I lay back in the plush leather I let the weed do its thing. I thought about Carlos again and how he'd fell for the okey-doke like a true *cone head.* True enough, I'd always known that every man has a thumbscrew, a weakness, and Carlos's weakness had always been pretty bitches with phat asses. But like that old school group BBD once sang "Never trust a big butt and a smile." That broad had really been *poison.* But I guessed that was just one of life's many curve balls that he just couldn't manage to duck. Ole girl had *really* rocked him to sleep.

I kicked my feet up on D.C.'s coffee table and looked over at Tan while she sang the last verse of R. Kelly's joint. I thought about what my sister had suggested about going back home and I came to the conclusion that it wasn't a bad idea. I hadn't been back to Chi-town since I was a kid and I was now kind of looking forward to the return trip. Justice was right, Charlotte had become too much for a nigga and I was getting tired of trying to maneuver while constantly having to look over my shoulder. It was bad enough that I had to worry about niggas who I'd robbed trying to get some get-back, but I had to be on point about a nigga who I *didn't* rob but wanted me dead. The game was starting to get deeper, and the more thought I gave it, the more I realized that I was getting burnt out on that shit.

"Did you hear me?" Tan asked. Apparently she'd been talking to me while I was lost in thought.

"Say what?" I was barely able to hold my eyes open.

"I said you look like a black Bruce Lee. I can't even see your eyes. Are they even open?" she joked.

"You got jokes tonight, huh?" I smiled at her.

We talked well into the night until at one point she checked her watch and told me that she had to get home but she'd see me again soon. I stopped her as she arose from the sofa to grab her purse.

Holding her hand, I said, "I'm leavin' in a few days. Me and my sister going to Cali for a minute, and I'on' even know if I'm comin' back." I lied with a straight face.

Tan gave me an inquisitive stare for a minute, and then said, "Just when we were getting to know one another."

She had a hint of disappointment in her voice.

I wanted to say, "Bitch, you don't even know my real name, so how we getting to know one another?" But what I actually said was, "Yeah, I know. But I wanna keep in touch wit' choo though." I was caressing her hand.

"No doubt," she responded. "But you betta not leave before we see each other again. Because I got something I wanna give you. I been waiting to let you have it for quite some time now, but I guess you can have it as a going away gift."

She licked her lips, running her tongue from one corner of her mouth to the other in slow motion. There was no misunderstanding her meaning because she was making it more than obvious.

I stood up and told her, "Hell, you can give it to me right now! Why make a nigga wait?" I was pulling her into my arms as I spoke.

She pulled away slowly and started towards the door, smiling, "Nah, I think I'll wait 'til I see you again. That way I'll be sure you won't leave without gettin' at me. Look at it this way, you've got something to look forward to next time we see each other."

With that said, she was out the door.

That girl had just teased the shit out of a nigga. But it was all good because the next time I would see her I'd be digging up in those guts. She had made it quite clear that the ass was only a phone call away, and I was anxious as hell to tear down those sugar walls. I'd always had a fantasy of hearing a bitch speak that Spanish shit in my ear and call me *Papi* while I fucked the shit out of her. Now, I was going to finally get that chance. I was thinking that maybe I'd get lucky and she'd bring ToWanda's tall ass with her for a threesome. It was wishful thinking, but I was just glad that things were starting to look up for me.

After Tan had left, I secured D.C.'s deadbolts, grabbed my two glocks and peeped out of both the front and back windows, Malcolm X-style, to make sure shit was still tranquil outside. Faded or not, I was still on point and conscious of my surroundings because I knew at any given time a foe could step out of the shadows and try to put a nigga to sleep. But I was on point, ready for whoever wanted it with me.

CHAPTER TWENTY-FOUR
JUSTICE

Ever since I had suggested that me and Monk take a trip back home I'd been looking forward to the day when we would leave. I had talked to J.T. and told him that I had been thinking about going back to Chicago for awhile and as expected, he didn't want me to leave. I really didn't want to leave him either, but I knew as long as I stayed in Charlotte I'd never be able to live a peaceful life. Besides, I couldn't stay cooped up in J.T.'s house forever.

Although Carlos had been met with an unfortunate circumstance, I knew his henchmen were still lurking in the cut, waiting for me to resurface. And I couldn't live my life constantly being paranoid, not knowing whether I'd catch a bullet while walking down the street or while pumping gas like the victims of the D.C. sniper, I couldn't live like that.

I was thrilled when Monk had told me that he'd made up his mind to go back home with me. With each day that passed without me hearing from him had me in suspended terror. I was worried about my brother's safety because Monk was the only family I had. I didn't know what I'd do if I was to lose him.

Everything had seemed to be getting better for me, until one morning I was laying in J.T.'s bed when his home phone rang. He'd already left for the day, and out of respect I still wasn't answering his phone so I just let it ring. After a few rings his answering machine picked up. Apparently he'd forgotten to turn the volume down because I heard a chick's voice loud and clear. I started to reach over and turn down the volume, but the voice sounded very familiar and it piqued my curiosity so I let it play.

"J.T., this is Joy *again*. I'm tired of callin' you and you ain't callin' a bitch back. I *wants* my money nigga! I ain't playin'! You an' Red ain't gonna play me like that. If you don't want me to call Lil' Joe and Supreme an' nem and tell 'em what *really* happened, you betta come up off my stacks and I mean *today* muthafucka!"

Anger crept up on me and I started to pick up the phone and blaze that heifer, but her next words made me sit straight up in the bed and gasp.

Joy said, "How you think Justice and Monk would feel if they knew the truth? Oh, you think I didn't know you been layin' up wit' that bitch? You betta get at me nigga!"

It was Sapphire's cousin Joy, and after she'd hung up I sat there spellbound, staring wide-eyed at that damn machine as if it would get up and walk away at any given second.

"What the hell!?" I said aloud.

What the fuck had she meant by *"how Justice would feel if she knew the truth?"* What fuckin' "truth"? And what did Carlos's boys have to do with J.T.? I didn't know that J.T. even knew those niggas. And why in the hell had my name just come outta this bitch's mouth?

I thought, *Oh hell nah, lemme call this bitch back!*

My tongue ring had unconsciously begun tapping my teeth.

I jumped my naked ass out of bed with a scarf tied around my head. Titties were bouncing everywhere as I reached for the phone and pressed *69 to return the call. I listened as a recording picked up and announced that the number would not accept incoming calls.

Damn! Think Justice! Think!

I sat back down on the bed, closed my eyes, and buried my forehead into my hands, trying to think of anyone I knew that may have had a way to contact Joy. The only person I could think of was my girl who was still lying comatose in that hospital bed. And Sapphire's mother had recently gotten her number changed so I was clueless.

Joy had told J.T. to call her back, so that meant he had *her* number, and maybe it was somewhere in the house. With this thought, I immediately began searching the bedroom.

187

After putting on one of J.T.'s oversized shirts I started combing through his drawers, searching through the pockets of his clothes, which were hanging in his closet, and looking any and everywhere I thought he would keep something he didn't want me to see. I tore that room apart like a Tsunami had been through it and still found *nada*.

However, this didn't deter me from continuing my search. I left the bedroom, went into the kitchen, and checked all the drawers. I went through all of his bills and scrap pieces of paper to see if maybe he'd scribbled Joy's number down and forgotten it. I found several numbers with names, but none of them were Joy's. I even checked the living room and came up empty. This nigga was good!

I was getting frustrated. I went back into the kitchen and walked over to the wall phone and dialed the first four digits of J.T.'s cell number, ready to wild out and see what the hell was going on! But I stopped myself and thought for a second, trying to come up with another alternative. After a few short seconds, I realized that there was still *one* room I hadn't checked.

His office!

I was sure that office would be the place I'd find Joy's number along with a lot more stuff he didn't want me to see. I hung up the kitchen phone and proceeded to head to the one room in the house I'd never been in.

I ran up the winding stairs until I reached the top. Winded, I hurried to the office door and tried the knob. As expected, it was locked. I stood before the door contemplating on what to do. I was wondering if I should've just calmed down and waited for J.T. to get home and let him explain what was going on, or if I should've tried to enter the room and find out on my own. True enough, I trusted J.T. and didn't think he would hide something that concerned me.

I thought, *Maybe I'm trippin' for nothing and over reacting.*

As I stood before that door I had to take a deep breath and let it marinate for a minute because I was sure my blood pressure had probably risen. But the longer I stood at that door the more my anger rose because Joy's message was replaying over and over in my head. I was becoming anxious as hell to find out what was going on. The fact that I knew Joy was a scandalous bitch that would do damn near anything for a dollar had my curiosity at peak level. A million scenarios swirled through my mind as I tried to justify J.T.'s reason for even dealing with a low-level, bottom feeder like her. I was thinking that maybe Red had done something to her and maybe she was also blaming J.T. because the two were cousins and known to be together frequently. But any way I looked at it, that bitch had mentioned me and my brother's names and in any case, I had to find out what *that* had been about!

Anger overpowered rationality and before I knew it I was beating on that door like I was trying to break that bitch down. I pounded on that door until my hands were sore and beet red. I soon tired myself out and realized what I was doing was fruitless. I turned my back to the door and slid to the floor with exhaustion. I *had* to get into that room and it looked like I definitely wasn't going to knock the door down, so I had to take another approach. I went back downstairs and called my brother, using my cell.

"What up, sis."

"Hey, you know Joy?" I asked.

"Phire's cousin?"

"Yeah. You know how to get in touch with her?" I was rambling through J.T.'s kitchen drawer again.

"Nah. You know I'on' fuck wit' that gutta bucket," Monk contested.

"Well, look, I need some help. You remember when we were little and you used to try to teach me how to pick locks?"

"Girl, what choo up to?" Monk was laughing.

"Just walk me through it right quick, okay?" I responded without explaining to him what I was up to because I knew Monk and how quick his hair-trigger temper was. I was gathering the tools I needed for the job as I spoke.

"You at that mark J.T.'s house?" he asked curiously.

"Yeah, but he ain't here right now," I replied while heading back upstairs towards the office.

"I kinda figured he wasn't there," he said sarcastically. "J.T. gonna kick that ass for fuckin' wit' his shit, 'cause I know your sneaky ass is up to no good." Monk was laughing again.

I was back at the office door in a matter of seconds, ready to receive instructions from my brother in Lock-Picking 101. I stuck the tiny tweezers in the lock and listened to Monk as he walked me through the process. After about fifty attempts to manipulate the lock I finally had the door open.

"Got it?" Monk asked, sounding a little frustrated with me because it had taken me so long.

"Yeah. Thanks lil' bruh. I'll hit ya' back."

"Aiight. And Justice...be careful, 'cause I know you up to something," Monk stated with genuine concern.

"I will be," I told him and we ended the call as I stepped inside J.T.'s private office. As I looked around I noticed that this room was nothing special. There was a large oak desk in the center of the room with a computer which was repeating, "You've got mail."

The only other item on the desk was a small CD player which sat next to the computer. A small, portable refrigerator sat in one corner and a burgundy lounge chair occupied the opposite side of the room. The walls were decorated with paintings of two older women whom I recognized as his mother and grandmother along with a family portrait of him and his mother when he was a young boy. There was a closet near the back of the room, so I walked over and tried the knob.

It was unlocked.

I twisted the knob and when the door was opened I saw a large safe. Just as I'd figured, this was where he kept his money. Why niggas don't put their money in the bank is beyond me, especially if it was being made legitimately. The safe was one of those with a digital combination and it was locked. But a sistah had to try anyway.

After trying every combination of numbers under the sun, I finally gave up. I closed the closet back and walked over to the desk and started rambling through the drawers. I expected to find some sort of business material like payroll stubs or time sheets from his businesses; instead, I found a stack of photos. I flipped through the stack and noticed he had a lot of flicks of naked women in compromising positions.

"Freaky ass nigga," I mumbled.

Halfway through the pile I saw three pictures of the bitch that had just left that nasty message on J.T.'s answering machine.

It was Joy!

She was sprawled out naked on a sofa that looked very much like the one that was downstairs in J.T.'s living room. In each of the photos she was being penetrated with a large dildo that was being held by someone else. As I took a closer look I saw the tattoo on the right wrist of the man who was screwing Joy with the toy.

It was J.T.'s hand!

Evidently he was the one who was taking the picture.

J.T. and Joy!?

I couldn't believe it! At that instance, I thought about the time the condom had broken when J.T. and I were once having sex. I immediately became worried because there was no telling what I might've contracted if he was screwing all of those girls, especially Joy's dirty ass.

I threw the photos onto the desk and stood up; ready to leave the room but another photo caught my eye. Beneath the stack of photos of women there were more photos of J.T. and his boys. On the back of the photos was J.T.'s handwriting, noting where the photos had been taken along with dates. He had pictures of himself with a few guys I'd seen only in passing, but I didn't know any of them except Red until I got to the last few pictures, then I saw a *real* familiar face.

The final few photos had me stunned! I couldn't believe who was in some of the pictures with J.T. and Red. I thought my eyes were playing tricks on me or maybe the dude just bared great resemblance to someone I knew. My mind was somersaulting as I flipped the photos over to see the names. The first one read THE TURNER BOYS—CLUB STIR JUNE 6TH. The next was a photo of J.T. and the familiar looking guy by themselves. It read ME AND LIL' CUZ--R.I.P. JULY 3RD. I flipped the picture back over, stared at the face again, and knew without a doubt that the guy I was seeing was indeed someone I knew.

There were a few more pictures of J.T., the guy, and Red at different clubs in Charlotte, Atlanta, Miami, and D.C. and all of them bared the same label THE TURNER BOYS—FAM' 4 LIFE!

I looked at the pictures again and noticed how much J.T. and this guy resembled and it dawned on me that these men were some kin. I dropped the photos to the desk and let out a loud sigh.

What in the hell is this man up to? I questioned silently just as I seen what looked like a pamphlet inside the drawer where the photos had been.

I picked it up and stared at it. It was an obituary. The same familiar face on the obituary stared back at me as I read the name under the picture aloud, confirming my speculation, "Croshawn Cross Turner!"

What type of game is J.T. playing? First, he'd fucked with nasty ass Joy, then he hadn't ever mentioned the fact that he knew Cross, let alone that they were family!

Thoughts swirled through my head like a cyclone and it made my temples throb.

I sat back in the large chair and closed my eyes while massaging my aching temples, then I began to think back to the day we'd found out about Cross's murder. No wonder J.T. had almost ran off the road when I told him about Cross getting shot at Sapphire's. He never meant to say "Ross"; he knew all along that I'd said it was "Cross." And Joy!? That skinny ass barfly. Damn! This nigga was trifling as hell!

After not finding anything else in the office, I placed the photos back inside the drawer just as I'd found them with the girls on top of the pile. Then as I closed the drawer and headed for the door, I glanced back and took one last look at that closet where the safe was hidden. I stepped out of the room and made sure the door was locked before I headed back downstairs to the bedroom so I could think.

I plopped back down on the bed and started trying to put the pieces of this puzzle together. Joy's message was playing in my head like a CD on repeat and I began to analyze her every word.

"I wants *my money nigga,"* but money for what?

"Tell Lil' Joe and Supreme and nem what really *happened."* What happened with what?

"If Justice and Monk knew the truth..." What truth?

I thought long and hard, trying to decipher what she had been talking about as I lay back on the bed with a pillow over my face. *Joy, Red, J.T.? What the fuck did they do? And how does Cross fit into all this? Cross? Cross? Cross?*

After about ten minutes of brainstorming I suddenly snatched the pillow away from my face and sat up on the bed as straight as a board. Finally, realization hit a bitch like a speeding Mack truck!

"OH, HELL NO! I *know* he didn't do that shit!" I screamed as my voice echoed throughout the entire house.

"Cross, two more niggas, and a female did it, it wasn't me." I heard my brother's voice speaking in my head as if he was standing right next to me. Now I really believed him. Tears began welling up in my eyes and I commenced to cry for the two hundredth time in the span of a month. I thought about the crazy ass twist my life had just encountered. I hoped all of this shit was just me misconstruing things, but everything was starting to add up too perfectly.

I needed to call Monk to tell him what I thought was going on. I struggled with weak, wobbly knees to make it to the dresser where my cell phone was at. I reached for my phone and glanced down at the dresser where my tears were falling and noticed the jewelry box where J.T. kept his jewels when he wasn't wearing them. I had never messed with his jewelry or any other personal items he'd ever left laying around, but something inside told me to open that box.

I lifted the lid off the wooden box and glanced at his platinum jewelry, which was sparkling with diamonds. His barrel link chain with the diamond encrusted J laid amongst his Patek Phillipe watch and platinum bracelet, along with a few other pieces I'd never seen him wear before.

I dialed Monk's number as I continued to browse over all of the ice that was staring back at me. I listened to Monk's phone ring and just as

I was about to close the box my eyebrows wrinkled as one of the rings inside caught my attention. I picked it up and lay it in the palm of my hand.

"Well I'll-be-damned," I muttered as I looked at the diamond ring with ruby and onyx settings.

I picked through the rest of the jewelry and saw a custom-made Invicta watch with Lucky Charm diamonds in the band and two more custom made rings that I had only ever seen one other person floss before. I picked up the watch and the rings and inspected them to make sure I wasn't trippin'. After looking over them, there was no doubt in my mind as to whom this jewelry belonged to. Just then, my brother answered his phone.

"What the bizness is? You finished wit' yo' lil' B&E," he joked.

I wiped my eyes and ran my hand under my nose as I sniffled, "M-Monk, I know who robbed Mark."

"Fuck you mean you know who robbed Mark? Cross did that shit."

"I meant, I know who else was with him," I reported as I cried into the phone.

"Who?" Monk was sounding anxious and angry all at the same time.

"J.T., Red, and Joy." Tears were now pouring.

"Where you hear that at? How you figure that?" he questioned skeptically.

I looked down at my hand and returned, "'Cause I'm lookin' at Mark's jewelry."

Monk was quiet for a moment. The silence was awkward until I commenced to relate to him how I'd put it all together, starting with Joy's message, and then with the pictures, and finally the jewelry.

"Give me directions! I'm on my way!" Monk was ready to come to my rescue but I stalled him. I thought about how J.T. had been playin' me like a fool. I thought about how he had me thinking he wasn't a street nigga while the whole time he had been knee deep in the game. I had to make this nigga feel me for trying to play me like that.

I told my brother, "Don't worry about J.T., I'ma take care of him."

"Nah, where you at Justice? Tell me where that nigga live."

I assured Monk that I'd be okay, but he was still ranting and raving as I disconnected the call. I should have let Monk touch that nigga a long time ago, but now I concluded that this would be one situation I would handle myself. I'd been used and this man had basically destroyed my life. My best friend was on her death bed; my brother and I were in hiding and running for our lives. All because of the man whose bed I'd been sharing for the past few weeks. A man I'd fallen head over heels for. J.T. had played me all the way out, but it was now my turn to play the game. And nobody plays the game better than a bitch that has been scorned!

A few minutes after I'd ended the call with my brother, I heard J.T.'s truck pulling up in the driveway. I hastily put the jewelry back inside the box like I'd found it, then looked into the mirror and wiped my eyes for the *last* time. There would be no more crying, and no more pain for me. I was all cried out.

My reflection had showed that the glow in my eyes had faded to black. Just that quickly, all the admiration I'd had for this man had transformed into straight up *hate*!

When I heard his key enter the lock in the front door I took off his shirt and headed to the bathroom to hop into the shower. I wanted to wash away all of the physical *and* emotional distress I'd accumulated while I'd been sleeping with the enemy!

CHAPTER TWENTY-FIVE
CARLOS

Lemme get that, Los," Winkie asked with a crooked smile. His teeth were brown and his breath smelled bad enough to gag a skunk.

"Get what?"

"That roastbeef. You know you ain't gonna eat it," he replied.

Winkie was a recovering crack addict who was only in rehab at the time because he had no choice but to be, considering where he was at. His appetite was humungous as hell because he was making up for all the meals he'd missed while chasing that "glass dick." He wasn't letting anything get pass him. I guessed he was trying to get his weight back up.

Looking down at the plastic tray I was holding, I decided that Winkie had been absolutely right; I didn't want *any* of that shit.

"Here, you can get *all* this shit," I told him while handing him the small tray.

Watching Winkie devour the meat that looked as if it had hues of green, pink, and blue in it made me realize where I was. I took a look around at all the niggas dressed in orange jumpsuits and flip flops, and it made me heated all over again. I was in the Charlotte Mecklenburg County Jail on some *bullshit*!

Those bitch ass homicide detectives had stepped their game up and ended up playing dirty with a nigga. Since they'd had such a hard time trying to pin bodies on a nigga in the past they'd decided to bring in reinforcements. They enlisted the ATF to try to rope a nigga off.

For the past month, I'd been sleeping on that hard ass slab of steel they called a bunk, having wet dreams and federal nightmares! They wouldn't give me a bond, stating that I was a "flight risk," meaning that once out, I'd probably disappear. So I was stuck!

They knew they'd never get me head up, so they decided to come at a nigga sideways by sending a woman at me. The more I thought about Janeka, or better yet "Agent Janice Waters" it made me feel as if molten lava was coursing through my veins. I had slipped with her because I should have followed up on her background. I should have also peeped the warning signs with her that was more than obvious. She had never told me the name of the salon she'd supposedly worked at nor had I even thought that maybe she'd lied about her job with Wells Fargo. That skunk had rocked a nigga all the way to sleep and when I'd finally woke up I was too far gone. Her words still rang in my head like the Liberty Bell.

"This pussy ain't heard enough yet."

I had joked with her about me talking to the pussy, but later I'd found out that I had been doing just that—literally. That broad had been wired up. Never would I have imagined her having a mini-transmitter taped to her fucking crotch area. Technology is a beast!

That fateful day, agents had been posted up all around my crib waiting for her to give the signal: *"My clit's throbbing."* As soon as the words had escaped her lips, my house was bombarded with feds!

So, there I was with my voice on tape, confessing to bodies and shit. But the bright side to all of it was the fact that my attorney, Ronnie Dobson, whom was known as the white Johnnie Cochran, was confident that I'd walk. He had said that the way the situation had gone down it had been entrapment. Furthermore, I had said that I'd only told Janice what I thought she wanted to hear because I thought it would lead to a sexual encounter. Niggas run game everyday, telling women what they want to hear just to get the ass. My situation was no different.

I said I'd had the gun, using Agent Waters as a shield because I thought some niggas were trying to rob me. She never once identified herself as an agent so I had assumed she was in on the robbery attempt. All I heard was the sound of my door being smashed, so I was trying to protect myself because I feared for my life. This was my story and I was sticking to it. Truth be told, if I could turn the clock back thirty-one days I would've broken that bitch Janice's neck in six different places!

In the four weeks I'd been off the streets things had gone berserk. Niggas had been stalling on payments of my cheddar and they had also been trying to spin Lil' Joe and Dave as well. Since Ali was dead and niggas thought I'd be gone for forever and a day, I guessed they felt they could try me like that. But little did they know they were sadly mistaken.

That nigga Monk had lost his fucking mind too. I had no idea which one of my niggas he'd caught slipping, but he had followed one of them to my condo and ended up blasting on them while they were all together. Face and Supreme had gotten hit but thankfully their injuries were nothing life threatening. But they were both still laid up in the hospital out of commission for a minute.

It seemed as soon as I'd gotten arrested, the niggas who used to harbor fear for me had suddenly grown some hair on their nuts. But it was all good because I was going to be back out there in no time. All I had to do was just lay it down, stay silent and ride that shit out.

"Los, you wanna play these niggas in spades?" Winkie asked.

I looked around and noticed that everyone had finished eating their so-called lunch and was now scattered out. Some were seated in the small television viewing area and a few were seated at the steel picnic-style tables playing chess, checkers, or card games. I was bored as hell and didn't feel like watching television so I decided to take Winkie up on his offer.

As we started towards the table Winkie whispered in my ear, "Watch my fingers, I'ma let you know how many spades I got on every deal, aiight." I smiled at the fact that it never stopped with that nigga. Even in jail, this nigga was gaming and scheming.

"I got cha," I told him as we sat at the table with two old school cats. "What we playin' for?" I asked as I shuffled the cards.

The old school cats looked at one another and the one to my right stated, "Five commissary items a head. That too steep for y'all?"

Evidently he had no idea of who I was so I said, "Fuck that. A hundred dollars a head. I got my man Winkie, so y'all ain't gotta worry about him."

I must've sounded like I was speaking Chinese or some other foreign language because the old heads looked at me like I was crazy, then they got up, leaving me and Winkie sitting there.

"Nigga you ain't on the streets no mo'. Niggas ain't got it like that up in here," Winkie stated with a hint of attitude because I'd run his "ducks" away. I had fucked up his hustle.

I watched as Winkie left to search for some more vics while I started playing solitary. I sat there and looked down at the orange suit I was wearing and thought *Ain't no way in the fuck I'm supposed to be sittin' up in here.*

I started thinking about everything that had happened in the past few months, from my spot getting jacked to Ali getting killed. And to top it off, I'd gotten knocked on some bogus ass shit. I got so frustrated I slung the cards across the table. Niggas looked at me like I was losing my mind. I ignored their stares, got up from the table, and left the cards scattered on the floor. I walked over to the television area and took a seat as the news was just coming on.

The headline was about missing persons and the first face I saw was a real familiar one. The name read JOY HARRIS and I squinted trying to place the face in my memory bank. I knew I knew her but I just couldn't put my finger on it.

"I used to fuck that bitch," one nigga said as he pointed at the girl's picture.

Another stated, "That broad used to set niggas up. Ain't no tellin' *what* happened to her ass. I'm willing to bet money they won't find that bitch alive."

It was then when I recognized her as Sapphire's cousin. The news was saying that somebody had snatched her ass. While watching the report about Joy I heard my name being called by the CO. He informed me that I had a visit. I wasn't expecting anyone so I had no idea who was waiting for me in the visitation room.

It took me fifteen minutes to get ready, and then I was escorted to the visitation area, which consisted of individual booths with one chair, a telephone mounted on the wall, and a thick pane of double-sided glass. On the other side of the glass was an identical booth reserved for the visitors. Once the cuffs were removed I rubbed my aching wrists before taking a seat. I looked across at my visitor through the glass and saw the beautiful woman motion for me to pick up the phone. We both took the phone off the wall at the same time and I spoke first.

"What it do, Mendoza?"

"Carlos," she nodded, then looked me over, inspecting the jump-suit. "Nice color. Matches your complexion."

"Oh, so you got jokes?" We both laughed, and then I asked, "What wind blew you this way?"

"You know I had to come check on my favorite client," she smiled.

"You sound like a lawyer talkin' like that," I smiled back.

"A lawyer? You know I don't like those crooked muthafuckas."

"What's good? What you doin' down here for real?" I asked my coke connect.

"Just wanted to come and see how you're doin', that's all."

"You mean you just wanted to see if I was keepin' my mouth shut, right?"

She nodded slowly while maintaining eye contact, "Papa sent me."

"I kinda figured that. Tell Papa Mendoza I got this shit whupped. And I don't appreciate him sending you to check a nigga like this either. How long y'all been knowing me?" My voice was rising a little.

"Simmer down Los. It's all love, baby," she stated with a calm voice. "Don't shoot the messenger, sweetheart," she teased with a smile. "Besides, I can't wait for you to get out so we can get back on track, I miss you." She crossed her thick legs.

"Yeah right, you miss my money. That's what you miss," I laughed.

Mendoza and I chatted about my predicament with the female agent until my visiting time was up, twenty minutes after it had begun. As she rose to leave, I watched her fine ass walk away and I was wondering what it would be like to hit that. My dick got hard as I watched her ass swing from side to side through the thick glass. I'd been away from women for a month and it was beginning to take its toll on me. However, I had to check myself because Mendoza and her family were nothing to be fucked with. Besides, chasing a fine bitch was the reason why I was in this situation.

After the visit with my connect I went back to my tiny one-man room and lay back on that hard ass bunk. I thought about how I was going to have to step the game up once good ole Ronnie sprang a nigga out of this shit. I couldn't believe that broad had come to see me like I had diarrhea at the mouth. If it hadn't been for her, Face and Preme would have never gone up in that restaurant like that, letting Monk get away. Their method of murder was far more cautious than that, but Mendoza had pressed the issue and they had gotten careless. I needed to get out so I could get my team back on point because it seemed like things were slowly falling apart.

CHAPTER TWENTY-SIX
JUSTICE

J.T.'s sleeping figure lay next to me as I sat upright in the bed with my arms folded across my naked breasts. My tongue ring wouldn't stop clacking as I looked over at him and tried to contain the anger that was seeping from my pores. So badly did I want to put a knife through this nigga's black heart, or pull an Al Green on his ass with some boiling grits. But instead, I eased from beneath the comforter and tip-toed into the restroom.

I hit the switch and waited for the room to be filled with light, and then I walked over and looked into the mirror. The first thing I noticed was how inanimate my eyes looked. Ever since I'd found out how much of a snake J.T. really was it seemed as if my entire world had turned morbid. I hated that nigga. I hated him for deceiving me. I also hated him for what he'd turned my life into. Everything about him made my stomach churn. Lately, I'd been trying not to cringe from his touch, but the just mere thought of his hands on me would literally make me sick!

I knew the charade I was playing would soon have to come to an end because I didn't know how long I could pretend everything was copasetic. But I had to wait until the time was right before I handled my business.

While still looking into my eyes in the mirror I thought back to that day I'd realized what J.T. and his cousins had done. When he had come home that afternoon I was trying my best to act like nothing had happened, as if nothing had changed. But just the sight of his face with that conniving ass smile; that smile that once made me melt, now had me ready to wild out! But I'd managed to hold my composure and I played my role to perfection.

When J.T. returned home I watched while he checked the answering machine and listened to Joy's message. I had just stepped from the shower and entered the room with one of his towels wrapped around me when I saw him standing by the nightstand, listening to the machine. The volume was still up until he'd heard me enter the room. That was when he turned down the volume. Joy's voice put him on blast! His back was to me but I was watching the movements in his body language and imagined what type of look was on his face at that moment.

I'd asked, "You okay over there?"

I was seated on the bed drying myself off.

He never turned around. "Yeah, I'm good. Listen, how long you been up?"

He was probably wondering if I'd heard the message, but he didn't ask.

"Not long," I lied as I lotioned my legs.

"I gotta go upstairs and write up a few contracts. I'll be down as soon as I'm done."

He erased the message, walked over and kissed me on the lips, then exited the room. I could hear his footsteps as he ascended the stairs. I looked toward the ceiling where the footsteps had settled and thought about how bad I wanted that nigga dead. But like a good girl, I just grinned and bared it.

After throwing on a pair of shorts and a tank top I let ten minutes pass before I tip-toed up the stairs behind J.T. He was already in his office when I reached the second story of the house so I walked over to the door and listened as he carried on a conversation. Apparently his was on his cell because I hadn't seen a telephone when I'd gone in there earlier. As I listened, I could only catch bits and pieces of what was being said.

I heard, "Fuck that bitch!...Hell yeah, milk carton material," then there was laughter. Then I heard, "New ski masks for that one," and then, "...yeah, I'm runnin' that right now as we speak."

I pressed my ear to the door a little harder and heard the faint mechanical sound of what seemed to be paper flipping at a rapid speed. It only took a hot second for me to realize it was the melodious sound of a money counting machine spitting out bills.

I immediately thought about the safe that was hidden inside the room. I knew it had to be open because J.T. had gone up the stairs empty handed and I definitely hadn't seen a counting machine, let alone any money when I'd been inside. So, I figured he had to have gotten it all from inside the safe. After listening for a few more minutes I heard him address the person on the other end of his phone.

"Red, lemme holla back."

Then apparently the conversation ended because there was no more talking.

I eased back downstairs to the living room and clicked on the television with the remote as I plopped down on the sofa and thought about what I'd heard J.T. say to his cousin. The mention of ski masks had confirmed everything I'd suspected, but I couldn't help but to wonder who he had referred to when he'd said *"Fuck that bitch"*

I wondered if he was talking about me and if so, did he have plans of trying to harm me, because I knew exactly what *"Milk carton material"* had meant!

A slight sense of fear had crept through me as I sat there and tried to figure out why I'd been so damn gullible. Then I realized that it had been the sex. It was said that, "Good dick will cause a bitch to turn a blind eye to all truths," and I believed that at that moment because I had actually allowed the dick to cloud my judgment.

The morning after I had learned the truth about J.T., I told him I was going out for a few hours while he was getting ready to leave for work. I told him I needed a relaxer and a professional manicure because it had been so long since I'd had either. I knew J.T. was ready to see the "old Justice" all dollied up again. I knew he wouldn't have any objections. Besides, those walls were driving a bitch bananas and I was in dire need of some fresh air.

I'd hopped in my Chrysler with hopes of not running into any of

Carlos's associates while out on the town. I pulled out of J.T.'s driveway and drove down the street from his house and parked. I could still see his house from where I was parked and minutes later, I saw J.T. climb into his truck and pull out and head in the opposite direction from which I'd driven.

I followed him and kept at least four cars between us as he made several stops. None of which were at an office nor any trucking companies. This nigga was flossing! He stopped by to pick up Red and they rode around for hours, frequenting pawn shops and gun stores. My brother used to do the same thing after a robbery. He'd try and pawn the jewelry he'd gotten from the stick up.

That first day after tailing him I beat him getting back home and promptly gave myself a store bought relaxer and did my own nails so he wouldn't have any suspicions. I followed J.T. for three days in a row and each day was just like the day before. The only thing he did was floss. It was then when I knew without a doubt that this man didn't even have a damn job. His occupation was the same as my brother's. J.T. was a stick-up kid. It was possible that he'd probably been selling drugs also, but from my observation I saw all the signs of "robbing" being his number one hustle. All of my suspicions had been confirmed. I had *no* doubt as to what J.T. had done.

My mind snapped back to the present when I heard J.T.'s sleep-filled voice call me from the bedroom.

"Justice! Come back to bed, baby."

I took a deep, frustrated breath and then flushed the toilet as if I'd been taking a tinkle, ran the water in the sink for a few moments while thinking of how bad I wanted to go back in there and pull a Lorena Bobbitt on that muthafucka!

After pulling myself together, I clicked off the bathroom light, re-entered the bedroom and climbed back in bed with this serpent. I was hoping he had fallen back asleep, but as soon as I was beneath the comforter his hands began groping my body and his lips was on my skin. He made me want to vomit. It was amazing as to how someone who used to be able to get me wet without even touching me now repulsed me to no end. I forced myself to reciprocate as the small, steel ball in my tongue clacked away.

He rolled over on top of me, climbed between my legs and spread my thighs so quickly I didn't even have time to protest as he entered me without protection.

"J.T., wait a min…"

I tried to stop him but it was too late, he was already inside and in full stroke. I couldn't push his weight off of me and he wasn't about to stop, so I raised my hips to meet him stroke for stroke and proceeded to grind harder and harder with each passing second, so he'd hurry up and finish and get the hell off of me!

"Yeah, throw that pussy baby!" J.T. commanded, stroking me faster and faster until his body jerked and his dick swelled inside me as he ejaculated. "Damn, baby, that shit was *like that,*" he whispered breathlessly in my ear, then rolled off me and moved back to his side of the bed. He was heaving and panting as if he'd just put in major work when in actuality he had just semi-raped me.

I pulled the comforter back up over my body, rolled over onto my side with my back to him, and stared into the darkness. A lone tear attempted to escape my eye, but I was determined not to cry again. My crying days were over.

A few minutes after J.T. had moved back to his side of the bed I heard his familiar light snore. He slept contently as if everything was lovely.

Only if you knew what I got planned for your ass, I thought silently as I felt his seed oozing from my vagina. *I can't take this shit no more." Tomorrow. It's gotta happen tomorrow. If I stay in this house with him one more day I'll lose my damn mind!*

The ball in my tongue was still clacking as I lay there, staring into black space.

CHAPTER TWENTY-SEVEN
JUSTICE

The next morning as soon as J.T. had left, I immediately began phase one of my plan. I packed all of my belongings and carried them to my car once again, just as I had done when I'd left my condo. After I was sure I had all of my clothes packed, I began gathering all the toiletries that I had scattered about in the bathroom. It took a little over an hour but I managed to pack everything and squeeze it into my trunk.

I called my brother to ask him if he was ready to make that trip.

He responded, "Am I ready? I *been* ready! I told you that last week," he yelled into the phone.

"Okay listen, when I call you back I'll be on the road and the only stop I'll make will be to pick you up. If you ain't ready, you just gonna have to meet me in Chicago." I took a deep breath and stated, "I'ma take care of this situation *today*!"

"Ice, I'on' know what you tryna prove, and I'on' know why you ain't just give a nigga directions so I can deal wit' that bitch ass nigga. You know I'm heated about that. Just tell me where that nigga live in case somethin' happen to you," Monk stated with concern.

"Trust me on this. I got this, okay Just be ready to go when I hit you," I replied while tying my hair back into a ponytail.

Monk was silent for a moment, then as if he realized he was fighting a lost cause, he sighed into the phone and reluctantly stated, "Aiight, sis. Well look, I promised Tan I'd see her before I leave so that's probably where I'll be when you hit me back."

"Rock Hill? You still seein' that girl?" I asked with surprise.

"I just need to take care of this one last thing wit' her, then it's a wrap," he replied, then added, "Ice, be careful baby girl. Love ya."

"Love you too, Monk. See ya later."

We ended the call on that note and I went to work.

Standing in the living room with my hands on my hips, I looked around with wrinkled eyebrows and wondered where I should start. Since the kitchen is where I'd stashed the rubber gloves, chemical mask, and multiple containers of Febreez, I decided I would start there first. Before putting in work, I pulled on the latex gloves and tied the mask around my face. I knew the chemical was a harmless disinfectant; however, as much as I was about to use would probably knock an elephant on his ass. So, I had to take precautions and try not to inhale it in excess.

I wiped down all of the appliances, cabinets, and even the sink and countertops. I scrubbed from top to bottom, making sure not to miss an inch. Sweat beaded up on my forehead as I moved about, but I continued to clean like a woman possessed. After putting all of the dishes in the dishwasher I walked around to inspect my work and made sure the kitchen was thoroughly spotless. Then I proceeded to the living room and commenced to clean just as diligently as I'd done the kitchen. I wiped down the leather furniture, the tables, lamps and even the remote just to make sure I wasn't missing anything.

Before I'd finished with the living room I had already gone through several containers of the cleaner and the strong scent was attacking my nose. I could even taste it in my throat through the mask. This didn't deter me nor did it slow me down because as soon as I'd wiped away the last traces of the cleaner from the coffee table I headed down the hall to do the same to the bedroom. I was wiping the walls and light switches en route.

The bedroom was by far the most time consuming because there were more items and more area to clean, but I made sure to clean it just as thoroughly as I had done the other two rooms.

Once the first floor was immaculate, I headed to the second level and wiped down the wooden stair rail and the table that sat in the middle of the hall. By this time, a bitch was winded!

After double-checking to make sure everything was painstakingly unblemished, I was satisfied with my work and I knew J.T. would be pleased to see the house totally sanitized.

I had purposely left the bathroom for last because I needed to take one last shower before scrubbing that area also. My back was aching and both of my arms were damn near numb as I climbed into the shower and let the pulsating water from the spraying showerhead massage my fatigued body. While showering, I closed my eyes and let the past couple months of my life play out like a movie. While looking back on things I began to wonder if this was just my karma coming back to bite me in the ass. I knew I'd done some trifling things to a lot of people and I knew one day all of it would catch up with me, but I never imagined it to be so extreme. However, karma or not, I had a mission to accomplish and I was halfway finished with phase one.

Once my shower was complete I wiped down the bathroom before getting dressed. My hair hang loosely down my back just the way J.T. liked it and I put on the skimpy Roberto Cavalli skirt he'd purchased for me a few weeks back. I had never worn the damn thing because I hadn't had anywhere to where it to, but today was a special occasion and I had decided to go all out and I was going to look my best while doing so.

The straps on my Prada sandals were wrapped around my leg, all the way up my calf and my freshly pedicured toes were looking oh so sexy with my toe ring sparkling. I applied a slight shadow of eyeliner to my eyes and a thin layer of gloss coated my luscious lips as I stood before the mirror, admiring my exotic beauty in the reflection. I looked like the "old Justice," the Justice before Sapphire was beaten; the Justice before my life had been threatened.

I grabbed my handbag with my "baby" in it and walked with confidence to the living room to watch television. The leather clung to the backs of my thighs as the skirt rose while I took a seat on the sofa. I then used a handkerchief to click on the television with the remote. I wanted to be the first thing J.T. would see when he stepped up in the house. I calmly sat there and watched an episode of the *Young and the Restless.*.

While watching television I vaguely thought about how long it had been since I'd been able to sit down and enjoy my favorite soap without wondering and worrying about what the day would bring. Since my mind was worry free today, I was able to enjoy Victor Newman doing his thing. White, black, or green, no matter what the race, any man with that much power makes my panties wet.

I sat through two soap operas and an episode of *Maury Povich* with a trifling chick who was trying to find out which of the six men onstage was her baby's daddy. I watched as Maury sounded like a scratched CD as he spat out "You are *not* the father" six times consecutively.

"Ooooh, nasty heifer," I muttered as the six men celebrated while the girl ran backstage crying with flailing arms.

Halfway through the episode of *Maury* I heard J.T.'s truck pulling up in the driveway. I sat there calmly and continued to watch television as I heard the engine die, then moments later, his truck door closed. I heard his key enter the front door, and then his voice echoed from the doorway.

"Damn, that shit strong!"

He had his nose turned up because of the loud smell of Febreez, which had hit him as soon as he'd opened the door.

"Hey, what's up, baby," he spoke as he closed the door behind him. When he walked in I noticed he was carrying a small surplus bag.

"Hey, Daddy," I smiled as I spoke to that snake!

"Daaaamn, you lookin' sexy as shit."

He walked over and took my hand, urging me to stand and slowly twirl around so he could check me out. I obliged with a wide, fake ass smile plastered on my face.

"You like?" I teased as I modeled for him.

"I *love*," he replied. His baldhead was shining and his pearly whites gleamed as he stood there admiring me with wanting eyes. Then he wrinkled his eyebrows for a second and asked, "Why that air freshener so loud? Lemme find out you been up in here blazin' without me," he laughed.

"No, I haven't been smoking. I just felt like cleaning up."

I sat back on the sofa and pretended like I was watching the rest of Maury.

"I'll be back down in a few. I think I wanna take you out this evening. 'Cause you look too damn good to be stuck up in here today. How that sound?" He was headed for the stairs as he spoke.

I smiled, "That'll be a nice change. I need a drink anyway."

I watched as he ascended the stairs with the bag in his hand just as I hoped he'd do.

"Think about where you wanna go, and let me know," his voice was fading as he neared the top of the staircase.

I yelled back, "Okay, baby!"

I was already sliding my "baby" from my purse as I answered him.

Moments after he'd climbed the stairs I heard his office door shut. That was my cue to move!

CHAPTER TWENTY-EIGHT

As I nervously climbed those winding stairs with my baby .380 clutched tightly in my sweaty palm I could feel beads of sweat trickling down between my breasts. With each step I climbed, my heart beat like jungle drums and I felt as if I would go into cardiac arrest at any given moment. Regardless, I knew I had to still my nerves, but I also knew there was no turning back. I was about to make this nigga pay for all of the pain and anguish he had put me through.

As I neared the door to his office I could hear the familiar melodious sound of his money counting machine as it rhythmically spit out bill after bill. I was hoping that I'd rocked him to sleep enough so that he'd be totally oblivious to what was about to happen. I was also hoping and praying that he had gotten so comfortable as to have left the door unlocked. He knew I'd never bothered him while he was in this office because I was aware of the fact that this was his private space. But today *his* space was about to become *mine* as well.

When I was directly in front of the large oak door I stood there and silently prayed my nerves would allow me to carry out my task. A million and one emotions began to well up in me all at once. So suddenly, it felt as if they were colliding and toppling over one another. I tried with all the restraint I could muster up to hold back the tears, which were fighting to be released, but it was to no avail because my eyes lost the battle and the water sprang free. Droplets of the eye water stained my blouse and a few drops hit the carpet at my feet. Mascara streaked down my chiseled cheekbones as the tears flowed freely.

Just the thought of how easily the man beyond that door had come into my life and turned it upside down made me really grasp the concept of what could happen when a man catches you at a vulnerable stage. I witnessed first hand how a woman's mind could really get twisted.

After taking a deep breath I reached for the cold knob and was thoroughly surprised to find it unlocked. I paused for a minute to muster up the courage I needed. Then with a trembling hand, I twisted the brass knob and hurriedly pushed the heavy door ajar just in time to witness J.T.'s eyes almost pop out of their sockets as he looked up from his desk where he sat.

"What the…"

His words were cut short when he saw the pistol I was holding and then he noticed the tears that were streaming down my cheeks.

J.T. was seated at his desk in front of the computer with a stack of money in each hand. There was another stack neatly piled on the desk and the counting machine was full, still spitting out money. I looked towards the closet where the safe was located and saw that the closet was open.

"Justice, what the fuck you doin'?" J.T. attempted to gain back some sense of control once the initial shock had worn off.

"Shut up, J.T.! Don't move or I swear I'll shoot!" I was still crying with trembling lips and my tongue ring wouldn't stop clacking.

J.T. started slowly backing away from the desk as he cut his eyes towards the safe for a split second.

I screamed, "Didn't I say don't move!? Matter of fact, drop that money and put yo' hands flat on the desk."

J.T. hesitated.

"Do it!" I screamed again as I sniffled and wiped a few tears from my eyes. I was standing on the opposite side of his desk and couldn't see all the way inside the closet, but I needed to know if the safe was open. I eased around the desk and moved slowly towards the closet while keeping my eyes on J.T. the whole time.

"Justice, just put the gun down so we can talk," J.T. stated calmly.

I ignored him and kept the pistol aimed at him as I neared the closet.

"Justice, just tell me what all this is about! What the hell's goin' on?" J.T. was trying to talk his way out of the situation he had suddenly found himself in. He tried to change tactics, "Baby, you know I love you. Why you actin' like—"

"*Love*!?" I asked, cutting him off. "Nigga, you 'on' know nothin' about *love*! If fuckin' my life up was *lovin'* me, then I'm gettin' ready to *love* the hell outta you!"

I aimed the .380 at his head. Tears were still streaming down my cheeks.

J.T. must have realized that his denial was getting him nowhere because I saw the change in his facial expression and his body language as he let out an exasperated sigh. His charade was up and he knew it. He could no longer act as if he had no idea why I had a gun aimed at his face, so he started trying to plead his case.

"Justice, I swear all this shit was just a misunderstanding. I mean, when I realized it had gotten outta hand it was too late." He looked as if he had tears in his eyes. "I never wanted this shit to go this far. I wanted to protect you, Justice. Why do you think I moved you in here with me?"

I was shaking my head, trying to keep my composure but he sounded *so* sincere!

"Baby, I knew them niggas was tryin' to get at you, that's why I had you here so they wouldn't find you. Justice, I never wanted you or anybody else to get hurt. You gotta believe me. Baby, I swear it's the truth."

J.T. was now shedding tears. I had never seen this man show any type of emotion before, yet now here he was crying with a genuinely sincere look in his eyes. I couldn't take it. The emotions that were flooding my soul all came rising to the surface at once. More tears streamed down cheeks and nervous convulsions had my entire body trembling. I was confused and didn't know *what* to believe at this point.

"Just, just shut up, J.T.! Shut up!" I screamed, while trying to regain my composure.

I told myself that regardless if what he was saying was true or not, the fact remained that he'd put me and Monk in danger and had played puppet-master with my life. Once I gathered a little composure, I stepped closer to the closet and out of the corner of my eye I saw that the safe's door was indeed open. Then I made the mistake of taking my eyes off of J.T. for a split second and it was then when all hell broke loose!

J.T. jumped up from the chair and lunged in my direction.

I flinched as I screamed, "Noooooooo!" If he was to get a hold of me I'd probably end up dead, so nervous reflexes had my finger squeezing the trigger as he threw his body at me.

How many times I pulled that trigger became a mystery to me because everything had happened so fast. It all seemed like a blur. I must have squeezed it more times than I could've imagined because when the ordeal had ended the gun was empty and I knew for a fact that the clip had been fully loaded.

Still trembling with fear, I looked down and saw J.T. lying at my feet where he had fallen. I could see the blood oozing from his body and spreading out into a pool around him. My blouse and skirt had splotches of his blood on it as did my legs. The sight of J.T.'s motionless, bloody body made me jolt with sudden anguish. I knew I'd killed him because I could smell the foul odor of his loose bowels mixing with the scent of the Febreez, which was pouring into the room. The contents of my stomach began rising in my throat but I choked back the vomit with my hand over my mouth. That acrid smell would be one I'd *never* forget, one that would haunt me for the rest of my life.

For what seemed like an eternity, I stood there mock still in the same spot with the gun in my hand, arms at my side and J.T.'s corpse at my feet. It would be later when I would realize that I'd momentarily been in shock.

When I finally came to my senses I ran back out of the office and headed downstairs to the kitchen, careful as not to leave any prints as I grabbed a trash bag. Then it was back up to the office while carefully avoiding the blood on the floor as I reentered. Hastily, I began filling the trash bag with the money from the desk and the counting machine. Then I walked over to the closet and looked inside the large safe. What I saw was unbelievable.

There was more money, and an assortment of platinum jewelry

along with several guns. With trembling hands and wet eyes, I filled the bag with money and jewelry and left the guns behind, because I had no use for them. Once the last bill had been stuffed inside the bag I stepped around J.T.'s body. His hand twitched and it caused me to scream out with fright! Live nerves still had his fingers twitching as I clutched the trash bag to my chest and ran out of that office. I gripped the knob with the bottom of my blouse and hurriedly pulled the door closed behind me.

When that office door was closed, separating me from J.T.'s lifeless body, part of me wanted to run back inside that room and try to save that man's life. I stood there staring at that closed door, having visions of J.T. with that sincere look in his eyes and those tears rolling down his face.

I thought, *What if he was telling the truth? What if he was only trying to get the gun away from me so that we could talk like civilized adults?*

Tears of confusion mixed with fear fell in droves onto the carpet as my mind flipped like a gymnast.

Justice, he's dead! He's dead! There's nothing you can do but put as many miles as possible between you and this house! rationality screamed through my head as I slowly backed away from the door with weak wobbly legs.

My next stop inside the house was the bedroom where the rest of the jewelry, including Mark's was stashed. I picked up the wooden box and dropped it inside the garbage bag along with the rest of the money and jewelry. When I was sure I hadn't missed anything I took a few minutes to clean myself up and change clothes. I made sure to cover all possible tracks. No prints? Check! No blood on me? Check! No signs of me ever being there? Double-check!

When everything was good to go I exited the house, lugging the trash bag behind me. I locked J.T.'s front door with a handkerchief and couldn't bring myself to look back as I opened my car door and tossed the bag into the backseat. I pulled out of J.T.'s driveway the same way I'd pulled in several weeks earlier; with tears in my eyes and a trunk full of clothes! Instead of being a chick on the run for her life, I was now on the run for my freedom.

When I got onto the highway I dialed my brother's number with trembling fingers and spoke with a shaky voice as I told him I was ready to go home. I was so scared and so paranoid it felt as if everyone on the road was staring at me like they knew exactly what I'd just done. My conscious was *already* killing me softly.

I kept trying to remind myself that I'd gotten away clean, but I couldn't stop the tears from flowing. I knew the only people who could link me with what I'd just done were Red and Joy. But all Red knew about me was my first name and what kind of car I drove. And not even the car could be traced back to me because it was in Sapphire's name. However, Joy knew a whole lot more. But unbeknownst to me at that time, Joy wouldn't be talking to anyone ever again unless it was during a séance.

I tried to force myself to relax by taking deep breaths and holding them for a few seconds before exhaling. After a few minutes of this I was finally halfway calm enough to almost concentrate on the road as I put in Keysha Cole's CD and slipped my Chanel shades over my puffy, bloodshot eyes.

"Two more stops, Justice, Rock Hill and Chicago. It's almost over," I kept repeating to myself as I rode down 1-77, heading towards South Carolina to meet my brother.

CHAPTER TWENTY-NINE
MONK

Hey, baby girl where you at?" I asked Tan as I turned down the volume on the radio. I was in D.C.'s Cutlass, headed to Rock Hill, South Carolina, to meet with Tan for the last time before Justice and I would leave for Chicago. My sister had called me earlier and told me that this would be the day. I was still heated because of what she had told me about J.T. and his cousins being the ones who had robbed Carlos's people. But I was even more vexed with her because she wouldn't tell a nigga where that muthafucka was living. She told me not to worry because she would handle it, but a nigga like me couldn't just lie down and take it like that. *Somebody* had to pay, and pay they did!

Tan's voice crooned through the phone, "Hey Chink! I'm on my way to the Long Shoreman on Johnston Place. Know where it is?"

I told her that I didn't know where the restaurant was located so she gave me directions. After jotting down what she was relaying to me, I ended the call and followed the simple route she'd given me to the restaurant.

Ten minutes later, I was pulling into the restaurant's parking lot next to Tan's BMW. As I parked, I observed her ride and noticed that the rims had been changed since I'd last seen it. The old rims had been replaced with brand new 24-inch Asanti rims, which were gleaming in the bright mid-afternoon sun.

"Damn, these bitches really doin' it big with that construction shit," I muttered as I exited the car and admired the rest of the BMW like it was my first time seeing it.

I was halfway to the entrance when I suddenly remembered that I'd left my money in the duffle bag inside the trunk of the Cutlass where

I had stashed it earlier. I walked back to D.C.'s ride, popped the trunk and moved a few bags aside until I found the one with the money in it, laying amongst the bags of clothes I'd packed for the trip. While reaching inside the bag for some money, something on the trunk's floor sparkled and caught my eyes.

I reached in, picked it up, and mumbled, "Damn, I'm slippin'."

Paranoia had me looking around to see if anyone was watching me as I held the tiny piece of memory in my palm. While looking down at the earring in my hand I thought about the girl whom it had belonged to. Then I had a flashback about the night I'd kidnapped her and stuffed her in the trunk of the Cutlass.

Since Justice wouldn't let me get that nigga J.T. and I hadn't been able to find Red, I'd decided to take it out on Joy! I had caught her coming home late one night from the club and I split her temple with my pistol, knocking her unconscious. After stuffing her inside the trunk I drove her to Mt. Holly, N.C. and found a secluded wooded area, which was miles from the nearest main road.

Once I pulled her from the trunk I smacked her with the gun a second time, breaking teeth and busting gums. Her pathetic pleading and weak ass attempt to explain what had happened only made me that much angrier. I ordered her to strip naked and lay in the dense soil as I held her at gunpoint. I wanted to humiliate this bitch and make her ass suffer for what she'd done, so I started unzipping my shorts. She cried, "Monk, Please! I'm so sorry! I'll do anything you wan—"

"Bitch, shut the fuck up." I kicked her in the stomach, and then pulled out my dick. "You'll do anything I want? You want this snake, huh?"

I was shaking my dick at her. She was crying and nodding with blood dripping from the corners of her mouth. I stood over her and pissed in her face and all over her head. I looked down at her and knew she thought I was getting ready to rape her trick ass, but raping that hoe with my dick would've been too good for her. So, I zipped my shorts back up, reached inside the trunk, and grabbed the crowbar.

When Joy saw me reach for the crowbar she got up off the ground and attempted to run while screaming at the top of her lungs. I chased her naked figure through a few trees and bushes, getting slapped in the face by a few hanging limbs, until I grabbed her by her ponytail and slammed her to the ground.

"HEEEEEEEEEELLLLLPPP!!!!" Her voice echoed through the darkness.

I struck her again with my gun to silence her cries. After picking her up from the ground where I had thrown her, I drug her back to the car as she kicked and pleaded for her life. Once I got her back to the car where I'd dropped the crowbar, I dropped her to the ground again and began kicking her in her head and chest until my legs got tired.

At this point, she had become subdued and had stopped trying to fight. She lay there as if she was dead, but I saw her still breathing as blood poured from her mouth and nostrils. I picked up the crowbar, spread her legs with my feet and then rammed the cold steel so far up into her pussy I would have sworn I'd seen the imprint of it in her belly.

Joy's eyes sprang open at the feel of the sudden infliction, then she let out a blood-shaking scream that made my ears ring. I continued to jam the crowbar up into her until blood cascaded from her vagina and coated the black piece of metal, painting it dark crimson. She was trying to escape the brutality, but I held her down and continued to rip her insides apart with the steel. Her body jerked and convulsed as her eyes rolled into the back of her head. I knew I'd punctured some internal organs because the crowbar was imbedded so far into her womb that the only part I could now grip was where it bent into a curve. I was thinking that this bitch deserved every ounce of pain she'd endured because of the shit she had caused me and my sister to go through.

When I looked down at Joy's bloody, motionless body I decided that she still hadn't suffered enough. D.C.'s face flashed in my mind for a moment, then I saw Sapphire lying in that hospital bed and fire arose in my eyes. I bent down and wrapped my hands around Joy's skinny ass neck.

"Go to sleep, bitch. Quit fighting it and embrace it," I whispered into her ear as I choked her until I felt her let go of what little bit of life she was trying to hold on to.

I let her head fall to the dense soil and then I pulled the dripping crowbar out of her because I was sure it was full of my prints. Seconds later, the crowbar was wrapped in her blouse and I tossed it onto the passenger's side of the Cutlass before grabbing the paper bag that had been lying on the floorboard.

Calmly, I walked back over to Joy's mutilated body and bent down to open her mouth. I pulled the dead snake from the paper bag and I stuffed as much of it as I could into her mouth with a few inches dangling from her lips.

"You said you wanted a snake? Now you got one. A snake for a snake ass bitch! Trifling hoe!"

I was talking to the mutilated corpse as if she could hear me. Then in a flash I'd hopped back into the Cutlass and peeled out. On the way back to Charlotte I tossed the crowbar into the Catawba River as I crossed the bridge, exiting Mt. Holly.

Back at the Long Shoreman, I shook off those thoughts of what I had done to Joy and shut the trunk before heading towards the entrance of the restaurant. As I approached the door, I casually tossed Joy's earring into a nearby trash can. I discarded that tiny piece of white gold just like the person who had owned it.

When I was finally inside the restaurant I saw Tan sitting in a corner booth looking sexy as hell in a short skirt and a sleeveless blouse. The open-toes she had on made a nigga want to suck her pretty, pedicured digits right there in the restaurant.

"Hōla Papi," Tan spoke with a smile as I approached the booth.

I was thinking, *Damn, she callin' a nigga "Papi" already.*

"What up, baby?" I spoke back as I slid into the booth next to her. Tan had the sexiest smile on her face and her whole aura was oozing sexuality. Even the way she was slurping her straw as she drank her iced tea was looking sensuous.

We ordered and enjoyed our seafood platters as we teased one another with sexual conversation until the tension was almost too much for either of us to bear. Just as I was paying the bill, my cell phone rang. It was Justice.

"Damn, not right now," I muttered under my breath at the thought of Justice calling just when it was about to go down.

I flipped open my phone.

"What up, sis?"

"Where you at?" Justice was sounding nervous as hell.

"I'm in Rock Hill at the Long Shoreman. Wuzzup?"

"It's time to bounce," she stated impatiently.

"Give me an hour," I suggested as I looked over at Tan sliding out of the booth as she headed to the restroom. The way her ass was swaying had me thinking of all the positions I was going to put her fine ass in. My dick got *brick*.

"No! We ain't got a hour Monk! You need to meet me *right now!*" my sister commanded.

I didn't know what it was that Justice had done, but whatever it was I assumed she had handled it because she sounded okay, a little apprehensive, but okay nonetheless.

"Girl, you aiight?" I asked curiously.

"I just…I just…I'm scared Monk!" she stammered.

I tried to calm Justice down.

"Aiight, look…calm down. Come this way and hit me when you get to Rock Hill. We'll leave from down here. Aiight?"

"Okay, I'm on my way." She sounded like she was crying.

"You sure you okay?"

"Yeah, I'll be okay when I see you. Love you, bruh."

"Love you too, sis."

As we ended the call I thought about Ice's well being. From the way she was acting I could tell she was spooked about something, but at least she was okay.

Only a few more hours and we'll be away from all this shit, I sighed.

Tan came back to the booth while I was sitting there lost in thought about my sister. I knew whatever me and Tan was going to do we'd have to do it soon because Justice was on her way. And I definitely couldn't let Tan see Justice's face because she'd surely recognize her from the robbery. I slid from the booth before she could sit back down and get comfortable.

I told her, "Look, that was my sister. She waitin' on me so we can bounce. So, what's the binness?"

I was holding her hands in mine while staring into those sexy ass eyes.

Tan was gazing in my eyes with a dreamy look as she smiled deviously like she'd just taken a triple-stack.

"Follow me. I told you I can't let you leave without giving you this. You deserve it."

She placed my palm on her ass as emphasis while she led me out into the parking lot.

We walked hand in hand to her BMW and she told me to follow her down the street because she knew the perfect deserted spot. As horny as I was, I couldn't have cared less if we'd fucked right there in that parking lot, but I let go of her hand and obliged with her request. I hopped in D.C.'s ride and followed as Tan drove a few blocks down the street. While driving behind her I was trying to pronounce the word that was on her custom-made license plate but it was in Spanish and I had no luck.

We ended up in a deserted alley that looked as if it had been designed specifically for the purpose of what we had in mind because there wasn't a soul in sight. I followed behind her until she slowed down, and then eventually came to a stop.

I was thinking, *This bitch wants a quickie! I wonder if she's fucked in this alley before. She looks totally comfortable with this shit.*

I watched as she got out of her car and sashayed her way back to the Cutlass while looking around with devilish eyes.

I stepped out and closed the door as I looked up and down the alley, noticing how serenely quiet it was. I walked to the front of the Cutlass and smiled, "Your ride or mine?"

Tan wrapped her arms around my neck and whispered in my ear, "I want it right here on the hood, Papi."

She leaned against the hood of D.C.'s ride while I stepped between her legs and started kissing on her neck while reaching beneath her short skirt. My fingers slid inside the elastic of her thong and I began tugging it south. The whole while, Tan was breathing deeply and whispering Spanish in my ear in between licks and nibbles of my ear lobe.

My dick was hard enough for a midget to do chin-ups on. I cupped her titties in my palm through her thin blouse while she stepped out of her thong with the skirt up around her waist. She raised her blouse and let her tanned breasts sprang free, inviting my lips. I wasted no time as I attached my mouth to her nipple and sucked away. As I continued to lick and suck on her hard nipples, I slid two of my fingers into her dripping wet pussy. She gasped and moaned seductively in my ear as I probed her wetness and stroked her clit. When she couldn't take it anymore she grabbed my hand and sucked her juices from my fingers as I fumbled with the zipper on my shorts, trying to free the slave!

I heard Tan's breathing get heavier as she lowered her head to my ear once again and began chanting something in whispered Spanish. I was getting so turned on it felt like I would bust off before I could even get my dick out. During her whispers and heavy breathing there was a slight pause in which she coughed once into her hand. Once she removed her hand from her mouth, the next thing I felt was the sharp sting of something slicing through the flesh of my throat.

The suddenness of it all caused me to look up into Tan's cold eyes one last time before realization of what had happened made me stumble away from her. In a feeble attempt to hold the loose flabs of flesh in my throat together, I saw the blood spurting from my wound like a lawn sprinkler as it escaped through my fingers.

I looked at Tan in disbelief as the pavement suddenly rushed up and slammed me in the face. Just that quickly, the blood loss was making me lose consciousness. In my state of semi-unconsciousness, I heard Tan speaking.

"Putá! Maricón! You think I didn't know it was *you* who tried to rob me!? You think I couldn't see those slanted eyes through the mask!? I'm a Jersey bitch and there's *nothing* slow about me! If you hadn't been so fuckin' stupid, you would've known the coke and the money was right under your fuckin' nose! You think I had Ralphie guarding that room for no reason!? You lil' Chinese-looking son-of-a-bitch! When those niggas missed you at that restaurant I knew I had to be the one to take care of you! Never send a man to do a lady's job."

I couldn't move an inch and I was getting weaker by the second, but I heard Tan's every word crystal clearly as she continued to rant and rave with a thick Spanish accent.

"Who do you think put the press on Carlos to make that hit on you and that bitch D.C.? Yeah, it was ME! Me and my family has been serving Carlos for years and he listens to us! Why do you look so surprised?"

My eyes must have unconsciously widened at the revelation of her being Carlos's supplier!

"After you killed Ali and stole my money he was bringing to me at the hotel, Carlos begged me for your location but I wouldn't give it to him because I wanted to take care of you myself. You got away at the restaurant, but you won't be getting away from this! By the way…"

She walked over to where I lay on the pavement trembling and struggling to breathe. I saw her bend down and she pressed the razor blade to my right temple and sliced all the way down to my chin. The blade went in so deep I could feel it scraping bone.

"That's for slapping me! You rice eating piece of shit!"

Tan was speaking with enough venom to kill a deadly cobra.

She hissed, "Now give *that* to God!"

She spat in my face and I watched helplessly as she picked up her panties, calmly walked back to her BMW and climbed into the driver's side.

I cut my weak eyes towards the Cutlass and thought about the pistol that was hidden beneath the driver's seat, then and I realized my limbs wouldn't move. The last thing I saw were those new rims spinning and that custom made plate with that Spanish word that spelled M-E-N-D-O-Z-A. Tan drove away and left me there on the asphalt spraying blood like a showerhead.

My last thought was, *Never in a million years would I have expected to go out at the hands of a bitch!*

Tan had been singing me the sweetest lullaby for weeks, now it was time for a nigga to sleep. My entire life flashed before my eyes just before I heard my mother's sweet voice telling her son to *"come home."*

CHAPTER THIRTY
JUSTICE

When I reached the Rock Hill city limits I called Monk back and listened as his phone rang six times before it went to voicemail. I hung up and re-dialed, waiting for him to pick up but he never did. This time I left a message.

"Boy, where you at? I told you I'm ready to go. I'm already in Rock hill, so hit me back as soon as you get this."

I hung up and sighed with frustration as I neared the Galleria Mall exit. I got off the highway and pulled into Applebee's parking lot, which was located across the street from the mall. Eating definitely wasn't on my mind at the time, actually I was feeling a little nauseous and I just needed to sit for a minute. I tried my brother again and got the same results—no answer!

"Shit! What the hell is this boy doin'?" I said aloud out of frustration.

I was wondering what was going on with him. He knew I'd been on my way so there should have been no reason for him not to answer his phone. I was willing to bet that he was somewhere laid up with that Mexican bitch. I made my mind up to cuss his ass out as soon as I got a hold of him.

A few minutes passed before I decided to wait inside the mall. From Applebee's to the mall was only a short drive so I was there in less than five minutes. The mall's parking area was crowded as hell and I had a hard time finding somewhere to park. I had to sit and wait for someone to leave before I could move into a space. I parked and put the empty gun into the glove compartment until I could figure out where to get rid of it.

I entered the mall through Belk's entrance and strolled through the department store, browsing clothes and shoes. I'd only been inside the store for a few minutes when my stomach began churning, and I fought to choke back the vomit that was rising, but I had to dash for the ladies' room. I barely made it to an empty stall before I lost whatever was in my system all over the seat of the toilet. Beads of sweat popped up on my forehead and I was light-headed as hell for a minute. Visions of J.T.'s bloody body had my insides all twisted up and the more I thought about what I'd done the sicker I felt.

I managed to make it to the sink and splashed some water on my face, and then I leaned against the sink for balance because I was so dizzy. I had to stay like this for awhile before I could regain my composure because my head was spinning like a tornado.

"Damn, I need to sit my ass down," I mumbled as the door opened and two young white girls entered, talking in a gossipy whisper. I ignored them while patting my forehead with a wet paper towel until I heard one of them mention something about a disturbance at the Long Shoreman restaurant. I was drying my face when one of the girls disappeared into an empty stall and the other stepped to the sink next to the one I was using.

I looked over at her and asked, "Excuse me, but did I just hear you say something happened at the Long Shoreman?"

"We were just down there. Someone got killed down the street from the Long Shoreman, not *at* the Long Shoreman," she replied and looked at me as if she wanted to say "Duh."

"Oh, okay Thanks," I stated, trying to hold my tongue from checking her because of her sarcasm.

I tossed the paper towel into the trash, hurriedly exited the restroom, and headed back towards Belk's to exit the same way I'd come in. I called my brother again while walking through the crowded parking lot, trying to remember where I'd parked. I prayed he would answer but to my dismay it went to voicemail again.

"Shit, Monk!" I cursed as I spotted my car.

I got inside and exited the mall's parking lot. When I got to the stop light I realized I had no idea where the restaurant was located. So I drove to the nearest convenience store to get directions. Something deep down inside was telling me that something had happened to my brother.

Thanks," I told the young man at the cash register inside the Handy Pantry I'd stopped at. He had just given me directions to the restaurant.

I was about to exit when I heard him ask me in a nervous tone, "You got a man?"

I was walking towards the door.

I smiled weakly, "Yeah, sweetie, I got a man." I lied as I opened the door and proceeded to my car.

The youngman's question made my stomach knot up again with thoughts of J.T.

The restaurant was only ten minutes away from the store and I had no problem finding it. When I did, I also found the spot where the murder had taken place. There were fire trucks, an ambulance, and several police cars all over the area. I immediately felt butterflies in the pit of my stomach. Female intuition was kicking in! I thought about the murder that I had committed and I decided to park the Chrysler at the restaurant because it had all the evidence in it. Down the street from where I parked was where all of the commotion was taking place. So that's where I headed.

As I neared the alley where all of the police cars were, I tried to see if I could get a glimpse of anything that looked familiar. The scene was totally blocked off and all I could see were the blue and white cruisers that obscured the view. Besides myself, there were a few other people who stood by observing the activity as well. One man, a middle-aged white guy with a pot belly, looked as if he had been there for quite some time.

I asked, "What happened, do you know?"

He stood there eating a foot-long hotdog. Traces of ketchup stained his T-shirt and he had dried up mustard in the corner of his mouth.

"Yeah, I know what happened. Somebody got iced, that's what happened," he stated non-chalantly, and then took another bite of his hotdog.

"Yeah, well, I can see that much," I replied, looking away from him and back at the police cars. "I mean, white, black, male, female? Walking? On a bicycle or what?" I asked, hoping I wasn't going to hear what I was already suspecting. My gut was telling me that my brother was somehow involved in whatever had taken place.

"A black guy in a white Chevy Cutlass. North Carolina plates," he said in between bites, dripping more ketchup onto his shirt.

At the mention of the Cutlass, my knees got weak and my hands began trembling! I knew Monk had been driving D.C.'s white Cutlass and that revelation scrambled my thought process. As if my body moved on its own accord, I started running straight towards the crime scene. I heard the man's voice behind me as I ran away from him.

"Hey! Where ya' goin'? You can't go in there!"

A few officers tried to stop me as well, screaming, "Hey lady! Hey you! Come back here!"

But when I got close enough to see that it was indeed D.C.'s car there was no stopping me. A hand grabbed me but I shook loose as I saw the body lying on the ground covered by a white sheet. The only thing that wasn't covered was the victim's feet, and I immediately recognized the blue and grey Prada sneakers I'd given Monk for his birthday a few months earlier.

I screamed at the top of my lungs, "MOOOOOOONK! NOOOOOOO!" and I fell to my knees. The next moment, there was blackness.

When I finally opened my eyes, I stared up at the ceiling. The unmistakable incandescence of the light that illuminated that room and the sanitized smell made me realize that I was in a hospital.

My body was so weak; it was an effort just for me to turn my head to the side to look at the IV that was attached to my arm. My eyes followed the tube from my arm to the bag that was hanging on a hook, dripping liquid. I tried to remember how I'd gotten there and all of a sudden, memories of Monk's body lying in that street came flashing back to my mind. I broke down crying as I faintly sat up and attempted to snatch the tubes out of my arms.

Just then, a short pale-faced doctor with a clipboard appeared inside the doorway and tried to calm me down as he approached the bed.

"Miss, Miss, please calm down," he stated as he grabbed my arms and tried to restrain me. "Nurse! Nurse!" he yelled out and then I saw a heavyset black female nurse enter the room and approach the bed as well.

"It's okay, darling. It's okay to let it out, but you don't wanna hurt yourself," she stated in a comforting tone as she gently grabbed my wrists and held on while I weakly struggled to break free from her grasp.

"My brother! My brother! They killed my brother!" I sobbed as what little strength I had was starting to fade. My struggles got weaker and weaker until my head hit the pillow and I couldn't raise it again. Tears stung my eyes and my lips were so dry it felt like they were cracking.

"Miss, you must try to stay calm. You were very dehydrated when the paramedics brought you in. You are not in a healthy state right now and that is very dangerous for the baby," the doctor stated with a calm, professional voice.

I thought I'd just heard him say, "Baby," so I slowly turned my head towards him and asked with a weak, cracking voice, "Baby?"

"Yes, you were unconscious when you were brought in so we ran a few tests and one of them revealed that you are a few weeks pregnant. Your iron is at a very..."

His lips were still moving but after the word *pregnant* had left his mouth everything else sounded like I was under twenty feet of water because once again, I faded to black.

CHAPTER THIRTY-ONE
JUSTICE

Ninety Days Later...

It had been ninety days since my visit to the hospital and I was finally back in Chicago, staying in the Palmer Hotel, downtown on Michigan Avenue. I'd put down a deposit on a residence that's on the ground floor of a large turn-of-the-century home in the Southeast section of Hinsdale, which had been transformed into a series of quaint condos. I was still awaiting a call back from management with a move-in date. That damn hotel was getting to be expensive as hell.

Once I'd gotten back in town I looked up my favorite aunt, my only aunt with any business sense, and we were in discussions about some business ventures. I was trying to invest some of the money I had into real estate and I also wanted to start some kind of business. Whatever we decided, I made sure that I would have total control of all decisions. I decided that it was time for a sistah to own something I could finally call *mine!*

Along with the money and jewelry I took from J.T., I also had the money Monk had taken from Ali. After I'd identified Monk's body, I was also able to get D.C.'s car because it had been confirmed that I was Monk's next of kin. I ended up finding the money in the trunk of the Cutlass along with his clothes and jewelry. All of that blood money I arrived in Chicago with had tallied up to more than a quarter of a million dollars, most of which had come from J.T.'s safe. I had the jewelry stashed away just in case I'd run into hard times, then the pawn shops and local dope boys would become my consumers.

Per my request, Monk's body was cremated. He had always told me that if he was to die before me, he wanted me to keep his ashes. That thought made me look over at the urn, which was placed on the coffee table in the living room area of the suite I was occupying.

As I reminisced back to that fateful day my brother was taken away from me, I wondered if it was God's way of making *me* pay for committing the ultimate sin. Maybe it was just his way of showing me that this world is all about the concept of a life for a life. Speaking of *life*, the one that was growing inside me was aborted the week after I'd returned home. There was *no way* I could bring a child into this crazy ass world. Without a doubt, I loved kids but I was in no hurry to give birth to one. Besides, I would have never been able to live with myself knowing that I had killed its father in cold blood.

I knew the baby had to have been J.T.'s because he was the only one I'd screwed during that time period. And although we had used condoms except for that last time, I was more than positive that it had to have happened the night the condom had broken, just before I had found out about him and trifling ass Joy.

As for my brother's killer? No suspects had been named, but I knew who did it. If that bitch Tan *didn't* do it, she definitely knew who was responsible. My brother's throat had been sliced open like a gutted pig and his face had been carved like a piece of wood! Those wounds would be etched into my memory for eternity. I hadn't forgotten where that bitch's house was located, and I had vowed that once I was situated she would be dealt with. It was crazy how everything in life always seemed to come full circle. Monk had escaped death in Charlotte only to get to Rock Hill and run straight into it.

I sighed as I got up from the bed where I'd been laying for the last thirty minutes. I walked over to the window and pulled the curtains back to look out over Michigan Avenue. The wind was blowing like crazy and everywhere I looked I saw people hovered over, trying to duck the hawk. While looking out, I thought about the phone call I received an hour earlier from my estranged father, Tyson. I hadn't seen him since my mother's funeral years earlier, and that had only been for a brief period.

My aunt had told him what had happened to Monk and she had given him my number. His trifling ass didn't even know his own son was dead. How fucked up is that? I thought that maybe if he had been in our lives things may have turned out much differently, but he wasn't there. Never had been. I was waiting on him to come over so we could talk; I wanted to hear his pathetic excuse for running out on me and Monk.

I walked back over to the bed to peruse the Harold's Chicken menu. Earlier on my way back from the mall I had picked it up so I could order some delivery. I wished Monk was there because that was his favorite chicken spot. As soon as I picked up the phone someone knocked at the door.

"Yes?" I yelled from the bedroom area.

"Justice? It's me, Tyson."

I heard my father's muffled voice on the other side of the door and I hesitated a minute before answering. Although I was heated with him I still had to acknowledge the fact that he was my father and I was his daughter.

I slowly got up from the bed, walked over to the door, and peeped through the peephole. I saw Tyson standing there looking the exact same as he did the last time I had seen him with his cleanly shaven head and those thick eyelashes.

Once the door was opened I stepped aside and allowed him to enter. He still wore the fragrance I remembered from when I was a child, and for a brief moment I became that little girl back when everything was fine; when Tyson and my mother were still together. Before his cheating and all of their fighting. Back when life was so simple.

Tyson took a good look at me and produced a weak smile.

"Hey Lil' Chyna. An old man can't get a hug?"

He called me the name he used to call me when I was younger, Lil' Chyna, and he held his arms wide for an embrace. He used to do the same thing everyday he came home from work, and I used to run into his big, strong arms and knew I would be safe from the world. But now, times were different.

"You don't deserve a hug, Tyson. Where were those hugs when I graduated high school? When I got my first job? When your wife died?"

I let a few tears fall, and then looked over at Monk's ashes.

"Where were the hugs when your son got killed?" I walked over to where he stood and looked him eye to eye.

"You still think you deserve that hug?" My eyes were soaked with tears as we stared each other down, trying to see who'd be the first to break eye contact. Tyson lost the battle and looked away.

"I guess I deserved that tongue lashing," he said as he slowly walked over to the sofa and took a seat.

I looked at my father and noticed how much Monk resembled him and it brought back painful memories.

"Tyson, why did you call? Why did you even come here? What's the real reason?" I asked as I took a seat opposite from him, staring into his eyes to see if he felt any kind of remorse for abandoning me.

"I...I really need to talk to you. I need you to know the reason why your mother and I had our differences," he stated while nervously fidgeting his hands.

I yelled at him, "*Differences?* Every couple has differences! That's no excuse for running out on your family!"

"I didn't run out, Justice. Kim put me out."

He spoke about my mother.

"What!? I don't believe that. That's low! Lying on a dead woman!" I stated defiantly as I crossed my arms across my chest. My tongue ring began clacking.

"It's true. She found out that I'd had an affair once," Tyson weakly explained.

"So you have an affair and she puts you out? If I recall correctly, you had more than one affair," I remarked sarcastically.

"This affair was different because it produced a child." With this revelation Tyson got up and walked over to the window where I'd been standing minutes earlier.

"Fuck you mean it produced a child?"

That was the first time my father ever heard me curse. He snapped his head away from the window and looked at me with a defeated look in his eyes. He began pacing back and forth near the window with his head down and arms behind his back as if he was deep in thought. I followed his movements with my eyes and wondered what the hell he was talking about.

A child? Hell to the nah! That meant I had a brother or sister out there that I had never met before!

"I had an affair when your mother and I had first gotten married. Right around the time she was pregnant with you, I had another woman pregnant also." I saw tears welling up in Tyson's eyes as he stopped pacing the floor and looked at me, searching my features for a reaction.

"You had another woman pregnant the same time mommy was pregnant with me? Damn, that's trifling. I see why she put you out," I said while shaking my head at the thought of how my mother probably had felt when all of this was going on.

"That's not when she put me out, Justice."

"Well, what happened?"

"I used to travel from state to state on business a lot and in one state, it just…it was something that just happened." Tears cascaded down his ebony cheeks.

All of this news had me in a state of disbelief as I sat there and tried to digest what my father was telling me. If what he was saying was true then I wanted to contact my long-lost sibling. But since Tyson never kept in touch with me and Monk I wondered if he kept in touch with his other child.

I asked, "Do you keep in touch with your other child?"

"No, because after your mother forgave me, I was hoping they'd just disappear. But the woman popped back up again around the time Monk was born and started pressing me for child support. Your mother thought I was still seeing the woman, but I swear to you, I wasn't. Your mother wouldn't hear anything I had to say and *that's* when she put me out."

Looking over at my father I saw the truth in his eyes. My mind traveled at light speed as confusion set in.

"But...but why didn't you ever come to see us? You could've at least came around every once in a while," I stated defensively.

Tyson looked distraught when he answered.

"I tried, but Kim wasn't having it. She even lied to the cops and got a restraining order against me. Do you remember seeing me at your school on your lunch breaks?"

I thought back to those days and remembered when Tyson used to show up at my school drunk. I used to be so embarrassed at times that I would not even acknowledge him. If what Tyson said was the truth, then that meant my mother was really the one to blame for his not being in my life.

"My drinking was the only way I could deal with the pain of losing my family." Wiping the liquid from his eyes with his fingers, he stated, "Lil' Chyna, I swear I never stopped loving you. Your mother turned you and Monk against me. I even tried to contact you when you moved down south and she threatened to have me arrested if I came anywhere near you two. When I saw you and your brother at the funeral, and saw how grown you two had gotten, it broke my heart that I hadn't been there to see you two grow up. You already know I tried to talk to you both but I got the cold shoulder. I kinda figured you all would come around when you felt like hearing me out. You're here now, so I guess I was right. I hate it took a tragedy like this to bring us together, but God works in mysterious ways."

The realization of what Tyson said hit me like a bolt of lightening.

The little girl in me silently screamed, *He still loves me! He didn't abandon me after all!*

Suddenly, I started to feel a little pity for him. For a long time, we were both silent until an idea hit me.

"Do you know how to get in touch with your other child? What is it a boy or girl?" I asked anxiously.

"You've got a brother." He looked over at the urn and shook his head. "I mean, you've got *another* brother. All I know is that his mother is still in the Maryland and D.C. area." Tyson looked distraught as he spoke.

I grabbed a pen and a scrap piece of paper.

"What's his name? I can go on the Internet and track him down. I wanna meet him."

I got a little excited knowing I still had a sibling out there I'd never even met before.

"He got our last name?" I inquired as I got ready to write down my long-lost brother's name with wishful thoughts of an immediate meeting running through my mind.

But then again, I thought, *What if he wants nothing to do with me because of Tyson's actions?*

That thought played in my mind as I sat and waited for my father to give me the name.

Seeing the anxiety in me along with the obvious twinkle that was now gleaming in my eye, Tyson attempted to perk up a little himself, and then he answered my question about the name.

"No, he's got his mother's last name. She wanted to name him after me, but she used to tease me something terrible about having the name *Tyson*. Said she didn't want her son to have two last names. She couldn't stand my name," he chuckled. Tyson smiled warmly and added, "So, she named him after my brother…your uncle Joaquin. His last name's Turner."

I started to jot it down when all of a sudden the name registered and began echoing in my head over and over. *Joaquin Turner…Joaquin Turner…*

As the finality of it all dawned on me, my head throbbed uncontrollably.

Oh my God! NO!

Those thick eye lashes. That baldhead and dark complexion.

"I'm originally from D.C., but I been staying in Charlotte for a minute…my father is somewhere in the Midwest…" I shook my head from side to side in utter disbelief as J.T.'s words haunted my thoughts.

The only thing I could do was stare off into space.

"Justice, baby girl, you okay? What's wrong?" my father asked as I closed my eyes. That acrid odor of Febreez and feces arose in my subconscious while my short-lived relationship with J.T. played in my head like a DVD. A blood-curling scream arose in my throat and slowly exited my mouth. The scream was so shrill Tyson had to cover his ears.

I felt myself spiraling downward as if I'd just been thrown off of a thirty-story building. The pen slipped from between my fingers. My bowels felt as if they were about to come loose. My entire world as I once knew it exploded into a thousand tiny pieces. After all those years, I suddenly realized that while relentlessly trying to quench that everlasting thirst, it had finally made me drown.

EPILOGUE

Coincidentally, on the same day Justice was meeting with her father, Carlos's case had been dismissed and he walked out of the Charlotte-Mecklenburg County Jail as a free man. Through jailhouse gossip he'd found out about J.T. and Red and his mind was set on evening the score once and for all. He'd just beaten the system *again* and was feeling like the "Teflon Don" because no one could link him and his crew to any wrong doings, especially not inflicting bodily harm.

Meanwhile, on this very same day at Carolina's Medical Center in room 426, Sapphire's mother was standing at her daughter's bedside. She'd just given the staff permission to pull the plug and put an end to her daughter's suffering. Her heart burned with pain and her soul was drowning in tears of despair with the thought of living a life without her only child. But she knew Sapphire would not want to continue to live this way. As soon as the life-support monitor was about to be disconnected, Sapphire's weak eyes slowly opened!

The detectives who had been patiently waiting for months for Sapphire to come around were immediately contacted. They wishfully hoped she would be able to remember what had happened that night and maybe she could identify at least one of her attackers. They were more than ready to apprehend the monsters that had been responsible for committing such a heinous act.

On Michigan Avenue, just down the street from the Palmer Hotel where Justice was staying, Red was checking into the Wingate. Instead of going to the police, he'd tracked Justice to Chicago. He knew she had been responsible for his cousin's death and she also had his money, which J.T. had been keeping for him in the safe. He wanted Justice to suffer the same painful death J.T. had suffered. He was laying and waiting for the right opportunity to strike, without having knowledge of the fact that *he* had been tracked down as well.

A READING GROUP GUIDE
THIRSTY
MIKE SANDERS

ABOUT THIS GUIDE
The suggested questions are intended to enhance
your group's reading of this book.

DISCUSSION QUESTIONS

1) Do you think Sapphire deserved to be beaten by Carlos's henchmen just because she was dating Cross?

2) Do you think Monk's death was justified? If so, why?

3) Did Carlos become Tan's puppet after it was learned that she had been violated by Monk?

4) Do you believe if their father had been in their lives Justice and Monk would have turned out differently?

5) If Sabrina had never told Carlos that Monk and D.C. were the ones hanging out with Cross, do you think the situation would have still gotten out of hand because of Tan being robbed by them?

6) Do you think Sapphire was more strong-willed than Justice?

7) If Cross had told Monk and D.C. about his involvement in robbing Carlos's people, based on their characteristics within the story what do you think Monk and D.C. would have done?

8) Do you think J.T. genuinely cared for Justice? Or was it all just a ruse to keep him from being exposed?

9) Should Justice have listened to J.T. and tried to reason with him or did she do the right thing by squeezing the trigger?

10) When Justice found out about J.T. being her brother do you believe her karma was well deserved?

Coming September 2009

Excerpt from *THIRSTY 2*
CHAPTER ONE

J ustice, we got a problem in the dressing room," Toni's high-pitched voice broke her train of thought for a brief moment. Standing in the doorway to Justice's office with the heavy oak frame door half-open, Toni was allowing the loud music from the club to pour in. Inside the office was expensive looking cherry wood furniture with photos of Justice's family and her best friend Sapphire adorning the walls.

Justice was seated at her desk tapping away at her keypad on her laptop. On the wall directly behind her hung a large family portrait of her, her deceased mother, and her deceased younger brother, Monk. Absent from the portrait was her father, Tyson, the only living member of her immediate family. Tyson had been estranged from her life since her early teenage years, but they had subsequently made amends two years ago when she'd first returned to Chicago from Charlotte, North Carolina. Tyson's photo sat alone on her desk next to the floral arrangement he'd sent two days ago for her birthday.

"What is it now?" Justice asked without looking up from her computer. She wasn't the slightest bit surprised at Toni's statement. There was always some sort of problem or another in the dressing room. Twenty-five girls running around in a confined area clad in nothing but bras and g-strings, sometimes even less, *would* cause an occasional problem or two.

Toni shifted her voluptuous five foot-two frame through the door, her honey-blonde dreadlocks and apple-bottom ass swinging in unison with every step. She closed the heavy door behind her, muffling the roar of Lil' Wayne's latest stripper anthem, which was blaring from the sound system. Leaning across Justice's desk, Toni huffed, "The girls you flew in from Memphis are complaining about Virgin and Precious."

Justice finally looked up from her monitor and sighed deeply as she pushed away from the desk and sank back further into the leather Queen Anne. Purely out of habit, her toned arms went up over her head and her slender fingers intertwined before coming to rest atop her silky mane of jet-black hair.

"Toni, if I ain't mistaking, you're the manager here last time I checked," her sarcasm was hard to miss.

She looked at Toni with a frustrated scowl. Sometimes dealing with Toni made Justice feel as if she was dealing with a child instead of a grown ass twenty-eight year old woman. Toni rolled her eyes at her boss and folded her arms across her ample bosom without replying.

"How many times have you had trouble with Virgin and that bitch Precious?" Justice asked, her jaw clenched tight and eyebrows knitted.

Toni hesitated as if she was actually trying to calculate the numerous times those two had caused problems at the club.

Without waiting for a response, Justice ejected, "Exactly. Too many times to count. Every time I bring in new girls from outta town to dance them two bitches start pmsin'. You know what...fire them bitches." Fire rose in Justice's tightly slanted eyes.

"Just like that?" Toni asked as if she couldn't grasp the finality of Justice's statement.

"Yeah, *just* like that. Tell them to keep their tips from tonight, gather their shit, and get off my prope...better yet, go get 'em. I'll do it myself."

Justice was fed up with Virgin and Precious. Those bitches were nothing but troublemakers.

Toni left Justice's office with an "*ooooh, somebody's ass is in trouble*" expression glued to her face. By the same token, she was also relieved that she didn't have to be the one to give the girls the boot.

Justice removed her scrunchie and shook out her long tresses while exhaling a deep-rooted sigh. She rubbed at her temples to relieve the slight migraine that was gradually building. For the past two days Justice had been under tremendous stress because the anniversary of her brother's death was fast approaching. Every time Justice thought about her brother it brought about a brain throbbing headache.

As she watched Toni's thick frame sashay its way out the door, Justice mumbled, "I need to be firing *your* incompetent ass." Then on second thought, Justice surmised that Toni had been there with her from the very beginning of her legitimate endeavor.

When Justice had first decided to invest some of the blood money she'd arrived back in Chicago with, Toni had been the one who had suggested she open the strip club. Initially, Justice had cringed at the idea because she'd never gotten along with other women, much less strippers with their asses on their shoulders. But to her astonishment, Justice discovered that dealing with the girls who had come through the doors of her establishment for auditions had been easier than she'd imagined. Mainly because of the fact that she realized most of the girls were just as fucked up in the head as she was. Each and every one of them had a story.

Justice had always prided herself on being a good judge of character, so with the girls who had come to her for an opportunity to work she looked beyond the surface. Beyond all of the D-cup titties, twenty-two inch waists, and porn star asses lay insecure opportunists willing to bear it all for a quick buck.

When Justice first opened Phire and Ice downtown on Michigan Avenue in the heart of Chicago, she had no idea it would become one of Chi-town's premiere spots for nightlife. The elite adult entertainment club attracted ballers from all around, especially local rappers and professional athletes. It was not unusual to see Twista or Ben Wallace in the VIP area, sipping champagne and making it rain on a weeknight.

Most of the time Justice's business ran smoothly, without any problems. But there were times when the estrogen level was at a boiling point and catfights were inevitable. Sometimes Justice felt like she had it all together, other times she felt as if she was running a circus like the late great Bernie Mac as Dollar Bill in the movie *Player's Club*. At those times, if it weren't for a caring staff, especially Toni, she felt like she'd lose it.

"Boss lady, here they go." Toni's voice brought Justice out of her lingering thoughts.

Justice rose from her chair and watched as Virgin and Precious entered her office reeking of cigarette smoke and fruity body oil. Looking at the two reminded Justice of that old school flick *Twins* with Arnold Swartzeneggar and Danny Devito. Precious was towering over Virgin by at least eight inches like Arnold had done Danny. Nevertheless, Precious's height didn't intimidate Justice in the least because if it weren't for Precious's heels, she and Justice would have been eye to eye. Justice had no idea where the pair had come up with their names because everybody in the Chi and the surrounding Metropolitan area knew the girls were anything *but* precious and virginal. It was even rumored that the two had used the VIP for occasional tricking. Turning tricks was a definite no-no in Phire and Ice.

After Toni had left the office and closed the door Justice stated, "Sit down." She was looking back and forth between the two girls with equal amounts of animosity so there would be no mistake as to whom she was speaking.

Virgin took a seat on the leather sofa near the door while Precious remained defiantly standing for a few seconds. Finally, she sucked her teeth and reluctantly sat her amazon ass down next to her partner.

Precious adjusted the garter on her thick thigh, which was stuffed with bills—tens and twenties, only a fraction of the tips she had earned for the night. Both girls were dressed in bras and matching g-strings along with expensive pumps. Virgin was wearing her signature color of all white, which symbolized purity. Her auburn-dyed hair was fixed in tight cornrows, which made her defined cheekbones even more pronounced than ever. Her creamy, peanut butter complexion was flawless without a trace of make-up. However, the glassy look in her eyes made Justice wonder if she was rollin' on X or jacked up on coke. There was no mistaking the fact that she was definitely high on something.

Precious was wearing fire engine red with gold-colored rhinestones decorating the nipple and crotch area of her outfit. This night she had her naturally short hair styled into a throwback Halle Berry number. Her ebony skin was glistening with a thin sheen of perspiration from the lap dance she was so rudely pulled away from.

With the bodies both Precious and Virgin possessed, Justice hated to admit the fact that they were both wearing their outfits damn well. Between Justice and the dancers, the confidence level in this room was at a record high and so thick you could taste it. Justice strolled over to her picture window and glanced out over the crowded, well-lit parking area before addressing the girls.

"Do y'all know the definition of the word *insanity?*" She had her back to them and could feel their eyes boring into the back of her head.

"What?" Precious asked with a hint of attitude and slight frustration as if she hadn't heard Justice's question correctly.

"You heard me," Justice said. She turned to face the girls, disdain evident in her exotic features. "If you don't know, lemme enlighten you. Insanity is when you constantly do the same thing but expect to get different results, different outcomes."

Precious and Virgin exchanged heated looks and rolled their eyes while twisting up their mouths as if they were sharing the same thought, *Yeah we know what insanity is. This Chinese looking, Kimora Lee wannabe bitch is the one insane. Sittin' up here lecturin' a bitch when it's niggas out there spendin' that dough.*

"I said that to say this: Every time I spend my hard earned money to bring new faces up in here so my customers won't get sick from seeing the same tired faces every night, you two always seem to be in the way. Tryin' to do all you can to make the featured girls as uncomfortable as possible. I don't understand you two."

Justice pointed towards the door.

"It's enough money out there for a hundred girls to eat and y'all wanna fuck that up every chance you get. You are the only two that hate like that! Y'all are just like cats, pissin' on a spot to try to claim turf!"

Justice's slanted eyes were boring into the girls.

"I'on' know what you talkin' 'bout 'cause I ain't—" Precious started, but Justice cut her off.

"You know *exactly* what I'm talking about, Precious! And I can do without your funky ass attitude right now." Justice's voice began to rise. "I got eighteen girls who dance here nightly along with ten I fly in every weekend from different cities. Tell me why I need you two!?"

Precious and Virgin were looking at one another dumbfounded as Justice calmly sat back down and began tapping her French manicured nails on her desk awaiting a response. She was silently sitting there waiting to see what type of justification the girls could come up with that would keep her from banning them from the hottest strip club in Chicago.

After a long uncomfortable silence, Precious responded, "So, you wanna play *that* game, huh?"

She arose from the sofa and slowly approached Justice's desk with a devious grin on her face.

She and Justice locked eyes, then Precious stated in a whisper, "You think a bitch don't know how you used to get your money back in the day in Carolina?" She waved her arms around as she looked about the spacious office. "A bitch know how you ended up with all this. I guess *nothing* was outta your realm when it came to gettin' dough, huh? Maybe not even murder."

Precious smiled devilishly as she read the look in Justice's eyes.

"So, Lucy Lu, you might wanna be mindful of who you threaten the next time you open your mouth 'cause you neva know who might know what you think they don't know, feel me?"

Justice stammered, "I...I don't know what you talkin' about. You need to get outta my office and outta my building before—"

"Oh, I think you do know what I'm talkin' about. But that's gonna just be between the three of us...for now." She looked back at Virgin and winked. "But right now, me and Virgin got a couple of VIPs lined up out there. So, we gonna finish out the rest of this night, and tomorrow night, and the next night, and the night after that, and...you get the idea." Precious scowled at Justice, then turned to Virgin, "You ready to finish getting this money?" Just that quickly, the tables had been turned a whole 360 degrees.

"No doubt," Virgin replied as she arose from the sofa and headed for the door with Precious right behind her.

When Precious reached the door she turned to look at Justice, "Holla at cha later, boss lady." The sarcasm was thick.

Then they were out the door.

Toni was standing outside the door waiting for the girls to exit. As soon as they came out, Toni went in.

"How much time you give them to get their shit and get out?" she asked Justice. Then she noticed the look on Justice's face. "Girl, what happened?"

Justice buried her head in her desk and ignored Toni's question. After a few minutes, Justice raised her head and stated a weak "They're staying."

"What?"

She looked at Toni and told her, "Lemme think for a minute. Come back in thirty minutes and we'll talk."

She watched as Toni reluctantly left the office. As soon as the door was closed Justice's mind began reeling. She tried to come up with scenarios as to how the two girls could possible know her secret.

After about twenty minutes of pondering over this, she came to the conclusion that the two girls couldn't possibly know what they were talking about. They had to be speculating on rumors. This wasn't the first time Justice had heard about her past of setting niggas up to be robbed, but it was the first time the word "murder" had been mentioned.

Speculation or not, Justice decided that she couldn't take the chance of letting those two bitches keep that secret dangling over her head. She opened her desk drawer and looked down at the .9mm she kept stashed there for protection. She picked it up and had flashbacks of the day she'd killed J.T. Never in a million years would she have thought that she would have to pull the trigger again to take a life, but the way she figured it, she had no choice.

WAHIDA CLARK PRESENTS
BEST SELLING TITLES

Trust No Man

Trust No Man II

Thirsty

Cheetah

Karma

The Ultimate Sacrifice

The Game of Deception

Karma 2: For The Love of Money

COMING SOON!

Thirsty 2

Country Boys

Lickin' License

Feenin'

Bonded by Blood

Uncle Yah Yah: 21st Century Man of Wisdom
And Under Pressure

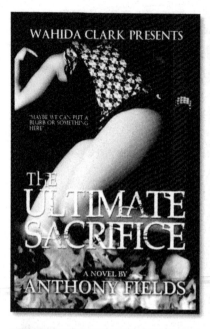

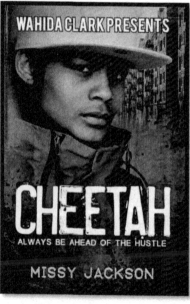

ON SALE NOW!

WWW.WCLARKPUBLISHING.COM

COMING SOON!

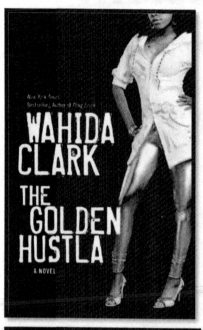

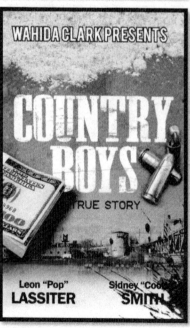

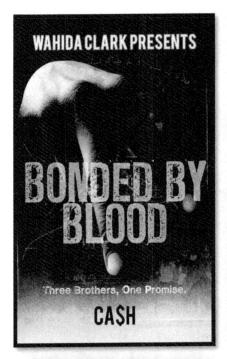

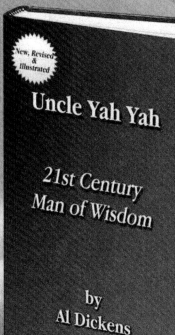

CPSIA information can be obtained
at www.ICGtesting.com
Printed in the USA
LVOW13s0518210718
584496LV00010B/319/P